Published by St. Frances Press
Copyright © 2016 by Gerri LeClerc

ISBN 978-0-9972631-0-7

Cover and book design by David M. Seager
Cover illustration by Donna Green
*A portion of the proceeds of Missing Emily
will be donated to Donna Green's foundation,
www.magicalmoon.org.*
Back cover image: Shutterstock

This book has been typeset in
Minion Pro Condensed
with heads in Ivory.

MISSING EMILY

GERRI LeCLERC

Gerri LeClerc

ST. FRANCES PRESS

Acknowlegements

*"WE DO NOT BELIEVE IN OURSELVES UNTIL SOMEONE
REVEALS THAT SOMETHING DEEP INSIDE US IS VALUABLE, WORTH
LISTENING TO, WORTHY OF OUR TRUST, SACRED TO OUR TOUCH..."*
E.E. CUMMINGS

*I have enormous gratitude for the myriad of people who supported my
writing journey. Yes, I'm going to list every one of them.*

*My family: Mom and Stepfather, Gerrie and Bob Bartruff. My sisters Pat Ray and Dennie
Costello; my children Ron and Jennifer LeClerc, and Renée and Erik Easton, and my two
sisters-in-law Brenda LeClerc and Laurel Seneca, my cousin Celeste LaRock all of whom
supported me by reading manuscripts and/or being my cheerleaders. I love you all.*

*I am overwhelmed by the generosity of friends who read for me, encouraged me, critiqued
my stories: Pat Collins, Mary and Dick Miller, Joan Earnhart, Jeff and Barbara Feldman,
(Jeff was a taskmaster who taught me an amazing amount), Anita Patchett, Annie Murphy,
Dana Dimier, Sue Ruben, Marian James, and Maria DeFrancisci, who selflessly read
and reread the same paragraphs until they were right! My newest readers, Louise Brady
and Susan Ferrara. Heartfelt thanks!*

*Suzanne Fox, author, teacher, coach, friend. You grew my fledgling writing to become my
vocation; spent endless hours redirecting my mistakes, sharing your amazing knowledge, and
sitting over salads at Applebees, just being my friend. Thank you!*

*My critique partner, Sandra Fontana. Published author, inventor, business woman
supreme, friend. We formed a delightful partnership, giving and taking criticism without
injury or insult, mutual cheerleaders with admiration for each other's work. What would
I do without you? Friends forever!*

*Freelance editor, Kathleen Marusak, for a fabulous job making my manuscript shine
and for unabashedly loving the book!*

*Donna Green, how can I thank you for taking precious time from your foundation,
Magical Moon, to make my publishing dream come true? You are an angel to the children
you help in so many ways deal with their cancer and other challenges; you are an angel to
this friend who will be forever grateful to know you.*

*Saving the love of my life for last, my husband Ron LeClerc. As I spent more and more
time at the computer, he spent more and more time in the kitchen. He supported me through
tearful rejections, frustrations, and shared all my joyful "firsts", contest wins, and
don't forget the paper and ink!*

This book is dedicated to my husband Ron,
my sun and moon and stars.

MISSING
EMILY

CHAPTER ONE

When Thea Connor drove across the Cape Cod Canal on the Sagamore Bridge, the tension eased out of her body. She looked down at the water, where toy-sized boats churned up fluffy white wakes.

She stuck her hand back between the bucket seats and tickled Emily's knee. "Hey, giggle girl, where are we?"

"Home," her four-year-old sang out, as she did every time they crossed the bridge.

They drove by Hannah's favorite Christmas Tree Shop, stoking Thea's grief. If only her mother were still with them. Why did she have to die before she saw Thea pass the bar and return home to practice law on the Cape?

Hannah had been so proud of Thea's accomplishments. That pride had helped support her through the hard times. How could Emily understand the loss of her grandmother, who had been an integral part of her life since the day she was born? Hannah had loved them both so dearly. Thea blinked her eyes against the tears.

It took another thirty minutes to arrive at their cottage. She woke Emily, unbuckled her car seat, and lifted her down to the gravel driveway.

Before she was fully awake, Emily began to talk. "Mommy, what's growing in my garden now?" Then she skipped toward the backyard, where her garden was planted, without waiting for an answer.

Thea stood looking after her until she remembered Star. "Oops. Sorry, girl." She walked around and opened the back of the car where Star—the German shepherd whom Emily had adored enough to wheedle away from Hannah—waited patiently in the way-back. Star flew out of the car and ran across the fresh-cut lawn to the woods. *Who mowed the lawn?* Thea wondered as she headed to the backyard.

"Mommy, look."

Thea knelt beside her as Emily pointed out the nubs of herbs pushing out of the rich brown soil. "Nana said the grass has enough room to grow in the lawn and it's not allowed in the garden," she said, pulling out each blade of grass that had begun to creep around the periphery of her garden. She hugged Emily's shoulders, left her daughter to her task, and walked back around to the front of the cottage.

She gazed at the quintessential Cape Cod cottage with its cedar shingles, hydrangea-blue shutters, and white picket fence. An arbor, laden with soon-to-bloom New Dawn roses, arched over the front door. A worn plaque next to it, placed by the original owner before street numbers existed, said Knoll Cottage. It was charming, but she saw the curl and split of the cedar shingles, mossy where the sun missed them, in need of replacement. The front door was in desperate need of a coat of paint; the chimney leaning so far to one side, Thea couldn't imagine what was keeping it up.

As she stepped onto the farmer's porch and pulled the key from her pocket, she heard Star's yelps of joy and saw her running flat out. She got the door open in time for Star to race inside, and kept it open for Emily, a few steps behind her. Star continued barking as she bolted through the kitchen, slipping and sliding as she turned down the hall. Emily followed her, bubbling with laughter.

Thea grinned as she pushed open the kitchen windows, freeing the lace curtains to dance in the breeze. *Home.*

Later, Thea sat in the old rocking chair on the sun porch, her flower-child mother's sacred space, waiting as Emily, bathed and in her nightie, pulled book after book from a shelf.

"Emily, please choose only one."

"But Nana reads me three." She held up two fingers and her thumb. "I want three books."

"Let's compromise. How about two?"

Emily pressed her full lips into a pout. *Too cute for words*, Thea thought, finding it all the more difficult to hold her ground.

"When's Nana coming back? I want her to read to me."

"Sweetie." Thea leaned forward and ran her hand over Emily's curls. "Remember, Nana isn't here anymore. She's gone to live with the angels," Thea said, feeling the pain of her words.

A frown briefly clouded Emily's face. She tilted her head to the side and looked around the sun porch. Her eyes seemed unfocused, as if she were listening to music. She blinked, then turned to look at her mother and giggled. "Nana's here, Mommy," she said, as she scooped up the pile of her chosen books. She climbed on Thea's lap, listened to her read the *three* books, sometimes pointing her index finger uncannily on the sentence.

Thea knew this joy they shared together would soon be part of the everyday in their permanent new life. At the thought, a pang of guilt shot through her. She'd been so busy the last three years that loving moments like this had been rare. But soon she would finish her last class, move away from the chaos of busy Boston and return to the serenity of the Cape. Almost there. Almost done.

Katherine Anderson was so absorbed watching the dance studio's pianist, she missed her little girl's fall. Only the sounds of worried, frightened voices alerted her.

She turned and saw Madison's inert body lying on the floor, and felt all the strength drain from her own body. She cried out, "Madison!" as she stumbled from her chair and scooped her pale, unconscious child into her arms. All around her subdued voices asked each other what was wrong with the child.

"Should we call someone?" the ballet teacher asked, wringing her hands and shaking them as if to cast off the drips of fear. "Should I call an ambulance?"

Madison stirred in Katherine's arms. Her light blue eyes flickered open and she looked around.

"Oh, thank goodness," the teacher said. "Are you feeling better, Madison? She must have fainted. Do you think she fainted?" the dance teacher asked Katherine.

But she couldn't answer. She'd turned icy cold. She gave her daughter a few sips from the glass of water one of the other mothers brought over. "Feel better, darling?"

Her daughter only nodded, as if she were too exhausted to speak.

Madison rested her head on Katherine's shoulder as she carried her to the car. She would go home and call the doctor the minute Madison fell asleep.

Maddy loved rock music. Katherine turned on the radio full blast for the ride home. Through the rearview mirror she watched Madison in her car seat, bobbing her head to the beat. Katherine held in the sobs that crowded together at the back of her throat. Something this terrible couldn't be happening to her daughter. These things happened to other people. Strangers. There had to be some mistake. But there wasn't. The doctor had warned her.

That afternoon, Doctor Thompson's expression, after he had examined Madison, told Katherine he suspected the worst, though he'd tried to sound encouraging. Madison's screams when they took blood for the tests he'd ordered echoed in her mother's mind. The results showed time was running out.

CHAPTER TWO

Thea could hear her daughter singing.

"Emily, what are you doing? Find your shoes. Mommy has to get to class." Thea stood by the door and knocked her briefcase rhythmically against the jamb. She hated the sharp sound of her voice. Being in Boston brought it all back, the tension and the exhaustion of her years there. She stared into her small apartment, one of several on the fringe of Beacon Hill rented year after year to college students. She could see the eat-in kitchen and the small living room, its furnishings worn and scarred by a succession of youthful tenants. The familiar embedded musty odor mixed with exhaust from the busy street filled her nostrils. Down the hall was a bedroom, a den—which was Emily's room—and a bathroom. Boxes were piled all around, packed and ready to go.

She *had* to get moving. Walk Emily to the house of a friend who had agreed to babysit these last Fridays, and then get some paralegal work done before her class. How she wished Diane Rimsa could be here. Emily's regular babysitter always had a knack of making the hectic mornings run smoothly. But she had her own troubles. She was in the hospital for surgery.

Emily skirted two boxes and entered the living room. She looked at her mother, her chubby hands raised, palms up. "Mommy, I can't find my shoes."

Thea flashed on the picture of Emily sitting in her car seat last night, her bunny-slippered feet kicking back and forth. She had forgotten to pack Emily's shoes. *Crap.*

"Wear your rain boots then. Hurry up."

"It's not rainy. I don't *want* to wear my boots." Emily frowned at her mother.

Thea went to the box in front of the closet and pulled out two pink rubber boots with bright yellow smiley faces. Her best friend, Annie, had given them to Emily, who was usually delighted to wear them. "Put your boots on and let's go. Mommy's going to be late."

Emily began to cry, but she pulled her boots on, one at a time, slowly. It was all Thea could do not to rush over and jam them onto Emily's feet. When she completed her task, Emily came toward her mother, crying louder now. "I don't want to wear my boots. There's no rain."

Thea, tight-lipped, slipped the end of Star's leash over her wrist and picked up her briefcase. The dog moved quickly to the door, her tail wagging wide behind her. Emily took Thea's other hand. They moved in a lurching procession down the brick sidewalk raised up in places by the roots of the ancient trees that lined the street.

Emily's rain boots might be needed after all; it was damp and gray outside. She continued to wail for several blocks as she walked, pulling on her mother's hand from behind, while an eager Star dragged Thea forward. For a moment, she sank into self-pity. She hated this feeling of frustration mixed with guilt for demanding so much of her child. And it seemed the closer they got to a saner life, the harder these last few months had become.

They turned and began to head down Tamerind Street—a short residential road lined with newer condominiums, constructed with the naked architecture born of need versus beauty.

Thea was distracted from her deliberations by a large black sedan that slowly cruised by them. She noticed the back door didn't appear to be completely closed. She glanced around her. It seemed the whole area was asleep at this hour, a few minutes past five-thirty. The sun had not begun its ascent and the lawns were still wet with dew. There was not a breath of wind. She looked at the windows of the condominium units that lined the right side of the street. She saw no activity and only a few lights were on. Some people should be heading out for their long commute soon, but the cars still sat idle in the lot. She shivered with the eerie feeling that she and Emily had slipped into another dimension.

When she looked again, she saw that the black car had pulled up, stopping at the curb several feet in front of them. It was parked at an odd angle. Now the back door on the curb side was open farther. She waited to see who would step out, and squeezed Emily's hand tighter.

When she heard footsteps, she felt relieved. They weren't the only people on the street after all. As she turned to see who was coming, she was stunned by a sharp blow to her back, knocking her to the ground and ripping Emily's hand from her grip. Star began frantically barking and yanking at the leash, which was trapped under Thea, along with her briefcase. She turned her head and saw a man wearing a black Yankees baseball cap, its brim pulled low over his brow, hoisting Emily over his shoulder. Her daughter was screaming, "Mommy! Mommy!"

Thea scrambled to get up, dropping the briefcase and freeing the leash. She saw Emily's strawberry-blond curls bouncing as the man ran the short distance to the black car. Star, now free, raced after them, barking and growling. Thea bolted forward, shouting loud enough to wake the city. "Emily! Help! Somebody help me!" She saw her daughter's head snap forward as the man holding her threw himself backward through the open car door. The car began to creep ahead.

Star had her jaw clamped on the man's pants, causing him to work to shake her off, and slowing the car's departure, giving Thea precious seconds to catch up. When the door slammed, her fingers were mere inches from the rear fender. Star let out a sharp yelp when the driver of the car swerved into her, then drove on. A high-pitched, scraping sound filled the otherwise silent street as the car sideswiped a parked vehicle. Thea raced around it and cut back into the street, grabbing the back door handle just as the sedan began to gain momentum. She hung onto the handle, taking jerky, loping steps to keep up. The sedan took the corner and sped up. Her fingers slipped from the handle.

"Emily!" She began to lose ground. Tears blinded her as she continued to run, sucking in deep breaths between shouts. "Somebody, help me!"

And then her daughter was gone.

Thea fell to her knees. A roar filled her ears, blocking out any coherent thought except one: Emily was gone.

She forced herself to move, to get help. She ran back for the briefcase she'd dropped on the sidewalk. People spilled from doorways toward her like an expanding puddle. They were touching her, asking her questions she couldn't understand. She pulled her phone from the briefcase and dialed 9-1-1 as she walked, bent over, one arm tight across her stomach, back to her dog lying still in the street. She knelt beside Star.

"Oh God, oh God, help me, help me!"

"What is your emergency?"

"My daughter, please, help me. Someone took my little girl." Her body curled into an arc of pain covering the soft fur of the dog. "Help me, please."

CHAPTER THREE

I had no other choice.
I had to do it.
Who am I now?
No one can judge me who hasn't walked in my shoes.
Madison's shoes.
I had to do it.

atherine closed her red leather journal and set down her pen. She'd kept journals since she was young, but from now on, she would add no new entries.

She stood up and began to pace in a loop around the spacious living room of her Boston home, the Tabriz Oriental muting her footsteps until she hit the hardwood floor and the sound broke into her frantic thoughts.

She raised her tight fists and pressed them against her mouth. *Why don't they call? What's taking so long?*

A minute later, the phone rang, jarring her to a standstill. It was her mother calling to chat. Katherine could hardly squeeze her voice past the lump in her throat. She had to work to sound calm. Her mother talked on without commenting on the sound of her tight voice, something she would never do if she thought something was wrong.

Her mother had not been a constant in her upbringing. She had a PhD in Archeology. When she wasn't off somewhere on a dig, she was writing one of her books. Then, she couldn't be disturbed. Katherine had nurses until she was old enough to attend pre-school. Her memories of her mother at home consisted of her sitting on Katherine's bed, smelling wonderful and looking beautiful, as she tucked her in before her evening social activity; saying goodbye before she went off for weeks at a time; phone calls from exotic places in the world, far from her daughter. Unlike her own childhood, relatively absent of a mother's presence, Katherine had promised herself to be a part of every step of Madison's life.

Katherine moved through the room, dragging her damp palms across the furniture, finally sitting on the edge of the rustic rush-seated bench. The room was decorated with eclectic French Country pieces she loved, a contrast to the formal English antiques of her childhood home. The colorful mixture of Provencal fabrics and patterns usually soothed her. But not today. She crossed the room to fluff the down cushions on the couch, then dropped down into it. *Why aren't they here?*

Drawn draperies blocked the dim morning light, keeping the room swathed in shadows. She thought of ghosts and shivered. She lit the three fat candles on the scarred wine-tasting table. Their warm glow eased only a little of her anxiety. The swaying flames reminded her of Madison's dance studio filled with little girls in pink tutus and white tights, twirling on tiptoes, dipping at the bar. The flames only held her attention for a few minutes.

Where are they now? Do they have her?

She slowed her breathing. Everything was going to be fine. She was taking a terrible risk, but what other choice did she have? This drastic measure was their last hope. If only she hadn't made that terrible call to the child's mother. If only the girl's grandmother had lived long enough to help.

She lifted the silver-framed picture of Madison from the coffee table. As she hugged the photograph to her breast, her mind replayed the black day a year ago, when four-year-old Maddy was diagnosed with Fanconi anemia.

The rumble of the garage door startled her. She dropped the picture and ran up the stairs to her bedroom, closing the door behind her.

Emily shrieked, kicking and swatting at the man who was holding her down on the back seat of the car. It wasn't like her mommy's car. The back seat felt cold where her jacket was pulled up underneath her. She was lying down, not in her car seat like she was supposed to be. It was slippery. She nearly slid to the floor when the car went around the corner, except the man held her tighter.

"It's okay, it's okay, I'm not going to hurt you," the strange man said. Emily turned her head so she couldn't see his black eyes or up his nose, which had ugly hairs in it.

"Let me go! I want my mommy."

"She'll be coming, don't worry. She'll come get you soon."

But Emily continued to yell. The man was hurting her, his big hands squeezing her shoulders. His mouth smelled bad when he talked, but she hardly noticed because she was so afraid. Where was her mommy? Who was this man?

She cried so hard she began to gag. The man jerked his head away from her.

"Where are we?" he demanded.

A woman's voice answered. "We're there. Just about to pull into the garage."

"Thank God. I can't stand this much longer."

The garage door slid closed, making the enclosed space almost dark. The man's hands released Emily, and she scooted up into the corner of the seat. She was sobbing and hiccoughing, which made it hard for her to breathe.

Emily heard a car door slam, then a lady opened the door behind her, and she lost her balance. The woman's hands didn't hurt her like the man's did. Emily turned away from the bad man to go to her. She had wrinkles in her cheeks like Nana.

"I've got you, sweet girl," the woman said, taking her arm. "Come on, we'll go into the house and see your new room."

"No! I won't!" Emily held fast to the car door. "I want my mommy. Please!"

The woman peeled Emily's fingers from the door and picked her up, locking her arms and legs in a tight grip so she couldn't fight. Emily screamed and screamed. The lady carried her into a house, through some rooms, then up stairs, then up more stairs. The lady was breathing loud as she bent over to open a door.

"You'll be all right, little girl," she said, setting Emily's feet on the floor. "I'll come back soon. Settle yourself down. It's going to be all right, little one." She gave Emily a light push into the room then closed the door.

Emily spun around and grabbed the knob, pulling with both fists, but the door wouldn't open. She kicked the door again and again. Finally, she was so tired she slid down to the floor. The barking of a dog that sounded a little like Star calmed her, and she closed her eyes.

Emily awoke and remembered the strange room as she looked around her. She stood and tried the door again, but it still wouldn't open. She had to go to the bathroom. The room was nearly dark, but she could see other doors. She walked over and found one door opened to a closet full of clothes, the other was a big bathroom with a tub that had bath toys sitting on the edge. She used the toilet and washed her hands.

Back in the big room, Emily went to the only window. She pulled back the heavy curtain, but couldn't see outside because the glass in the window was black. She could smell the paint.

Folding her arms over the hurt in her tummy, she turned and scanned the room. It was bigger than any room she'd ever seen. It had slanted ceilings like Nana's cottage. On shelves, she saw a lot of toys that she could reach. The bed was big like mommy's and it had dolls and stuffed animals on it. But she hated the dolls and toys. She didn't want them, she wanted to go home.

"Mommy," Emily whispered. Then she called out as loud as she could, "I want to go home!" She went to the bed and threw the toys on the floor. "I want my mommy," she shouted, and began to cry.

She stopped suddenly. Was someone coming? A stuffed frog was the only toy left on the bed. She pulled it close to her, looking around the shadowy room. She rubbed the goose bumps on her arms, but she didn't feel afraid anymore.

Then, over the sound of her own breathing, she heard the softest voice. She looked around again, sniffling. The voice was so tiny she could hardly hear it. Then she felt happy inside.

"Nana?"

"Shhh, sweet baby, Nana's here."

 She was standing at the foot of the bed. Emily was so glad to see her grandmother, who would hug her and kiss her. Nana would open the door so they could go home together. She smiled at her like she always did, making Emily want to giggle. She was so excited; she wanted to run into Nana's arms. But she couldn't move her legs, which made her afraid again. "Nana, take me home. I want to go home."

"Not yet, dear heart. But I have a new book for us to read. It's called *The Lost Bear.*" She held it up for Emily to see the front cover. "Hop in bed and snuggle under the blanket."

When Emily was settled, holding the soft green frog, Nana sat on the bed next to Emily and began to read the book, making all the funny voices like she always did.

CHAPTER FOUR

Tamerind Street was jammed with uniformed police officers, patrol cars with flashing lights, Animal Control vehicles, and a rescue truck. Thea was sitting sideways in the backseat of one of the Boston Police Department's blue-and-white cruisers. She was bent over, her feet on the pavement and her head in her hands. Her hair fell forward, draping about her face like privacy curtains. A young police officer, clean shaven and smelling of citrus, stooped beside her, quiet while she wept. She couldn't stop, would never be able to stop. *Emily, Emily, where are you?*

"Ma'am, the timing is urgent." The officer spoke with a hint of a Spanish accent. "We need you to help us find your daughter. We have to work quickly. I know how upsetting—"

Thea focused on him with her wet, burning eyes.

"I didn't mean—I can't begin to imagine what you're going through, but we need information to help find your daughter. Can you call your husband? A relative or a friend?"

She took a deep, shuddering breath. "I'm sorry. Tell me what you need," she said, then pressed her eyelids tight to try to stop the tears.

The officer's face relaxed. He took up the notebook and pen he was holding and prepared to write. "First, your daughter's name, her age, and as detailed a description as you can give. Including any scars or birthmarks."

"Emily Connor. She just turned four years old . . . what else did you need?" Thea said, shaking her head as if to dispel this nightmare.

"Birthmarks, her weight and height. Can you give me an estimate?"

"No, no scars or birthmarks. At her last appointment, maybe three weeks ago, she was forty-three and a half inches—no forty-three and a half *pounds* and forty-two and a quarter inches."

"What was she wearing today?"

"Boots." Thea broke down, sobbing again. What had happened to Emily? Why did he take her? A million stories of horror popped into her head, and she thought she would die from anguish.

"Listen to me, Mrs. Connor. Look at me now. We have to find your daughter. We *will* find her, but we need your help. You've heard of the Amber Alert, haven't you, Mrs. Connor?"

"Yes, I'm sorry. Um, I'm not married." A flash of the man who was Emily's father sent a shot of the old anger through her. Thea rubbed her face with the heels of her hands, but silent tears continued to roll down her cheeks. "Yes, the Amber Alert." She nodded, took a deep breath, and concentrated. "Em was wearing blue denim jeans with pink flowers embroidered on the pockets. I think she wore her Dora shirt. Her boots—"

"Ma'am? Dora shirt? Can you give me a description of that?"

"No, no, not her Dora shirt. She had on an orange shirt with a pink pumpkin." Thea paused, a tiny smile on her lips. "She's learning to match her own clothes. You're supposed to allow wide latitude in their choices at this time. You know, she matched pink flowers with a pink pumpkin." She looked away for a moment, covering her mouth with her hand. "And she had on a pink zip-up jacket."

"Does she take any medicine?"

"No."

"Are her fingerprints on file?"

A moan escaped Thea. Fingerprints would help identify a body. "Yes, they are." She remembered when she took Emily to have her prints registered. She never thought she was doing it in case Emily was kidnapped. It was just something a responsible mother would do, especially one studying the law. This present reality was bitter in her mouth.

"That's good. Now, ma'am, tell me what she looks like. Hair color, eyes."

"Emily has strawberry-blond hair. It's on the long side, but it looks shorter because it's so curly." She swallowed hard. "Her eyes are blue. She's a very pretty little girl. People stop and tell me that."

"You're doing well. You said she was wearing boots?"

"I made her wear her rain boots," Thea sobbed, wiping her eyes with the tissue he'd given her, which was already sodden. "I forgot to pack her shoes and I was in a hurry. Oh God, she was crying, I couldn't wait, I was in such a *goddamn* hurry." The words came out with building force.

The officer gave her a minute to compose herself, before he asked, "Do you have a picture of your daughter with you?"

Thea sniffed and rubbed her nose with the back of her hand. "On my phone—" She looked around the back seat. Her phone was on the floor with her briefcase. She handed the phone to the officer. "It has plenty of pictures of her. Take what you need."

The officer stood up and leaned into the front seat of the cruiser for another tissue. He gave it to her.

"Thanks." She blew her nose.

He asked her about the car, the plate, the man, anything she could remember.

"It was a big, black sedan. Maybe a Lincoln or—no, not a Cadillac. It had four doors. The engine was quiet. I could hardly hear it even when Star stopped barking." She looked up, pushing her hair back from her face. "Oh no! I didn't get the plate. I didn't even think of it. How could I not get the damn license plate?"

"It happens. It's okay."

"It's not okay. Oh my God, that could have changed everything." She closed her eyes, tried to see it in her mind. "I don't know. I think it could have been a Massachusetts plate. Could I have noticed something other than that? I just don't know." She squeezed her fists tight. How could she not think of the plate!

"How about the man? Can you describe him?"

Thea thought; she tried to picture him. "He came up behind me and knocked me down. I turned and saw him, but it all happened so fast." She looked away with an unfocused gaze. "I couldn't see much of his face because he wore a baseball hat with the brim pulled down over his forehead." She closed her eyes, trying to see him again. "He was clean-shaven, and from what I could see of his lower face, he had a swarthy complexion." She looked at the officer, widened her eyes. "He had short, dark hair, black, with gray in it. I could see it at the nape of his neck when he ran back to the car." Then the mental image shifted and all she could see was her daughter's face. Hear her piercing cry, "Mommeeee!"

"Oh, please, are we finished? We have to find her."

"We're not losing any time here, ma'am. The Boston police force is working right now to get officers out walking the area. They'll set up road blocks and get a helicopter out to search. They'll use every available resource to find her. The Crime Lab Unit's already here and working," the officer said, pointing across a sea of people. Thea looked in the direction he indicated. Yellow tape was being unrolled around what she knew was the crime scene. Other officers were herding people, already gathered, farther back. She saw two uniformed men still hovering over her dog. Please, God, Emily loves that dog. They'd told her Star had multiple injuries, but they hoped she'd recover. What was taking them so long to get her treatment?

The officer stood up slowly. Thea realized how long he'd been stooped beside her. "You sit tight a minute while we get this information out."

He handed her the tissue box. "I'll be back in a few minutes. Ask anyone if you need something."

"Officer? My name doesn't go out on the Amber Alert, does it?"

"No, Ma'am," he asserted, with a momentary creased brow at the thought.

She nodded, and then he walked away. She didn't want her name out there. Would she be able to remain anonymous? She couldn't think; her mind wouldn't function. She pulled out a fresh tissue and wiped her face. What did it matter? For so long she'd kept Emily's parentage from the world—from the father—it had become a habit. Nothing mattered now except Emily. God, God, God, where was she? Who was the man who took her?

Thea looked out at the scudding gray clouds. She wrapped her arms around herself, trying to ward off the chill of the damp morning—the cold that penetrated her soul. What she desperately needed was a time machine. A do-over. If only she'd taken the time to check the boxes for Emily's other shoes, would the car have already gone around the corner? If only her usual babysitter didn't need surgery, Emily would not have been on the sidewalk with her mother, but safe in her house playing. If only she had stayed home with Emily today, said the hell with everything else. What was so goddamn important? She squeezed her eyes shut, focused on Emily's face, burning it into her mind. She remembered the promise she made on the day Emily was born: to give her all the love she could possibly need. A pain stabbed her heart. She turned around to sit facing front, pulling her feet back into the cruiser. She bent over with her elbows on her knees, her head in her hands. *Please God, don't let him hurt my baby.*

"Ms. Connor, I'm Detective McIntyre," a man said, leaning into the police car where she sat. When she looked up, he went on. "I'm going to do everything in my power to find Emily and bring her home." He enunciated each word. She felt herself grasping at every syllable.

"Excuse me, sir," an officer from the Crime Lab Unit interrupted them. "Ma'am, does this belong to your daughter?" His large hand nearly swallowed one little pink and yellow boot inside a plastic bag.

Thea got out of the car, reaching both hands out for Emily's boot, but the officer pulled it away. "I'm sorry, Ma'am, I can't give this back to you right now. Can you identify it?"

"Yes, it's one of my daughter's boots," she said, raising her hands to her mouth to smother her sob. She began to cry again as the officer left.

After a few minutes, she composed herself, wiping her eyes and nose with her shredded tissue. She looked up at the detective standing beside the car. "I'm sorry. I can't seem to stop crying."

"Don't worry, it's understandable. Just trust that we're doing everything possible to find your daughter. If you're up to it, we have work for you to do." When Thea nodded, he went on. "We need some additional information and some items from your home. I'm going to have an officer drive you there now. She'll stay with you to help make this easier for you, keep you informed of what's going on. I'll be there in a little while, also. Okay? Are you ready to go?"

Thea hesitated, looking toward the group of reporters and cameras outside the yellow tape. When she didn't answer, the detective turned to see what she was focused on. "Right. Don't worry about them. We'll arrange for you to speak with them later."

She frowned and bit her lip. The detective added, "They look like a pack of wolves, I agree, but reporters have been a huge help in finding missing children, Ms. Connor. We want to use every opportunity to find your daughter." He turned and raised his hand. A female officer walked over to them.

"This is Officer Mary Jo Pallino."

"Hello, Ms. Connor," the officer said, looking at Thea with large brown eyes filled with compassion. She wore a dark-blue long-sleeved uniform shirt with a black tie. Her shiny black curls were mostly covered by her silver-banded cap. Thea looked down at the gun handle protruding from the holster on her belt. She couldn't look away. The gun made the nightmare real. She forced her eyes closed and stood still, her arms hanging loose at her sides. She felt as fragile as glass, and was afraid if she moved one inch, she might burst into a million shards.

CHAPTER FIVE

Katherine sat on the edge of the chair in her bedroom suite, her hands clasping her knees. She'd heard her housekeeper carrying Thea Connor's child up to the maid's quarters. She'd held her hands over her ears, but it hadn't drowned out the little girl's cries for her mother.

She looked up when she heard the quick knock at her door before it opened and Dee Reyes entered the suite.

"We did it. We have her," Dee said.

Katherine's body went limp. She closed her eyes. "What does she look like?" Why had she asked that question first? There was so much more to know.

"She's cute. A scrapper, though. Don't think this is going to be easy. It'll take some work to get this one to accept her fate. Still, she's four, she'll come around."

"Does she look healthy?"

"Well, from what I saw, she looks solid. She can sure belt out the noise." Dee's eyes darted around the room as if she couldn't bear to look at Katherine.

A pang of guilt shot through Katherine. What had she done to her housekeeper, such a warm and kind woman? She wanted to apologize. Instead she said, "How are we going to keep her quiet? Someone could hear her and call the police."

"No one will hear her. Your house is too far away from the others. And the maid's quarters are on the third floor. You can't hear her anywhere on the lower level."

"I worry about my parents. They can't go up to Madison's room."

"We'll watch for that. Anyway, the girl will settle down, don't worry. Besides, if anyone could hear her, she sounds just like Madison throwing a fit. Who could tell the difference?" Dee looked up as if she could see the new child through the ceiling.

"We have to do this for Madison. We have to make it work," Katherine said, her voice breaking. She took a deep breath. It was done. Not the way they'd planned, but they'd been forced to move quickly when they realized the child's mother was ready to leave Boston. They couldn't lose track of her.

Now, Katherine just had to keep her head and avoid thinking about the enormity of the horrible act they'd committed. Keep her eyes focused forward on the new plan. On her daughter's future.

"We're doing it for the little miss. It's the only way." Dee's eyes glistened as if she might break down and cry. But Katherine couldn't cry. She felt shattered, guilty, and overwhelmed. She stared at the woman before her. Dee was as shaken as she was, emotional in a way Katherine had rarely seen her.

Dee checked her watch. "Artie should be almost home by now, six-ten, right about the time he's usually coming in with my take-out breakfast." She paused then spoke again with a slight tremor in her voice. "It was touch and go. We didn't count on the dog. We should have. It got a hold of Artie's pants and hung on. The mother caught up with us, but I don't think she saw me, she was focused on the girl."

The warning she heard in Dee's voice made her shiver.

"I sideswiped a car trying to drive away," Dee went on. "I was afraid I'd killed the mother, but she's unharmed. I might have killed her dog, though. I hope I didn't, but I had to pull out fast. The mother ran with us for a good long time. It seemed like forever before I could take the corner and lose her."

"Did you see anyone else?"

"I was too busy to notice, and Artie was down low, holding the little girl. Don't worry. Artie can fix the scratches, and that car won't surface again until it's all over and we're on our way for good."

Katherine didn't move. She could feel the pulse of her rapid heartbeat in her neck.

"When are Mimi and Gramps bringing the little missy back home?" Dee asked.

Katherine rarely let Madison out of her sight now, but she'd needed her parents to take her away until they had the new child settled in. "Not until Sunday night."

"We'll be ready by then. We can do this."

When Dee left the room, Katherine dropped her head into her hands. She'd heard the trepidation in Dee's voice and it frightened her. Dee had always been strong, both physically and mentally. She could work a dinner party for sixteen guests without missing a beat. In the past few years, though, as Dee aged, Katherine had worried how she would manage when Dee retired. Madison's illness made those concerns seem frivolous. The same dependability Dee had shown through the years, handling any job she was given, was what Katherine counted on now. They had entered into an unholy pact. Dee would help save her daughter's life in exchange for a comfortable retirement.

Dee had been her housekeeper for over ten years, serving faithfully through dinner parties, meetings, and special celebrations. She kept the house sparkling clean. Katherine could invite a friend for lunch with no notice, and Dee would produce a fabulous meal. And sing while she did it. She and Artie were of Cape Verdean descent. She loved to cook, not only for Katherine, but also for herself and her husband. She'd come to work loaded down with a big pot of caldo verde soup, thick with kale, potatoes, and Portuguese sausage, or rice pudding with nutmeg, Madison's favorite.

Dee was a few inches taller than Katherine. She was lean and strong from a lifetime of hard physical work. Over the past few years, her hair had turned gray. Her nearly black eyes were deep set over high cheek-bones. Laugh lines gave her face character. Over time, she'd grown close to Katherine and Madison, whom she adored. But it was only when she found out how sick Madison was that she showed how much she loved them. That was the day Dee had colored her hair.

Katherine had been practicing her planned pitch to the housekeeper, but all the words flew from her mind when she saw the ash blond shade of Dee's hair. It had been pouring outside, and when she pulled back the hood of her rain slicker, she smiled at Katherine. "Like it? If I was going to do it, I decided to do it up right. Better than black, don't you think?"

Katherine had stared, and Dee laughed.

They always started the day together over coffee to discuss the list of items for Dee's workday. That morning, there was no list.

"Dee, you've been with me a long time. It's been good for both of us, hasn't it?"

"I knew something was wrong. Are you going to fire me?"

"No, of course not. I need you now more than I ever have."

Dee squinted. "What's wrong? It's the little missy, isn't it?"

"If she's going to get better, I'm afraid I'm going to need some special help." Katherine rubbed her aching right temple. "What I'm going to ask you to do is extremely risky. For both of us. It will have to be our secret, and it will require a great trust between us."

Dee pulled her chair closer and folded her hands on the table. "Do what?"

"We need to kidnap a child," Katherine said, then bowed her head over her tightly laced fingers. When she raised her head back up, Dee's mouth was open, and she was staring at Katherine as if she were crazy.

"God in heaven! You're serious?" she said when Katherine didn't deny it.

"I am. It's the only way. It won't be for long. And we would never hurt her." Tears burned her eyes. "There are reasons why her mother wouldn't let her come willingly."

Katherine's hard swallow was the only sound in the room for a moment. "Believe me, Dee, if there were any other way, I'd never ask you." Her words began to come faster. "And I am only asking. You can say no and we'll never speak of it again." She paused, watching Dee. "Say something."

"I know you wouldn't ask me unless Maddy was really sick again. But—"

"I want you to think it over. Please, take your time. Be certain of your decision," Katherine said, extending her hand across the table to cover Dee's. "I won't think badly of you for refusing. Kidnapping is a serious crime, but it's our only hope." She held her breath. If Dee said no, what could she do?

Dee remained silent, tapping the fingers of her right hand over her heart. After a few minutes she spoke. "I tell Artie everything. I couldn't help you without talking to him about it."

"Yes. I want you to do so. I think we'd need him, too." She bit her lip. "He won't say anything, will he?"

"No. Artie and I would *never* tell anyone something that would harm you or our girl."

"Thank you, Dee. If there were any way in the world I could do it alone, I'd never ask you."

"I—I don't know," Dee said, opening and closing both fists. "I love the little missy, and I want to do anything that would help her. I just don't know. I'll talk to Artie tonight."

Katherine thought she heard a fragment of hope in Dee's voice. "It can't be one-sided. I'll tell you what I need, and you can decide if you can do it. No pressure. If you do agree to help me, I will give you and Artie enough money to retire." They'd discussed more than once Artie's love of the Greyhound races. With a big family, but no children of their own, Dee worried about their future.

Katherine named a figure.

Dee's eyes filled and she rubbed them with her arthritic hands. "Can I let you know tomorrow?"

Three days later, the planning had begun.

The morning dragged on, until at ten-thirty Katherine showered and dressed. She sat at her vanity and began to apply her makeup. Her hand shook as she worked with her eyeliner. She stopped, intertwined her fingers, and rested them on her lap. She had to get over the shock. She whispered a Hail Mary. She would lean on her faith.

She returned to her makeup, her hands steadier. She had to maintain the usual activities. Today she was hosting a benefit luncheon for one of her charities, The Sunflower Children's Center.

The success of the benefit warmed Katherine's heart, but she could hardly swallow the glazed salmon salad. When her friends commented on her edginess, she told them she had a headache. No one questioned her. They were becoming accustomed to the changes in her behavior, probably whispered about her behind her back.

Madison's dire situation had changed her world. Katherine had tried to change with it. But she didn't know how to be this other person.

When she entered her house a few minutes after one-thirty, she felt limp and exhausted. All was quiet. She dropped her purse on the table in the foyer and covered her face with her hands, picturing the little girl in the room two stories up.

Katherine paced the foyer. So much was riding on the little child upstairs.

The private detective she'd hired when she suspected John was having an affair after Madison was born was the smartest thing she'd ever done. Even before they were married John had women troubles. He couldn't help himself; he'd been born a womanizer and what he didn't know instinctively, his father taught him. John was a devastatingly handsome man.

She needed to see the child. She climbed the two sets of stairs as quietly as possible. Not a sound from the room; the little girl must be exhausted, and was probably asleep. At the top of the attic steps, Katherine saw the key in the door and couldn't look away. The locked door highlighted the horror of what she had done.

She knew the child couldn't see her face until they were sure. She tucked her hair behind her ears and rubbed her face with her palms. If this didn't work. . . .

She moved one hand to the key, the other to the knob, and opened the door a few inches to peek in the room. The little girl was in bed, curled up in a ball, sound asleep. Katherine took small steps across the carpet until she was standing by the child called Emily. She was as beautiful as her own daughter. *Madison.*

Merely thinking of her daughter's name caused the weight of sorrow to bear down hard on her chest. How could God allow a child to suffer so? She knelt down, bent over, and lowered her head until her forehead rested on the carpet. She stayed that way until she felt stronger then raised herself up to look at Emily.

The little girl's full lips were slightly parted; long blond lashes rested on apple-red cheeks. Strawberry blond curls framed her face. When Madison slept now, her fair skin became so pale it took on a bluish tinge, the color of skim milk. For the millionth time, Katherine asked herself why. Why *her* daughter?

Even with her knees pulled up, she could see that Emily was taller than Madison, heavier, too, even though she was a year younger. There was a healing scrape on her knee, partially covered by a Spiderman Band-Aid. This beautiful child she had stolen was the picture of hardy good health.

Madison had always been small for her age. Katherine had never thought much about it; she'd been petite herself. But now her daughter's size had taken on a different connotation. The doctor had said small stature was a characteristic of her genetic disease. A disease that would follow a relentless path that even the most loving mother could not impede.

The child stirred, and Katherine quickly dropped back out of her eye level. Emily moaned but didn't awaken. When her breathing was regular again, Katherine rose and stared at the helpless and vulnerable child. She was another woman's daughter. A woman who loved her as much as she loved Madison. Katherine's knees grew weak as she realized how devastated she would feel if Madison had been the child kidnapped. How could she have done this terrible act? She pinched her arm hard. She couldn't think this way. She'd done what she had to do. She would take care of this sweet child as if she were her own daughter.

She walked across the room, stepped out, and closed the door. She turned the key in the lock then ran down the stairs as if the devil himself were chasing her.

CHAPTER SIX

The police car pulled up before the small Boston apartment Thea and Emily had lived in for three years. Thea and Officer Pallino—Mary Jo, she'd told Thea to call her—stepped out of the car. She froze at the foot of the three steps to the front door. It was the last Friday she and Emily would have been in Boston. Only one more class and this had happened. A class in bar exam preparation that wasn't even necessary for her to graduate. It was merely a safety net.

If only she'd skipped the class, stayed on the Cape.

Her knees grew weak. She was trembling and reached for the metal railing. Mary Jo moved to her side. Thea handed her the key that her shaking hand could not control, and then climbed the steps. When the door was open, Thea nearly fainted as her eyes landed on Emily's little red chair, a bright accent in a room filled with shades of brown. She held onto the door jamb, tight enough to turn her fingers white, as she stared into the small apartment, at the packed boxes. So close. They'd been so close to avoiding disaster.

Mary Jo spoke in soothing tones, "Come and sit down. Give yourself a minute."

While the officer went to check the rooms in the small apartment, Thea sat on the couch in a numb heap, at last dry-eyed. Outside the window behind her, she could hear the banter of youthful voices. Suffolk University students walking to class; ignorant of their vulnerability, unaware they were surrounded by a fragile bubble whose flimsy, shimmering membrane could rupture at any second, exposing them to the horror in the world.

Mary Jo brought a kitchen chair into the living room and sat in front of her.

"Okay if I call you Thea?"

She nodded.

"Okay, Thea. First, we'll—"

A heavy knock sounded right before the door opened, and several uniformed officers came in, some carrying equipment.

"Thea, these officers are going to set up the trace for your phones and email, and add some recording electronics," Mary Jo said. "They'll also set up a separate phone line for police use, so yours is clear for any incoming calls. Also, with your permission, the officers will conduct a search of the apartment. It's going to be a little crazy, but just ask me if you have any questions about what's going on."

"Ms. Connor, we need you to give us Emily's dentist's name, address, and phone number," another female officer said.

Thea felt as if she was crawling through heavy fog as she made her way to the kitchen. She couldn't stop the thought, the picture in her mind of why a medical examiner needed dental records. She scribbled the information she'd found in her address book on a sheet of paper and handed it to the officer.

"Thank you." The officer paused then spoke softly, saying, "We need something with Emily's DNA on it. A hairbrush or toothbrush. Can you get that for me?"

Thea felt as if her heart was being ripped from her chest as she handed the officer Emily's hairbrush and toothbrush. She wept as she watched them they carry the items away.

The first time the phone rang every sound and movement in the apartment ceased. Mary Jo had earlier reviewed the trap-and-trace procedure in her soft, gravelly voice. When they gave her the sign, Thea answered the phone. Her heart was banging so loud in her ears she was afraid she wouldn't be able to hear, but she took a deep breath and said, "Hello."

It was the friend who was going to babysit for Emily, wondering where they were. An officer handled the rest of the call, asking questions and taking notes.

In the next two hours, there were moments when Thea desperately wanted to run out into the street to look for Emily. To walk around the neighborhood, calling her daughter's name. Then there were times when she couldn't move under the weight of loss pressing her to the couch where she sat with her head back and her eyes closed.

Mary Jo saved her from losing her grip. She explained everything the uniformed officers were doing. In between, she asked Thea more questions. Sometimes she just made conversation to keep Thea engaged.

"Thea is a beautiful name. You can't believe what my parents did to me."

When Thea focused on the officer's pretty face, she went on. "Okay, I have five older brothers. My parents are devout Catholics. They made novenas to the Holy Family for a baby girl the whole time my mother carried me. They named me Mary Josephina in heartfelt gratitude." She shook her head. "It's quite a burden."

Detective McIntyre came in to interview her. He was very tall so she had to look up to view his serious face. He wore a suit the same shade of brown as his hair. The jacket was unbuttoned. The gold detective badge clipped to his belt was gleaming.

"It's important we keep records of everyone we interview for later review," he explained, as another officer set up a video camera. He extended his hand, gesturing toward the officer. "Ms. Connor, this is Detective Haddon. He'll be working closely with me to find your daughter." The second detective was dark-complexioned. His mustache was a thick shelf over thin lips.

The questions ran together in a repeated sequence: What time did the car stop; how many people were in the car; what color was it; do you remember anything about the plate, the man, his clothes? Then: Where were you going; why did you change your babysitter; who is the person you were going to leave your daughter with; had she babysat the child before?

Once again Thea iterated every single detail she could remember about the kidnapping. She knew from her law studies the first three hours post-abduction were crucial—the length of time before a killer would have done his work. *Emily. God, please keep her safe.*

There were times during the questioning when she crashed, sobbing. Then Mary Jo would come and speak a few words of encouragement to her. When McIntyre asked if she knew anyone who might harm her daughter, Thea broke down. Mary Jo handed her a glass of ice water. She took a few sips, then set the glass down and looked back at the detectives.

Detective Haddon explained, "We're going to change it up a bit here. First, I'm going to give you an important fact: Most of the time, children are abducted by a family member or close friend, not a random predator. So we'll cover Emily's family first."

"Let's start with Emily's father," Detective McIntyre said.

The anger response that always came when she thought of Emily's father surged through her. It felt comfortable, an old enemy that gave her new misery a moment of respite. But she had to focus. The goal was to find Emily, and she wanted to give them all the help she could. She took a minute to collect her thoughts.

"Detective McIntyre, Emily's father has nothing to do with this. He doesn't even know he *is* her father."

He held her gaze, but remained quiet.

Thea filled the silence. "He doesn't even know she exists. I never told him. I never saw him again. It's not him. It's got to be someone else."

She just wanted to scream; to get up and run from this suffocating room. Go somewhere. *Do* something. They were wasting precious time. They had to find Emily!

"Who do you think it might be? Is there anyone who's threatened you? Is there a man in your life who's friendly with Emily?" he asked.

The thought turned her blood cold. Was there? Certainly no significant other. She couldn't think of anyone. Few people in Boston had even met Emily. Thea's schedule was too tight during the week to add visitors to the list.

"Thea?"

She looked up. "Oh . . . no, no one."

Detective Haddon spoke in his low voice. "Did you ever notice any men paying attention to your daughter? Have you seen anyone suspicious, a man who worried or scared you? Maybe someone taking pictures, or talking to Emily?"

"I would certainly notice something like that. I'm about to graduate from law school. I've focused on criminal law. I'm aware of a pedophile's behavior pattern," Thea said, then pressed her lips together. Diane usually took care of Em in their apartment. Thea couldn't afford pre-school for Emily but Diane occasionally took her on outings to parks or stores. She kept an eagle-eye on Emily. Diane would have told her if she'd seen anyone suspicious, wouldn't she?

"Okay," Detective McIntyre said, "we're going to make a list of every-one who's been randomly or routinely in contact with Emily."

Finally, something she could do. But before she could begin to think, Detective McIntyre caught her off guard.

"Thea, before we get started on this, I noticed your reluctance earlier when I mentioned you should meet with the press. It's extremely import-ant to get a statement out to the public. The sooner the better. I under-stand how stressful it can be. If that's your reason, don't worry, it's okay to let people see how distraught you are."

"No, I—I just can't do it right now."

He hesitated. She saw something in his eyes that shocked her. Did he suspect her? *Just great.* She was only making things worse for Emily. But as she watched him, his face seemed to relax.

"Is there someone who can step in for you?"

She tried to think of some friend here in Boston. The people she saw most often were Suffolk University students and professors, but she didn't know any of them well enough to ask for this kind of help. She considered the lawyers at Hebert & Massey where she did paralegal work. Would Will Hebert act as her spokesperson?

Detective McIntyre came to stand before her. A two-inch scar that bracketed the outside of his right eye stood out on his face. He wore his brown hair short. His dark brows arched over slate-blue eyes, oddly opaque eyes that made him harder to read.

"Having trouble figuring out who to ask? It's not an easy job. Do you have a family member who would do it?"

"No. Emily is my only family now."

"How about a distant cousin, aunt or uncle, a relative to speak for you? You'd be amazed how willing people are to step up to the plate when there's trouble."

"No, there's no one."

"One of your friends or an acquaintance you trust? Don't over-think it. Pick someone and make the call." Detective McIntyre raised his eyebrows and looked down into her face. "It would be best if you did it yourself, but it's critical to get the news out there. We need the public's help. Every minute counts."

There was no other choice; she would call Will Hebert. He was a fair man, a great lawyer, tough, and Thea was sure she could depend on him now to support her.

ill was a short, stout African-American man who looked as
gentle as Santa, a trait of which he took full advantage in the
courtroom. He rushed into the apartment dressed in slacks
and a sports coat—which would have to stretch a size up to button—
toting a scarred brown briefcase. He looked at the video camera, the
detectives, and then at Thea. She felt a sense of relief that Will was
involved, in spite of his frown, which made it clear he was already upset
that she had spoken to the police without him.

Will handed his card to Detective McIntyre. Thea noticed the detective
glance at her with an intense expression after he scanned Will's card. He
turned back to the lawyer. "What's next?"

"I think Thea's answered enough questions for now. I'll need time
to confer with my client," Will said, then turned his scowl on Thea.
Her short-lived comfort began to fade as a thought broke though her
numbness: He was not here to handle a press conference; he was going to
represent her. Is that what she wanted? There would be a price to pay for
Will's help, besides money.

Detective McIntyre nodded, flicking Will's card with his thumb.
"We'll talk more later," he said to Thea, then nodded to the videographer.
Thea watched with relief the as the door closed behind them.

Will sat in the chair the detective had abandoned. His back was to the
kitchen, which was filled with police officers. He leaned forward, taking
Thea's hands in his.

"I am so sorry about this. I'm going to do everything I can to help."

"Thank you, Will. I just can't believe what's happened. Why would
anybody take Emily? Kidnap her. For what?" She bowed her head, shaking
it. "Stupid questions."

He squeezed her hands then released them. He put on his half glasses
and took a pen and legal pad from the briefcase he'd set on the floor
beside his chair.

"I'm going to represent you, of course."

"Will, I—"

"You're a smart woman, I know, but you can't handle this yourself."
He scowled at her. "You should have called me right away. You know better
than to talk to the police alone. You're a suspect, Thea."

Before Thea could get in a word in her defense, he got right to business, for which she was grateful.

"Now, let's look at the big picture. Tell me everything that happened. Don't leave anything out. Your feelings, anything you saw, everything you did."

She told her story once again, stopping from time to time to calm herself. At times she broke down. When she described the man who took Emily, rage set in and gave her momentary relief from her helplessness.

Will waited until she finished, then asked her several questions, making notes as she answered. After a pause, he said, "You're a single mom, right?"

Thea pressed her lips together and nodded. "Yes. The detective wants to know the father's name."

She understood the look Will gave her; he was sizing up the ramifications of her statement. "You won't answer any questions that make you feel uncomfortable from the detective or any law officers. Remember, the police are looking at you as a suspect, a given, based on kidnapping statistics. Accept that fact and don't panic. They'll also ask you to take a polygraph test."

"Why would they waste time with me? It's clear in this case someone else took Emily. Several people on Tamerind Street came outside when it happened. They must have seen *something*."

"Maybe they did, but the police will still follow standard operating procedure. You know that, Thea. It feels different when you're on the other side of the law, doesn't it? I advise you to offer to take the polygraph. But not right now. You're too upset, and that can skew the test."

"I'll do it whenever. I don't care. I'll do anything they ask. Time is slipping away and taking Emily with it. We have to do something. I have to help, but . . . they want me to meet with reporters," she said.

"And? You will, of course," Will said, looking at her over his glasses.

"I—I can't do it. I was hoping you would act as the spokesperson for me."

"Why?"

Thea didn't answer. She tried to sort out the swirling thoughts in her brain. What did it matter now if the world knew?

"Thea, what's this about?"

"It's about a horrible mistake, that's all."

"I need to know everything, Thea."

Will would have to keep her confidence, she decided. But she didn't want to tell him. She didn't want anyone to know. "I don't want her father to see me."

"Why?"

She sighed. "Because he has no right to know anything about us."

"Married man?"

"It turned out that he was. Look, he has no idea I had her. He couldn't have taken her."

A muscle worked in Will's jaw. "He couldn't? How can you be sure he doesn't know you had his child?"

His words hit hard. Had she been wrong? "I—I don't know how he could. Are you saying you think he took her?"

"Why not?" Will asked.

"But he couldn't have. He doesn't know she's alive."

"Calm yourself. All I'm saying is maybe you should let the police do their work. Are you afraid of what this man might do? Did he threaten you?"

"No. I'm sure he wouldn't be happy, but, no." Thea stood up, took a few steps. "What are they doing now? I need to get out of here. I have to help find her."

"They're doing everything they should. You can help them later. What we're doing right here is more important."

She sat down again.

Loud voices, police radio spurts, doors opening and closing blended into white noise drowning out their conversation. Still, Will kept his voice low. "Tell me this: Would it put your daughter in danger if he knew?"

Think. Think. Would it? No, not danger. Wasn't her reason for keeping him out of the loop more about her loathing of the man who had used her? Who had paid her off and dumped her? He had been adamant he did not want the child to be born. But years had passed since then. How could she be sure what he might do? She really had no idea how he'd react if he found out that she had given birth to his child.

Thea looked up at Will's stern face. He would go in front of the cameras for her if she asked. Did she want him to speak for her?

It was suddenly clear to her, the answer was no. She would do the press conference in spite of the risk of Emily's father seeing her. She would do everything she could to help Emily. She would go public for her daughter's sake. And she would do it as soon as possible.

"I'm going to do the press conference myself," Thea said, standing up again.

In his quiet, bullying voice, Will said, "I think you need to tell me the complete truth about this before I decide if you should get out there. It won't end this, you know. You'll be hounded by reporters, and you could make a mistake."

"Thank you, Will. But I need to do this. It's the best thing for Emily."

"I hope you're making a good-lawyer decision and not an impulsive, emotional one. If there's something I should know about this man—"

"It's nothing like that. I have to think that part out. I won't do anything until we talk about it. As far as the press conference goes, I know I can count on you if I feel I need help. That's a great relief, really, but just talking to you makes me see this is something I have to do myself."

n Sunday morning, they were ready to take the next step. Yesterday, the kit had arrived by overnight mail at the post office box Katherine had rented and listed under Cruickshank Enterprises.

At the kitchen table, Katherine and Dee read the instructions once again.

"What if they check on our phony Peter Cruickshank to see if he really is her father?" Dee said.

"I'm going to fill out the forms with the names we chose, and hope they don't check. They won't find a record to check anyway, since the names are false. If they do check, they'll probably ask for more information. I'll just put them off, and then I'll have to find another way to get the test done. These forms may just be a way for the lab to have a record of permission on file. I'm not too worried."

Dee nodded. She pulled out the wrapped swabs from the kit. "This is it? It seems too simple."

"It's supposed to be easy. It's just that you have to do a thorough rubbing." She studied Dee's worried face. "Do you think you're up for it? I mean, I can't help you. She can't see me. I could cover my face, but then she'd be frightened, and become uncooperative. You seem to have made inroads with her."

"She's a good girl, but stubborn. It won't be easy. But I've learned how to get around her. One thing I know, she loves chocolate. I've got a Hershey's bar in my pocket." She nodded. "Okay. I can do it."

They climbed the stairs, Dee first, then Katherine. Dee went inside and locked the door. Katherine could hear her speaking. When the subsequent quiet stretched out, she put her ear to the door. She heard Emily say, "No. I don't want to."

Dee crooned on, then, amazingly, Emily laughed.

Soon, she heard the key jiggle in the lock and Dee stepped out.

"Piece of cake," she whispered. "No, a piece of chocolate bar."

Katherine sunk to the floor because her knees couldn't hold her up another second.

"What's wrong? Are you okay?"

"I don't know what I would have done without you, Dee."

"Here, let me help you up. You'll feel better now. It's just a natural reaction, considering how worried you were. Huh! So was I. My hands were shaking like butterflies in a windstorm. But I got it, and little Emmie is eating chocolate for breakfast."

Sunday evening, Katherine's parents brought Madison home, pale and tired, setting off a sense of panic Katherine tried to hide.

"We had the best time, didn't we, sweetie?" her grandmother said to Maddy.

"Mommy, I rode a white pony named Powder!"

"You did? I wish I could have seen that," Katherine said, picking up her daughter and kissing her cheek.

"Mimi took pictures for you. And Gramps fell down," Maddy said and chuckled.

"You promised you wouldn't tell."

"Oops." Maddy covered her mouth with her hand then turned her face into Katherine's shoulder when Gramps hustled over and playfully poked Maddy with his finger.

Katherine managed to convince Mimi and Gramps to leave shortly after they'd arrived.

"I hope we didn't tire her too much," her mother said on the way out the door.

"She's due for a treatment. She's fine. The doctor's very happy with her progress. Don't worry."

Lies. And many more to come before this was over. The doctor had told her only the hard truth: Madison's illness would be unrelenting, a bone marrow transplant the only possible cure. She could still remember his frightening words.

"I'm afraid this is a very serious condition," Doctor Thompson, her oncologist, had said. "I'm going to tell you a little about it, but I'll have the nurse give you more information to review. Fanconi anemia is a rare genetic disease. It leads to what we call aplastic anemia. That's when the bone marrow fails to do its job, which is to make new blood cells. Maddy isn't there yet, which is good. It gives us much-needed, valuable time."

Katherine held up her hand as if to stop the conversation, and shook her head. "What do you mean 'leads to'? Does she necessarily have to get it? Can't you treat her anemia?"

"I think it would be a good idea for you to come in later with your husband. It's a lot to take in, and you must prepare yourself."

She felt a creeping freeze radiate out from her core. "I'm divorced."

"If you're co-parenting, you'll want to bring Maddy's father into the discussion. He should know what's going on, and you'll need the emotional support."

"Wait, wait. You are scaring me to death. What are you telling me? Is Maddy—" She looked down at the two-year-old child in her lap, then back to the doctor. She raised her eyebrows, asking the question she couldn't put into words.

"Let's not get ahead of ourselves. Is your ex-husband local? Are you able to get in touch with him?"

Katherine began to tremble. This was no simple matter. Why didn't he just spit it out? But did she want to hear it? Alone? "I'll call him. He's in the area."

The doctor had made an appointment for Katherine and her ex-husband that evening to explain the disease process in greater detail.

But John hadn't made the meeting. He hadn't heard the discussion on how the aplastic anemia most likely would become leukemia. A bone marrow transplant was the only cure. When the doctor discussed the need for the family to be tested as donors, he explained siblings had the best chance of a perfect match. If not, testing would proceed to extended family including parents, half siblings, cousins, aunts and uncles. Since Maddy was her only child, Katherine had immediately focused on the half sibling mentioned, even though the doctor had said the extended family was less likely to have a solid match.

John had been present for a few of Maddy's transfusions, but he'd depended on Katherine to inform him about her doctor visits and her progress. Since none of the family had been a donor match, Katherine had begun to alter the truth to John and others about Madison's disease progression. A sleight of hand while she'd begun to implement plan B.

Now she took Maddy's hand and led her upstairs. "Let's have a sleepover," she said, while inside she was burning with shame at how blithely she'd lied to her mother. Such a tangled web had to take its toll. What would she have become when this was over?

She sat on the bed beside her daughter. They were watching a DVD, and drinking hot chocolate. Maddy's head began to nod.

"Time to tuck you in, baby."

"No. I'm not sleepy."

Katherine stood up and took her cup. "We'll have more fun tomorrow. Mimi and Gramps tuckered you out." She pulled up Maddy's sheet and flannel blanket then lay down beside her. She traced soft circles with her finger on Maddy's forehead. When her eyes closed, Katherine could count the tiny blue veins in her eyelids, easy to see through her pale skin. Maddy slept, but Katherine stayed beside her for an hour longer. She prayed the whole time.

In the morning, after sleeping twelve hours, Madison's color was improved, so Katherine took her to kindergarten. But she knew time was running out.

After she dropped Madison off at school, Katherine went online and researched transplant centers in Brazil. She knew she couldn't bring Emily to any US hospital. There was a huge risk that someone would recognize her from the news coverage of her kidnapping. She hoped the risk in Brazil would be less than here. The country had multiple well-regarded, accredited transplant centers, but she found one in Sao Paulo that had an added treatment found to increase the bone marrow transplant success rates from 40 percent to 70 percent—an edge Maddy would need.

Next, she researched oncologists who performed BMT, bone marrow transplants, at the center. She chose one and recorded his phone number on a slip of paper. As she folded up the paper and slid it into her jewelry box, her heart was bursting with the hope she would soon be calling this doctor to request his services. Having this hope bolstered her courage. Kidnapping a child was overwhelming. It seemed almost impossible to accomplish. But they'd done it.

Now, the wait.

CHAPTER NINE

It seemed to Thea a sense of dread so heavy she could barely move had filled her body, leaving no room for anything else, blocking even her deepest fears for Emily. She almost felt as if she were asleep, or more like she was close to dying. And in spite of the people crammed into the apartment, she felt isolated, alone. No one could enter this black place of her gloom.

The sound of the ringing phone shot a spurt of adrenaline through her, pulling her out of her near trance. She watched as Mary Jo read the name on the caller ID and turned to her.

"Anne Rimsa?"

Thea jumped up. "It's Annie, my friend." Mary Jo extended the phone and Thea gripped it like a lifeline.

"Annie."

"Thea. Oh honey. I'm here. I'm outside."

Thea's heart was pounding from the rush of the call. "She's outside. Please, can you bring her in?" she said to the officer.

Annie Rimsa was her best friend. They'd known each other since elementary school, had grown up on Cape Cod together. It was Annie's grandmother, Diane, who was Emily's regular babysitter.

She came through the door and sloughed off her rain slicker. Annie, the Gwyneth Paltrow of Cape Cod, was a beautiful sight. She gripped Thea in a bear hug and they both wept together.

"I'm staying in Boston at my grandmother's house," Annie said through tears. "She's still in the hospital and I was sitting with her. When I got back in the car, I heard the Amber Alert. Thea, I can't believe this. Tell me what happened."

They sat side by side on the couch while Thea told her story once again.

"This is terrible," Annie said with fresh tears streaming down her face. She hugged Thea again. "They'll find her, I know it. I'll be right here as long as you need me."

An Information Services officer explained how the press conference would work. They were sitting in a room at Police Headquarters. The press conference would take place outside on the steps of the Tremont Street entrance.

"The Chief of Police will speak. Then he'll call on the lead detective, Detective McIntyre. He'll take questions. You'll go last. All we want you to do is give a short statement. Do you think you can handle that?"

"Yes. I'll do it."

"I understand you will have your friend," he checked his notes, "Anne Rimsa, with you. Can you spell her name for me?"

He followed each spoken letter with the point of his pencil to the name on his sheet. He nodded. "Okay, you'll make a short statement in your own words. Whatever you feel comfortable saying, whatever comes from your heart. People will be motivated to help when they see your face, hear your voice. Just let them know you love your daughter, and ask them for help in bringing her home. Use her name. Tell them something about her personality. Don't mention any details of the kidnapping even if they ask you. They'll have handouts with Emily's picture and a detailed description, but tell them about her in your own words."

The rain came down steadily, as if all the angels in heaven were crying, which delayed the press conference for a half hour. When it stopped the group assembled outside. Thea stood on the steps, shivering. Annie stood beside her with an arm around Thea's waist, supporting her. She looked out at the group of reporters standing before her with microphones and recorders. Behind them were cameramen, television vans, and trucks with dish antennae. Bright lights were aimed at the podium. Flashes went off everywhere like bolts of lightning.

Thea had seen other parents talk to the press on television, but it had never seemed real. They were strangers. Their missing children were simply stories you read about in a book. There was no connection to reality. A gust of wind blew a soft mist at her face, and for a minute, everything seemed surreal to her, as if she might wake up and find the abduction had never happened.

Detective McIntyre broke the spell when he motioned for her to come forward. She wasn't sure she could walk. Annie nudged her forward until she was standing at the podium.

Thea looked out at the pool of faces scrutinizing her with intense curiosity. These were the people who would help the police find her daughter. From somewhere within, she found the courage to speak.

She tightened her grip on the picture of Emily that she held facing them.

"This is my daughter, Emily. She's a happy, outgoing child. We recently celebrated Emily's fourth birthday. She sang the birthday song louder than anyone at her party." Some of the reporters smiled. Thea swallowed and went on. "Her hair is reddish blond, very curly, so it looks shorter than it really is. Her skin is fair. She has a few freckles on her nose." She watched the reporters' faces and knew she was right to speak to them herself. She could see in their eyes that they were going to do their best for her. "Emily loves books. She's very smart. She can already recognize several words."

She had to stop, hold her breath for a minute, and overcome the urge to cry. Annie rubbed her back and whispered in her ear, "You're doing fine."

And then she found she could continue. "Emily's feisty and she's strong. She'll be putting up a fight. Please, help me find her. Look for her in your travels. Maybe in a store or at a playground. She's fearless on the monkey bars. Please, if you think for a second you might have seen her, call the tip line. She's my baby, and she needs her mother's care." Her voice broke. "Thank you all for listening." Tears she'd worked to hold off ran down her cheeks as she turned away from the microphones.

When the detective came back inside police headquarters, he smiled at her. "You did well. How are you?"

"I feel a little better, less numb. It helps to be doing something."

"Good, good. Mary Jo will drive you both back to the apartment." His smile faded. "I'll need to ask you more questions later. We'll set up a time with your lawyer. Get some rest and remember, every resource the Boston Police Department has—and it has plenty—is in play to find Emily. The FBI is fully onboard. If you think of anything, at any time, call me." He gave her a card. "All my numbers are here. Call me even if you just want to talk."

Thea was lying on top of the covers on her bed in the apartment. No one had bothered her. If only she could sleep, but she couldn't. Her eyes felt glazed and gritty. She was as still as a corpse. Was Emily dead? Too much time had passed for a positive outcome. Tomorrow was the first day of June.

She stared at the bulls-eye molding over the closet door, but saw only her daughter's beautiful face. Thea couldn't even cry.

The door opened and Annie's face appeared. "You're awake. Did you sleep at all?"

"No."

"Well, I have a little good news." Annie held up a hand when Thea widened her eyes. "No, honey, it's not about Emily. The vet called. Star's going to be fine."

Thea's small smile felt as if it split her lips. Annie tried to talk to her but Thea couldn't respond. There was nothing to say, and she didn't want to think.

Mary Jo was back on duty today. She came in a few minutes after Annie left. "Thea? Detective McIntyre needs to speak with you."

Thea lifted her head and looked at the officer. "Is there news?" she asked, her voice sounding rusty to her ears.

Mary Jo's expression held pity, which filled Thea with horror. "Did they find—something?"

"No. It's nothing like that. He's been conducting interviews, and he has a few questions. He's sending an officer to drive you to his office."

"How can I leave? What if the phone rings? What if the call comes?"

Mary Jo raised her hand, as if to stop the fear-filled words from tumbling out. "I think it will be all right. But don't worry. I'll be taking the calls myself, and every call will be recorded and investigated."

Thea heard the undertone: It probably doesn't matter anymore. She collapsed back on the bed. "I'll have to call Will."

"He knows that. But he asked if you could both get there as soon as possible."

It didn't sound good, but at least it was a reason to move. She went to the bathroom, washed her face and hands and combed her hair. She avoided the mirror, which reflected a woman she'd never seen before.

Will agreed to meet her at Detective McIntyre's office. Before they hung up, he reviewed some rules of engagement, which Thea already understood.

CHAPTER TEN

"It was your dog's blood on the street, not the kidnapper's, unfortunately," Detective McIntyre began, once he had identified the session. She knew the built-in camera was running. On the way in, she'd seen other detectives watching activity in one of these rooms on a computer screen.

Thea and Will were seated at the rectangular oak table in the cold interview room. Detective Haddon stood against the wall at the end of the table.

"Star," Thea said.

"Excuse me?"

"My dog's name is Star."

McIntyre nodded and went on. "They picked up car paint from Star's collar which identified the vehicle as a 2008 Mercury Marquis. Since we don't have information on the plate, and there are hundreds of these cars in the Boston environs alone, it doesn't give us any immediate answers. But it's a good lead. We'll track down every one of them. We've notified all local, state, and federal law enforcement to be on the lookout for the car. Star also had some threads from the man's pants in her teeth. Off the rack, common brand. But again, it's something to work with."

Thea breathed. Finally, there was some physical evidence.

"I've interviewed several people who know you. Some of whom didn't know you had a daughter." Tim sat back in the chair, looking relaxed and untroubled, but there was an undefined element in his voice. Something cold.

"Who did you talk to?"

"Employees of Hebert and Massey. A couple of law professors from Suffolk."

"Oh. Well, they know me, but not much about me. Those people are not close. They're work and school related."

"Still, it seems odd to me that having been involved with them for a long time, you never mentioned you had a daughter. I mean, women are always chatting about their kids, aren't they?"

Thea bolted upright, ignoring the hand Will placed on her wrist. A rush of deep anger at the horrid injustice of being a suspect in her own daughter's kidnapping surged through her. "Maybe women playing Mah

Jong, or lunching in the Italian north end. But women who are carrying a heavy schedule of classes, working part-time, and raising a child? Those women don't chat, they don't have time." She glanced at Detective Haddon, whose expression gave nothing away.

McIntyre went on. "I can imagine how hard it would be for a woman, a single mom, to make it through law school. But you must have had conversations sometimes. I mean, do you fly out the door the minute class is over? If you speak to a professor, there's never time for a little personal conversation?" He stopped, tilting his head to one side, as if he was waiting for Thea to defend herself. She didn't, and he went on. "Don't you see how it makes this look?"

Will cleared his throat. "Do you have a point, Detective?"

"When you think about it, it seems odd." He went on as if Will had not spoken. "Maybe you were stretched too thin. Or maybe your daughter was an impediment to your career plans. It looks like you purposely kept her out of your life away from home."

Thea sat rigid and tight with her knees pressed together. No. Will knew she had a daughter. So did some of his employees, and a few students. Including the one who was going to watch Emily that horrific morning.

Thea pursed her lips. She would always be the prime suspect. It wouldn't be the first time a mother killed her children for a reason as simple as she wanted her freedom. She knew why the detective was baiting her, though it was frustrating as hell that she couldn't prove her innocence. Still, guilt raised its ugly head. She should have talked about Emily to anyone who would listen, but she hadn't. Was it only because she didn't want the father to find out Emily existed? Or was she so busy with everything else that Emily didn't get the attention she should have?

"If you have something to present, do so, please," Will said.

Detective McIntyre nodded to Will, and then looked back at Thea. "I also spoke with Mrs. Rimsa."

It took her a second to refocus. "You saw her at the hospital?"

He nodded. "She's going to be fine."

"I know. Annie told me. I'm so glad."

"Thea, how well do you know her? How do you keep tabs on what she and Emily do all day? Do you discuss their activities with her?"

"Of course. She treats Emily like a granddaughter. She told me she was so happy to have Emily in her life, because she was sure she wouldn't live long enough to see her great grandchildren." Something in his tone started a pulse throbbing in Thea's neck. *Now what?* Both detectives remained quiet, looking at her. She went on, her words coming faster. "They pretty much stayed home. Sometimes Annie took them somewhere. It was rare that Mrs. Rimsa took Em anywhere but to the park or an occasional play date. And she always asked me first if she could. We talked several times a day on the phone." Thea paused and looked at Detective McIntyre's face, reading something ugly there. "Why? Tell me why you're asking these things," she said, her voice registering at a higher pitch. "Do you think she was somehow involved in the kidnapping? Oh my God. Did I leave my daughter with someone who could hurt her?" Thea leaned forward, clutching the edge of the table.

The detective flipped the pages in the black notebook he pulled from his pocket. He read: " 'It kills me to say this, but there wasn't much affection shown to Emily by her mother.' " He looked up at her, then back at his notes. "Also: 'I was with Emily every day, and I like minding her. But Thea called more often than not to ask me if I could stay longer. It was a lot to ask. I'm nearly sixty-six. But I stayed. I can't tell you the number of times I was the one who tucked in the little girl.' "

She couldn't stop the tears that stung her eyes. She had no idea Mrs. Rimsa felt that way. Thea hoped the woman hadn't given Emily any indication of her feelings. "I . . . I can't believe she said that. I hardly spent any time with Mrs. Rimsa. How could she know about the way Emily and I interacted? She showed up each morning, and I went off to work. I came home, and she left. We talked on the phone in between."

"This is upsetting to you."

"Of course it is. You know it is. And you can stop trying to build it into something it isn't. There must have been some people who witnessed Emily's kidnapping from the condo windows along Tamerind Street. Why aren't you working on that?"

"We have corroboration of your account of the events."

"So?" Thea raised her hands, palms up, as if in supplication.

"Witnesses can't tell us if the kidnappers were acting alone."

Will interrupted. "I think that's enough. Unless you have something substantial to offer, Thea's answered your questions sufficiently."

Detective McIntyre continued to stare at Thea. Haddon leaned against the wall, his hands in his pockets jingling keys or coins.

McIntyre had caught her off guard, exactly as he must have planned. She had no defense on the tip of her tongue. What else had Mrs. Rimsa told him about her? She had to convince him of her innocence, or he would stop looking for Emily's kidnapper.

"Are we finished?" Will asked.

Detective McIntyre stood and looked down at Will. "I strongly suggest you advise your client to take the polygraph."

It was still going wrong. *She* wasn't the suspect. They were wasting time interrogating her. They had to find Emily. What horror might be happening to her while they were investigating Thea instead of the kidnapper? Anger swelled inside her. She was losing her grip.

"Listen to me, Detective. You're on the wrong track," she said, her voice strong. "I'm not involved. I *will* take your damn polygraph, but please, get busy finding my daughter. Find the man who took her!"

Again, Will reached over and put a hand on her arm. "Stay calm. We're leaving now."

She stood up, and the detective handed her his card. "Call me with your available times, and we'll set up the exam."

Back at the apartment, Thea and Annie sat on the edge of the bed. The door was closed. Thea told Annie about the session. She watched her friend's expression grow furious. "How could he think you had anything to do with this? Good Lord. Anyone could just look at you and see how much you're suffering."

"I could never hurt her, Annie. You know I couldn't."

Annie moved closer and put her hand over Thea's. "Of course, I know. You couldn't possibly hurt her. You don't have a mean bone in your body."

Thea said, her voice low and breathless, "If he thinks I'm guilty, he'll never find her. Oh God. Where is she? I just want to hold her and kiss her cheeks and tell her how much her mommy loves her." Thea rolled back onto the bed into a fetal position and cried.

Annie went around the other side of the bed and lay down facing her friend. She draped an arm over Thea's shoulder and looked into her eyes. "Have I ever told you my grandmother is a dick?"

Thea looked at Annie. Suddenly they were laughing. Guffawing. Thea nearly choked, she laughed so hard.

Annie pointed. "Snot alert." She went out to the bathroom, still chuckling, and got a wet washcloth for Thea to wipe her face.

"Oh Annie, what would I do without you?" Thea scrubbed her face with the cloth and smiled at her friend. "So now you tell me?"

"Yeah, she's a total dick, but she would never hurt Emily. She's just got this lord-it-over-the-world complex, and no one can live up to her lofty standards. I remember once my mother told me that nothing she did was ever good enough for her mother. Tough woman, but she keeps a damn clean house."

They both laughed again. Mary Jo opened the door and peeked in. Her face was smooth, amused. "Everybody sane in here?"

They both smiled, and the officer retreated again, leaving the room.

"I was afraid of what would happen when my grandmother instructed me to leave the hospital room while she talked to the detective. I had a bad feeling she was into her judgmental, self-righteous state. But if I tried to prevent him from talking to her, it would have seemed suspicious."

"You have an idea what she told him, don't you?"

"Yeah. She bent my ear about how you don't show affection to Emily like she does. I'd tell her how difficult it was for a single mom, and how hard you were working to make a good life for Em." Annie's eyes were gentle as she looked at her friend, but Thea was aware of her worries about the implications of the interview.

"He wants me to take the polygraph. Will says to wait."

"Are you going to wait?"

"I'll see how long he thinks I should forego it. I know being an emotional wreck can influence the test. That's why Will wants me to put it off. But I can't wait too long. I can see how not doing it puts the focus on me, not on the man who took my daughter."

"What about Emily's father? Did you tell the detective about him?"

Thea raised the washcloth, folded it up, and held its coolness against her swollen, burning eyes. "I'll have to tell him." Thea's eyelids grew heavy. Maybe if she could sleep a little her head would clear. "I think I hate that man."

"John?"

"No—yes, that's his name, but I mean the detective." Thea felt the heaviness of impending sleep, and succumbed to the fading of conscious thought.

CHAPTER ELEVEN

Thea woke to a cacophony of chirping birds, which told her she had slept through the night for the first time since Emily's kidnapping. She got out of bed and stood by the window. She felt a new strength, and with that, a resurgence of indignation. She'd fallen into a deep hole filled with overwhelming sorrow. And self-blame. If she'd only held on to her daughter's hand tighter, run after the man sooner, gotten the license plate, maybe Emily would not have been taken.

She would never know. One thing she did know was that she had to get busy. She had to clear her mind of what-ifs and make a plan. What the hell was she doing; was she doing enough? This morning she was scheduled to meet with reporters again. After the press interview, she had an appointment with Will at his office. Thea would give him Emily's father's name to pass on to the police. Her delay was only making the detectives suspect her more. She grabbed some clean clothes and headed to the shower with new resolve.

The second press conference was easier. At ten o'clock, she was ushered into Will's' office. He sat in his high, smooth-leather desk chair, known around the water cooler as "the throne."

Will had made up his mind—without an answer from Thea—that she would join his firm once she passed the bar. But she'd decided to accept an offer on the Cape, where she preferred to live and raise Emily. The fact that he would be difficult to work with had also played into her decision. Will bulldozed any opinion he didn't agree with, especially if it came from a woman.

She began the session with him by stating her intention to take the polygraph sooner rather than later.

"Why? I thought we discussed the perils of taking the test too soon."

"I want to do it because Detective McIntyre is wasting time with his suspicions centered on me instead of focusing on the kidnappers. You heard him."

"You should have expected that. He's following SOP. He doesn't really have anything, so he was baiting you. But adding a bad polygraph *could* make him suspect you. Give yourself more time."

"How much time?"

"We'll know when you're ready. Nothing will be lost by delaying the test. The police are proceeding with the investigation. They're not waiting for your poly results. Let it go another few days. What about the father?"

"I'm going tell Detective McIntyre who Emily's father is. First I'm going to talk to him myself." Thea returned Will's direct gaze.

"This is *exactly* why you shouldn't take the polygraph. You're making decisions based on emotion, not intellect. It would be legal suicide to talk to the man who might be involved in the kidnapping. What if he did it and you gave him a head's up. You think you're a suspect now? And what if he's dangerous? No. Very bad idea. Let the police do their job. And let me do mine. It's time to tell me about him."

Thea cringed. She knew he was right. She wasn't thinking clearly.

"Thea, tell me, who is this man, Emily's father?"

She nodded. "John Henry Warren. He's a lawyer—"

"Warren? From one of the most prestigious law firms in the country? US Senator Warren's brother? No wonder you were reluctant to divulge his name. Warren has no idea Emily is his child? God, the man must be sixty, Thea, how did this happen?"

"No, not that Warren, the son, John Warren, the third."

"Oh, I see. I wasn't aware his son was a lawyer, too. Doesn't matter. They are a very powerful family. I hope this detective can handle what's about to befall him. These guys will eat him alive. They are very connected. Okay, I'll let the detective know the father's identity."

It was a relief to Thea that the decision was made. She wished she could be there when they told John he had a child. But she was sure that giving the police Emily's father's name was the right choice. Thanks to Will.

When they first heard about Emily's abduction, the employees of Hebert & Massey banded together to help. They solicited the assistance of a local office store that graciously provided all paper products and the use of their machines to make up posters of Emily. The law firm employees were in the process of distributing the posters around Boston. Before she left the office, Thea made a point of thanking everyone, accepting their kind words and a few hugs. As she walked back to her apartment, she thought about how many people were performing quiet acts of kindness to help find Emily. She was overwhelmed with gratitude. For the first time since the abduction, she felt more positive.

She came into the apartment through the backyard to avoid the reporters.

Mary Jo's only news to report was that the tip line had heated up after Thea's morning press conference.

Thea brought her computer into her bedroom, closing the door to drown out the incessant ringing phone. There were so many calls from reporters, psychics, and cranks, the sound no longer set her nerves zinging with hope.

She sat on the comforter with her back against the wall and settled the computer on her lap. She needed to research John Warren. A shiver ran though her as she waited for her Google response. What if John had taken her daughter—his daughter? Is that why he hadn't surfaced with Emily's kidnapping all over the news? Thea took a deep breath. She still couldn't buy it. He'd never tried to hide his feelings about her pregnancy. He'd been adamantly against her giving birth.

She lifted her fingers from the keyboard, remembering the last time she saw John.

She'd just stepped out of the T station when John broke through the rush-hour throng and enveloped her in a hug. "Let's skip the meal, we'll just eat each other," he'd said, nuzzling her neck.

"John, we have to talk," Thea said, tamping down her body's lightning-fast reaction to his kiss.

He pulled back and looked at her. "What's wrong, Thea? You look upset."

"Not here. Can we go for coffee?" she asked, glancing around at the crowd. When her eyes landed on John again, she knew he knew. In that second, everything changed.

He didn't say a word as he led her to his car and opened the door. It was a luxurious Acura TL sedan. She sank into the soft leather passenger seat. He got behind the wheel and turned to her. Thea was wondering why he'd never picked her up in this car. Why he always had her meet him somewhere along the T line.

"Jesus, tell me you're not pregnant," John said, his voice pleading.

"How did you know? Do I look it?"

"No, but you look worried." He stared out the windshield while he bounced his closed fist on the steering wheel. "Damn it, we were having so much fun."

It was as if biblical scales fell from her eyes, but she still couldn't accept it. This was their child, conceived in love. "What are we going to do?" she asked, her heart knocking against her ribs as if to escape her chest.

"What everybody else does: Get rid of it." He turned and took her hand in his. "Listen, you can get an abortion. Nobody needs to know. Money's no object."

She stared at him, a slow freeze creeping through her body. "What are you saying? I can't do that. This is our baby, alive in me."

"Thea, I never made you any promises." He looked away from her.

"So what?" She had to force the words through her throat, which was aching with her attempt to hold back tears. "It's your child, John."

"Look. It was sex—no, it was *terrific* sex. If you were looking to rope me into marriage, you've got to understand, that was never my intention. I'm sorry if I misled you."

She slowly pulled her hand from his grasp. She was in love. In mad, passionate love with a man who was *fucking* her. For such a smart girl, she sure was stupid. A quick review of their courtship told her he was right. He'd never intended a long-term relationship. She was not in his echelon. He was rich, she wasn't. They lived in two different worlds. As much as she hated to, she began to cry.

He'd never moved. He'd sat stoically until she composed herself. "Hey, I'm sorry, Thea. I thought you were having fun, too."

It was only when his *wife* called that she found out John was married. The woman was hysterical, saying Thea was a slut and a home-wrecker and a whore, and to leave her husband alone. That if Thea ever hoped to practice law in Boston she could think again. Her family had the means to destroy her.

It had taken her hours to stop sobbing.

When Emily was born, Thea had vowed John would never know about her, never share in the joy of his daughter. With Hannah's help, she'd managed without his child support. She'd kept the knowledge of Emily's birth from him. Now, all that seemed foolish. She shook her head. How had she gotten this so wrong? She'd wasted too much energy and emotion over the circumstances of Emily's conception, detracting from the joy she had brought to Thea and Hannah.

She clicked on the Google search results, read about the successes of some of John's cases and articles he'd published. Next, she checked for a Facebook page and found one. His new wife, Sondra, had posted their whole life on their wall. *He's married a second time.* Thea felt the old anger and rejection rise as she scrolled through the page.

John and his new bride had arrived home from their honeymoon three weeks before Emily's kidnapping. Sondra posted every detail of their marriage ceremony, and a complete itinerary of their European trip, replete with photographs. The very public display of their life supported her belief that John had not kidnapped Emily.

Thea turned off the computer and slipped down to lie stretched out on the bed. The old loathing of the man tightened her jaw and sped up her breathing. She was happy she gave his name to Will. The police needed to rule out John in order to concentrate on other areas. She wondered what would be on his Facebook page after the police questioned him. A small frisson of satisfaction went through her.

How would John react? Would he revel in the notoriety of being the unknown father of a kidnapped child? She remembered his enormous ego. Was he imagining the new business the attention would bring? Or would the truth of his relationship with her hurt him? What image would he have as a man who had fathered a child he knew nothing about?

She didn't give a damn.

She must have dozed. Annie was back, Thea could hear her talking. And something else. A happy, doggy whine. Star was home! Thea opened the bedroom door, and Star rushed in, with Annie behind her.

"The animal hospital called before I left this morning and said she was ready to come home. I wanted to surprise you," Annie gushed happily.

Thea wrapped her arms around Star's neck and dropped kisses on her soft head. "Oh puppy, I'm so happy you're home." She looked up at her friend to say, "Thank you for bringing her."

Star pulled out of Thea's embrace and began to sniff around the room, then went out and into Emily's room, which was no longer sealed. She moved through the small apartment, her nose to the ground like a vacuum cleaner, stopping to greet the officer in the kitchen. Thea put out her food and water while Star supervised all the activity in the small home, but she didn't eat or drink.

Her fur was shaved with the skin stitched in several places, and she moved with unusual caution. Thea had no idea how badly Star had been hurt. The veterinarian report listed broken ribs, a mild concussion, and multiple lacerations resulting from her fight to save Emily. After a few more minutes of tolerating Thea's petting, Star walked into Emily's room and lay down next to her bed. She released a long sigh. Thea interpreted the sound to mean the dog was settling in for as long as it took to have Emily home again.

octor Thompson, Maddy's oncologist, called a few minutes before four p.m. "Are you sitting down, Katherine?"

"Oh my God. What is it?"

"It's good news. The variation in Madison's HLA, which has been making it so difficult to find a donor, is present in her relative's HLA. That is a very good thing."

She couldn't speak. There was more. Her hand gripped the phone so tight, her fingers were white.

"Are you there?" He chuckled.

"I'm here."

"The match isn't perfect, but it might be the best we'll find." He paused. "Katherine, there's a good chance this donor match will work. You're allowed to be happy right now."

As they talked on, she worked hard to keep her story straight; to remember to breathe. She was walking a high wire, woven of lies, and any misstep could bring her crashing down.

She amazed herself at how calmly she listened as Doctor Thompson went on about the wonder of finding a 'needle in a haystack.' Finally, he was ready to sign off. "Let's see, it's June fifth, we'll need time to do more testing and get everything organized. Madison may need another transfusion before you leave. Meanwhile, go celebrate with your daughter, Katherine. We'll talk more later."

She felt like her chest was in a vice; she could hardly squeeze out the word goodbye. When she hung up, she couldn't catch her breath. She walked around the conservatory, making tiny hand claps and taking nips of breaths that were part laugh and part cry.

She'd seen Doctor Thompson in his office yesterday. He called her in after he'd received a call that one Emma Cruickshank's Human Leukocyte Antigen, HLA, results were pending.

The detailed lie she'd told him was: She'd hired a company who researched extended family members for donors. They had found a distant cousin, Emma Cruickshank, whose father agreed to have her tested as a possible donor. The lab they'd used would send the results of her HLA testing directly to Dr. Thompson. If by any wonderful chance this child was a donor match for Madison, they would have the transplant done in

Brazil. The young child's mother was deceased, and her father worked on an offshore oil rig and couldn't take time off to bring her to the United States.

Doctor Thompson seemed surprised, but not suspicious. He said he'd get an answer about the quality of the match back to her as soon as possible. Katherine hadn't stopped shaking the whole way home. In between whispered Hail Marys, she had pleaded in a soft voice, "Please, God, let it be a match."

Now, God had answered her prayers. She couldn't tell Madison, or anyone else but Dee. She checked the clock. Since the time in Sao Paulo was one hour ahead of Boston, she still had time to call Doctor Cabral. She went to her bedroom, pulled the slip of paper with his number from her jewelry box. She tucked it into her pocket. Next, she settled Madison in front of one of her favorite TV shows. She poured a glass of red wine for herself, and carried it to the phone in the conservatory.

She was finishing her second glass of wine, and Madison was playing in her bath, when the doctor finally returned her call. By then Katherine was quite relaxed.

Because any reason to bring two children to Brazil for a transplant that could be easily done in the US would be suspicious, she told her lie to Doctor Cabral: The donor was an American child currently living in Brazil with her father, who worked offshore in the Santos Basin. Doctor Cabral agreed to take Madison as his patient and perform the bone marrow transplant, if the BMT center approved the match.

For the first time in a long time, Katherine slept all the way through the night.

This morning, she'd called Doctor Thompson and given him Doctor Rodrigo Cabral's information.

She was bursting with joy, anxious to tell Dee as soon as she walked in the kitchen door.

"Emily's a match!"

"Praise God! I can see that all over your face. Oh God. Little missy." Tears rolled down her cheeks and she pulled a tissue from her pocket. They hugged each other for the first time in their relationship.

"I've been working this out in my head. I'm not sure I ever believed it would work, but I started to plan anyway," Katherine said, as she poured them both a cup of coffee, and then sat down at the table. "We're going to call her Emmie from now on, since it's closer to Emily if we make a mistake, and it works for Emma, too. If she fights it, tell her Emily is her special name that only her mommy can use." Katherine jumped up. "Maybe we should write this down?" She answered her own question before Dee could reply. "No, we can't have anything in writing. We have to keep it in our heads."

"Settle down, Katherine. We'll get it all straight." Dee took a sip of her coffee.

"I'm just so excited." She took a deep breath. "Okay. From now on, Dee, only speak Portuguese to her. Children pick up languages quickly, so Emma Cruickshank will soon have enough Portuguese words to make her year of life in Brazil a more plausible story."

They brainstormed for an hour and a half on what Katherine prayed was a logical premise to allow her to take Emily to Brazil under the name of Emma Cruickshank. Since a mother would normally accompany a child undergoing surgery, she told Dee she'd decided to list Emma's mother as deceased. Dee liked Katherine's idea of the father as an employee of an American oil company, working on the Santos Basin drill platforms. It would make it feasible that he couldn't come to the transplant center himself, but would allow Katherine to pay for a nurse he hired to be with her.

"I have to go play tennis. Keep going over it and see if it holds together. I'll be back right after the game," Katherine instructed the housekeeper.

The door slammed behind Katherine. She asked, "Is everything all right?"

"Everything's fine. Your friend brought Missy home. I gave her lunch and she's having a nice nap now."

"Oh, good. I hated to play tennis, but people are beginning to wonder out loud about me. It didn't help that I played so badly. I'm such a wreck."

Dee was folding laundry at the kitchen table. Her face scrunched up in worry as she listened to Katherine.

"They're wondering about you because they remember what happened when you got divorced," Dee said. "You can't let that happen again. You have to keep your nerve. You have a lot of work to do. Right now, you have to be sensible when you make the call."

"Yes, I know," Katherine said, then bit her lip as a spurt of fear shot through her.

"Go do it. Get it over with," Dee said.

Katherine went up to her bedroom on shaking legs and made the call. She'd jumped the first hurdle when he answered at the number she'd found for him. They spoke briefly. She hung up, and wiped the sweat from her palms onto her tennis skirt.

Dee was sitting at the kitchen table with her hands folded. "How'd it go? Is he going to help?"

"We didn't discuss anything over the phone. Obviously, his time in prison hasn't set him straight. He seemed eager for my business. He agreed to meet me this afternoon."

"Did he remember who you were?"

"I think so. If the meeting runs late, will you be able to stay longer?"

Dee nodded. "You just settle on what you're going to say and all. Quiet yourself. You have to do a good job. Without him we're lost."

Katherine closed the double doors of her room. She flopped down onto her bed, heedless of her still sweat-damp tennis clothes rubbing against the silk duvet. She lay on her back and raised her hands to her head, tangling her fingers in her hair.

The lies rolled around in her overstressed brain. Again and again, she searched for inconsistencies. She turned on her side, sliding her hand under the decorative pillow. She needed help from the computer hacker to make the lies work. He was the only hope she had. This man could make the documents she needed to pull off the transplant that would save Maddy's life.

He was a criminal himself, but would he turn her in to the police when she laid out her plan? She pulled her knees up close to her chest and wrapped her arms around them. She had no other way to pull it off. She had to take the risk. God help her, there was no other way.

Once she was settled in the booth, Katherine checked her cell phone. It was on. The battery was charged. Dee would call if she needed her. She looked around the bar. It was already noisy at three-thirty, with people sitting around the horseshoe-shaped bar, chatting and laughing. She chose the Irish pub for the meeting place, where she'd had lunch once, because the lighting was dim and the walls were covered in dark wood paneling. When the server appeared, she ordered a glass of white wine.

She'd dressed in jeans and a loose t-shirt she'd found in a thrift shop, white with a faded image of Mount Rushmore. Her hair was pulled back under a baseball cap, and she wore no makeup.

She recognized him right away. His light brown hair had receded from his forehead, but he was still a striking man with his square jaw and hazel eyes. He was coming right to her booth, with no slowing or hesitation. He must have remembered her, too, in spite of her bland appearance. He slid in and nodded at her. He then waited.

Katherine had a Bachelor's degree in Childhood Education, a Master's in Education, and had been working on her Doctorate at Harvard before Madison was diagnosed. She was a smart woman.

She'd learned a lot about cyber crime when she'd interviewed this man before his trial. It was research for her Master's thesis question: How has the education system failed some very intelligent children?

By the look of his expensive clothing, he was doing quite well for himself. That fact assured her of his dependability and the quality of his work.

"Thank you for coming. Um . . . we met before. Remember?"

His demeanor remained cool. "I remember."

"I'm sorry it didn't go well for you."

"I had a lousy lawyer." He shifted in his seat. "I don't have a lot of time."

Katherine was squeezing the soft edge of the bench cushion under the table. She began her prepared speech. "A friend of mine needs help. Her daughter is very sick and needs a transplant. There's a donor who can save her life, but the child's mother won't allow it."

"Hey, what are you asking? I don't want anything to do with this." He began to get up, and Katherine panicked.

"No. Wait." She put a hand out as if to hold him there. "It's not what you think." She took a breath once he was seated across from her again. "It's only paperwork. She needs documents. You know; an easy fix."

The server returned, and he ordered a Guinness, and then stared at Katherine long enough for her to feel like running from the bar. Finally, he asked, "What kind of documents?"

"A lot of them. A passport, birth certificate. The treatment has to be done in Brazil. It's not easy to take a child out of the country now." Her glass was dripping condensation. She couldn't take a sip.

"No kidding." He pursed his lips, making Katherine fear she'd lost him.

"So, you probably know," she said in a rush, "she'll need permission from her father on a notarized form. I have to have proof of at least ninety day's residency for him, a gas bill or other similar bill. The mother has to be deceased. She'll need a death certificate. All of these false documents have to be good enough to stand up to authentication at their consulate before they'll issue a visa."

"Is that all?" Sarcasm tainted his words. He took several swallows of his beer.

"I need you to access the donor's real medical records, change the name to Emma Cruickshank, and alter the birth date. They have to be sent to both the US and Brazilian oncologists." She slid an index card toward him. "All the information is on the card, including the full names for the mother and father. Use the fake address from the gas bill if you need it for the medical records. The records must *appear* to come from another doctor in Brazil with a backed-up email address. Can you do all that?"

"Wow, lady, do you have any idea what you're asking? How deep you're getting, in a really bad place?"

Katherine leaned toward him. "Can you help me? If not, just tell me and I'll leave." Below the table, her hands were gripped so tightly together there was no blood getting to her fingers. They began to tingle. *He's going to say no.* She didn't really expect him to do otherwise. Even if he agreed, would he change his mind when he recognized Emily's name? What if he went to the police? She was faint. If he said no, she didn't know where else to turn to save her child.

He sat still, looking at her through half-closed eyes. Katherine knew he was choosing the words he would use to tell her he wouldn't do it.

"I'll consider it. But lady, this won't be cheap. What you're asking for is a huge risk for me. It's going to set you back some big bucks."

The air whooshed out of her lungs. "I'm prepared to pay."

"I don't think you are, but give me a few days to line up the preliminaries. I'll need the whole scenario, and you'll probably have to provide additional information." He looked down at his hands, his eyes blinking rapidly. "First, to hack her medical records, I'll need the child's real name, stats, and her doctor's information."

"I don't know the name of her pediatrician," Katherine said, then covered her mouth with a hand. This was a detail she'd missed. Were there more?

He took several more gulps of beer then wiped his mouth with the napkin. "Do you know where she was born? The hospital record will list the pediatrician."

"Cape Cod Hospital, but she lives in Boston now."

"The hospital records are probably digitalized, and should include a Records Release to have the child's records sent to the new doctor. If I can't find the information, I'll let you know." He paused. "When do you need this?"

"As soon as you can do it."

"I'm going to have to bring in some help. Some of this I don't do."

"Can you trust these people?"

They had kept their voices low. When he laughed loudly at her question, a woman at the bar looked over. He leaned closer to Katherine. "No one in this business trusts each other. But I've worked with them before, and for the right amount of money, they can be counted on."

He slid out of the booth, dropped some cash on the table, and promised to call her on the pre-paid cell phone he passed to her. He instructed her to use only the name Dirk when she addressed him.

When the door closed behind him, Katherine went to the ladies room and threw up.

CHAPTER THIRTEEN

Thea leaned her back against the elevator wall, both hands grasping the railing behind her. She struggled to keep her emotions in sync when her world had just collapsed around her feet. Will had informed her an hour ago that John did not keep the appointment Tim had set up to interview him. The police were looking for him. How could she think John's disappearance did not have something to do with Emily? She had to push these thoughts out of her mind, calm herself before taking the polygraph on the fifteenth floor.

She was scheduled to meet with Will after the polygraph test. By then he should have more information. She attempted to control her breathing. She'd waited long enough to take the test, and she was ready. Until this new worry had cropped up.

The polygraph examiner was all business. He looked to be in his fifties, someone's father, husband, a nice ordinary man with thinning hair and a boring tie.

An hour after she was strapped up and answering questions, Thea broke down and cried. By the time the examiner released her, she knew she'd failed the test.

She stood in the ladies room holding a wet paper towel over her face. How could she screw up something so important? She looked at her watch and confirmed she had to move fast, or she might miss her appointment with Will. The day was turning out to be a disaster.

When she arrived at Hebert & Massey, Will was about to leave.

"I can't talk long. I'm on my way to court. Tell me quickly, how did it go?"

"I started worrying that John disappeared because he had Emily. I tried to calm myself enough to take the polygraph. But I couldn't."

"Collect your thoughts, Thea. You didn't take the poly?"

"No. I mean I couldn't relax, and I know I didn't pass it."

A sigh from Will said it all: You should have waited longer. But he didn't say it out loud.

Her normally logical brain was muddled by fear and anxiety, and she wasn't thinking straight. Now she was sick with worry that John had taken Emily. What did she really know about the man who fathered her daughter? She knew he was a liar, a philanderer, an egotist. During their time together, he never spoke about his family's wealth or standing. Later, when she was alone and pregnant, she'd had time to learn about him. Learn every-thing except what she desperately needed to know right now. Was he a bad or dangerous person? She *had* to know.

"I have to go see the detective. I'll never rest unless I know what he found out about John."

"You mustn't go alone."

She agreed to have one of Will's associates, Jason Brown, accompany her to Tim's office.

At the police station, Detective McIntyre kept them waiting. Thea sat gnawing on her bottom lip. The lawyer sat beside her, reading a brief.

Finally, the detective leaned out the door. He studied Thea for a moment then said, "Come on back." He led them to an interview room and turned on the video.

"Detective McIntyre, I have to know what you found out about John Warren," she said once they were sitting down, and then, to her complete surprise, she cried again. *Damn.* It made her so angry to lose control, but the day had sapped all her bravado. She was just plain spent. Jason asked her if she wanted to postpone the interview. She didn't.

"Sorry, Detective McIntyre. I just had to let off a little pressure."

He waited until she finished blowing her nose. "It's easier if you call me Tim. Now, tell me why you're here."

"I've been so worried that John might have taken Emily. And it probably skewed the results of the polygraph I just took. I should have told you about him earlier." She took a deep breath. "Have you found him?"

"It would help us if you told me more about John Warren and your relationship," Tim said, ignoring her question.

"Hold on. I need a moment with my client," Jason interrupted.

A few minutes later, they resumed the interview.

Tim leaned back in his chair, and Thea saw the toes of his shoes poke out on her side of the table. He was tall and substantial and stalwart. He suspected her, but he was clearly professional.

She told him the bare bones of how she and John met, and how their relationship ended.

"Why didn't you want to disclose this information?"

Jason whispered instructions in her ear.

"It wasn't that. I was sure John Warren didn't know about his daughter. And that's how I wanted it to remain. I've taken measures to keep it that way."

"Why didn't you want him to know?"

"Because he made it clear he didn't want her when I told him I was pregnant. He didn't even care whether or not I wanted her. He just wrote me a check to cover the abortion." She swiped away the helpless tears. "I couldn't end her life, so I went home and gave birth to my daughter. It was love at first sight." Thea remembered the joy of those first moments. "I was so happy I'd made the right decision. I never told John she was born. I didn't want him to have a thing to do with her. The check he gave wasn't just for the abortion, it included a large *payoff*. I used the money for law school."

Tim hardly moved while she spoke, and he never took his eyes away from her face. He was like a computer, receiving information without emotion or reaction. Then he sat up straighter and nodded. "When did you see him last?"

"That night. In 2007, August-something."

"Have you been in touch with him at all since?"

"No. I told you, in no way did I want to talk to him or see him. Ever!"

"You never considered asking him for child support? It couldn't be easy being a single mom and attending law school."

She could feel anger redden her face. "No. As I said, I wanted nothing from him. I managed law school with help from my mother and scholarships. I worked, too. John was not needed or wanted."

The interview had backfired on her. She'd received no answers to her questions; instead, she'd bared her soul. And now she was being dismissed. It was impossible to read what Tim thought about her story. Probably decided that she was bitter. She wished she could have answered his questions with equanimity, but she'd reached her limit of restraint for the day. She must look like a crazed lunatic, too, after such a harrowing day. Thea raised a hand to her hair, but let it drop to her lap. Why would she even care how she looked?

The police would tell John he was the father of the kidnapped child. Tim wouldn't hide his suspicions. What if they hauled John in for questioning? He would be furious. Thea knew how dirt stuck. If it was reported that a member of a family as important as the Warrens was being questioned about a kidnapping, it could harm their firm. Thea didn't care. If there was one iota of a possibility that John had anything to do with

Emily's abduction, she would go on television herself and blast that news to the world. She looked up at Tim who was watching her. She had to leave the matter in his hands. She pushed back her chair and stood up. "Please let me know what you find. I have to know."

"We'll be in touch."

He had told her nothing. She would go home and listen for every ring of the phone until he called. The wait would be torture.

CHAPTER FOURTEEN

When she got home from dropping off Maddy at school the next morning, Katherine sent Dee to the drug store to buy what they needed to take the next step. While she was gone, Katherine went to the attic to meet the child they'd abducted.

She climbed the stairs, unlocked the door, and stepped into the attic room. With shaking fingers, she locked the door behind her. In her heart, she didn't want to meet this child. But she couldn't avoid it. The plan wouldn't work unless she bonded with the girl. Dee had done a good job. Now it was Katherine's turn. She couldn't let herself think of what it meant that the child would now know her abductor.

"I'm your Auntie Kay. Please don't be afraid. I want you to be happy here with us."

The child stared at her with huge eyes, nearly violet blue.

"You see all the wonderful toys and books we have for you? And such a lovely room."

Tears filled the girl's eyes. "I want my mommy."

"I know, dear. And you'll be going home before you know it. My goodness, this is just a short visit to your cousin's house."

Emily's face remained fearful, but Katherine could see a tiny glimmer of hope dawn in her eyes. Only it couldn't last. She'd be with them for a long time. A wave of guilt swept over Katherine. What kind of person could abduct a child and watch her suffer like this?

"I don't want to visit. I want to go home. Please take me home now."

Katherine moved closer to the bed. "Who's this?" she said, picking up a stuffed green frog.

Emily raised her hands, and Katherine gave her the frog. The little girl squeezed it in her arms. "It's Froggy," she said so low, Katherine could barely hear her.

"What, sweetie? What's his name?"

But Emily wouldn't answer. She began to cry. Katherine knelt beside the bed and put her arm over the child and frog, felt the child's body go rigid. "No, don't cry." Katherine's own eyes filled. What had she done? This little angel was loved by her mother, who must be suffering so much. "I promise you, I'll bring you back to your mommy. I promise." The words felt like a knife piercing her heart.

The child began to get up as if to leave.

"Not yet. Not right now, sweetie. There are a few things we have to do first. You have to be a brave girl for a little while, but then it will all be over, and you'll be back with your mommy."

The little girl's eyes seemed to burn right through to Katherine's soul. She could feel the heat searing her inside. It was too much. She stood up and hurried to the door. Katherine was going to lose it. She rushed out, relocked the door, and clambered down the steps. She had to get away, didn't want the child to hear her cry. It would only make matters worse.

Dee was coming up the stairs from the first floor. She took one look at Katherine's face and rushed to her. "What is it? Is the child all right?" The older woman placed a strong arm over Katherine's shoulders.

"She's okay," Katherine murmured.

"You scared me to death. What happened?"

Katherine couldn't contain the emotion as her tears overflowed. She bowed her head and ran her fingers through her hair. "We did an awful thing to her and her mother."

"We won't hurt her. And we don't have a choice, now, do we? It's for the little miss."

Katherine nodded. "Are you ready?" She wiped her tears away with the back of her hand then took a deep breath.

Dee showed her the package. "Same as I use. Works good."

They climbed back up the attic stairs.

Katherine bit her lip, turned the key, and opened Emily's door. Dee waited behind her. They went in and Katherine relocked the door.

The child was sitting on the bed, her round eyes fearful, and her arms in a strangle-hold around the neck of her adopted stuffed frog.

"We won't hurt you, honey. Everything is going to be all right," Katherine said, slowly approaching the child. She held a hand out behind her to warn Dee to stay put. "Don't be afraid."

Emily's eyes followed Katherine's progress, but she didn't move, except to press her cheek to the frog's soft head.

Katherine knelt down beside the bed looking at the poor heartbroken and frightened child. Realizing what she about to do pushed Katherine to the edge of hysteria. Before she could stop herself, she began to sob. Then Emily began to cry, scooting across the bed away from her.

Dee came over and placed a hand on Katherine's shoulder. "Stop it now. You're scaring the child. She thinks we're going to hurt her." Dee spoke a few words of Portuguese to Emily in a soothing voice.

Katherine rose, more composed. She smiled at Emily. "I came to ask you to help me."

Emily didn't move.

"You see, I have a little girl like you. She's five years old. Her name is Madison, but sometimes we call her Maddy."

Emily looked back and forth between Katherine and Dee as she slowly scooted off the bed and backed into the corner of the room.

"Maddy has a princess castle." Something lit up in the child's eyes, and Katherine pressed her advantage. "It's a big castle with three princesses who live in it. Would you like to play with it?"

The little girl appeared torn, but then she nodded. After a few moments, Katherine extended her hand, and Emily slowly moved toward her. When she put her small hand in Katherine's, she thought she would break down again. This daughter of another woman was reaching out in trust to the person who had kidnapped her. The guilt was cutting her breath short, but she couldn't break down and frighten her again. They had to get through this.

"First we have to do something else, and then, if you're very good, Dee will bring the castle to your room." Katherine led Emily into the bathroom.

"We have to cut your hair, sweetie."

Emily raised her arms over her head in protection of her hair. "No!"

"Don't try to bargain with her. We just have to do it fast." Dee was fumbling with the scissors, her hands shaking. "Get a towel around her."

Emily began to scream. "Stop! No!"

Dee leaned over and put her face close to Emily's. "You have to be quiet like I taught you. Be a good girl. We won't hurt you, little one."

But Emily continued to wail as Katherine held her and Dee cut off the long red tresses. Katherine tried to comfort her, but Emily thrashed about and screamed through the ordeal. The act finally finished, Katherine released her. Emily, her chest heaving with stuttering gasps, knelt down on the bathroom floor, littered with her curls, and tried to scoop them up.

Katherine shook all over as she tried to pull the child up into a hug. "We can't do the color now. She's far too upset." Emily was slapping at her, trying to get free to pick up her shorn locks.

Dee shook her head. She eased Emily close to her and began to undress her with gentle but firm hands. "She won't trust us again, and she's not going to get any better. We have to do it quickly then we'll comfort her."

Katherine turned on the tub faucet and adjusted the water temperature.

"Almost done, little one. Don't cry anymore. Your hair will grow back in no time," Dee assured her, then lifted a kicking Emily into the tub. All three were soaking wet in seconds. Dee turned to Katherine. "You get the color started. I'll go get the castle." She said something to Emily in Portuguese, loud enough for her to hear over her weeping, then hurried out of the bathroom.

After a few minutes of sitting in the warm water, Emily stopped fighting. She allowed Katherine to wet her boy-cut hair and rub in the bleaching agent. Emily stopped crying, except for some intermittent dry sobs. She became docile as Katherine counted down the minutes listed on the directions.

She could hear Dee's heavy breathing when she entered the bedroom carrying the castle.

"Dee, come into the bathroom." She noticed the tinge of panic in her voice. This lack of reaction from the child was more unnerving than all the screaming and weeping.

Dee stood in the doorframe. "What's wrong?"

"Look at her. Do you think she's all right?"

Emily didn't move. She was growing as pale as Madison.

Dee ran her fingers through Emily's pixie-cut hair. "It's done. Rinse her quick and get her out."

Katherine dried Emily, who stood like a ragdoll, and dressed her in clean clothes. She carried her to the bed and nestled the frog close to her, but Emily didn't seem to notice. She lay on her side, pale and listless. Her eyes never focused on the castle at the foot of her bed. She continued to stare straight ahead.

"Oh my God, what's wrong with her?"

"I don't know. Maybe she's just worn herself out," Dee said, pressing her fisted hands to her chin. "I'll go make her some nice cocoa. She loves that, and it'll bring her right back."

CHAPTER FIFTEEN

The next morning, Thea carried a cup of fresh-brewed coffee to the couch. Her muscles lagged, as if she'd spent the night in the gym instead of her bed. The rain had awakened her during the night, and she couldn't get back to sleep. Before she went to bed, Will had called to tell her that John had gone fishing. *Gone fishing.* Nothing exciting, he just went on an outing and missed his appointment. According to Tim, he'd taken a spot on a charter on short notice and wouldn't be back for two more days. Tim would meet with him then. She'd lain in bed for hours wondering what John would have to say.

The apartment was eerily quiet now that the police officers were gone. She turned around on the couch to gaze out the window. The grass was wet and steaming where the warm morning sun hit it. She frowned. Three purple irises were blooming beside the top step. She'd been lost in another world and hadn't noticed them until now. Thea had bought the bulbs last fall, but never took the time to plant them. Mrs. Rimsa must have planted them with Emily. Thea smiled. Emily was a born gardener, like Hannah. The bright blooms looked out of place in the weedy lawn, next to the crumbling cement steps, and rusty railing. The apartment had been a necessity, never home sweet home. It was the antithesis of the cottage on the Cape, scented by gardens of flowers, surrounded by fresh air sweetened by locust trees, pines, maples, and washed with salt water breezes. The cottage called to her, but how could she leave this place without Emily? Thea rubbed her face with both hands. *Please, God, bring her home.*

Annie came into the living room, carrying her bag. "I'll be back late tonight, probably around eight."

"Annie, don't bother. I'll be all right. You have to work."

"I don't mind. I'll get caught up at the office, get some clean clothes for both of us, and be back tonight. Maybe I could stay here now? My grandmother's feeling better and I'm starting to annoy her." Annie grinned. "And vice versa."

When Annie left, Thea put down her cold coffee and continued her musing. She may *have* to go home without Emily, as much as she couldn't bear the thought. Her apartment was probably already rented to someone else, since she had given notice months ago. Even if she could find another reasonable place in Boston, it might be difficult financially. She now had bills to pay for the cottage, too, with no money coming in. Still, she'd find a way to hang on forever if it would help bring Emily home.

She watched a large UPS truck navigate the narrow street, lined with parked cars, then took a deep breath and stood up. Nothing mattered except Emily. There was still no sign of her anywhere. Thea decided she should stay in Boston. There might be a way she could help by being here. She would check with Will and the detectives. Her mind went round and round.

Thea felt a gray pall threatening to descend on her. She couldn't give in. She had to get out, couldn't stand this prison another second. Hebert & Massey employees had put aside a stack of new Emily posters for her. Thea had told them she wanted to personally distribute them to store fronts around her neighborhood. Today she would do that.

The vet said Star should walk daily, so Thea took her along. The Boston sidewalk shimmered under the unusually hot June sun. The familiar acrid odor of exhaust assailed Thea's nostrils. She looked down the street, bustling with pedestrians. "Come on, Star. Let's get to work." Thea would place the Emily posters in any agreeable neighborhood shops, and around Suffolk University, starting on the busy stretch of Cambridge Street.

Her heart lurched when she saw her daughter's face on posters already displayed on the street's lamp posts and telephone poles.

"This is your daughter?" the owner of a pizza restaurant asked, wiping her hands on her apron before taking Emily's poster. She stared at the picture a minute then looked at Thea. "I'm so sorry. Of course I'll put this in the window. Do you have extras? Know where people pay attention? In the bathrooms."

The proprietor of an upscale antique shop was a tall man with white hair. He looked at Thea with such compassion she had to hold back tears. He reached out to shake her hand. "I'm Peter Goodpastor. I've seen you on the news, Ms. Connor. How are you managing?"

"Not very well, I'm afraid."

"I lost a son—from cancer, not kidnapping—when he was only six years old. He had leukemia. That was a long time ago. Now things have changed, and a youngster with leukemia has a good shot at living." He shook his head. "Sorry, you don't need to hear this. I didn't mean to go on about my son. It's just that it's something you never get over. I hope they find your child." He glanced around his shop. "Give me two of these. I'll put one in the window, but I have a lot of regulars coming in to check new stock every week. Those are the people you want to target. They live in the area."

He went over to a decorative brass easel with an old oil painting on it. He set the painting on a nearby chair, and set the poster in its place. Then he moved the easel, positioning it so anyone coming in through the door would be face to face with Emily.

A man in the hardware store patted Thea on the shoulder with a big hand gnarled from arthritis. He nodded. "I'm sure the boss would be happy to hang this for you." He looked at the shop window, and Thea noted the area had little room between all the signs and posters already there.

"Can't think of a better time to clean this up." In five minutes he'd cleared a large area of the plate glass window, then hung Emily's poster.

"I'll be watching the news. They'll get the bastard. We got the best damn police department in the country. When they get him, I hope he fries. You keep your strength up, Mrs."

When she arrived at Suffolk University, a large sign inviting everyone to a candlelight vigil for Emily lifted her spirits. But only a little.

After another two days had elapsed, Tim came to the apartment to report on his meeting with John. She was surprised to see his sport coat glistening with raindrops. She didn't seem to notice the weather these days.

"You talked with him? What did he say?" Thea asked as he lowered himself into the kitchen chair that was now permanently stationed in front of the couch, and pulled out a small recorder.

Tim took a breath. "Mr. Warren was clearly shocked at hearing he was the father of your child. As a matter of fact, he refused to accept the fact."

"He denies being Emily's father?" Of all the things she expected to hear, this had never occurred to her.

"Yes, but he was also very angry. He accused you of being a gold-digger, his words, and he attempted to tarnish your character. He denied giving you any money."

"You can double-check that."

He nodded. "Once we explained the child was Emily Connor, the victim of a recent kidnapping, he redeemed himself." Tim pressed his lips together and lowered his head, but maintained eye contact. "I doubt very much John Warren had anything to do with the kidnapping."

She didn't realize how desperately she'd clung to the hope that John was involved in Emily's abduction. The letdown, topped with John's demeaning of her character, made her light-headed, but her anger kept her upright. She sat back, leaning her head on the top of the couch. "I can't believe this. Are you sure he wasn't lying? He was damn good at it when I knew him."

"As a matter of fact, when we first told him your name, he couldn't place it."

Thea clamped her teeth together, partly out of fury, but also to keep herself from saying something she'd be sorry for later. How could he not remember her? It wasn't about ego, and it wasn't about how memorable she thought she was, this was about Thea being pregnant with his child. How many women he'd charmed out of their panties told him they were pregnant, for God's sake?

But even if John had heard about Emily's kidnapping, would it necessarily occur to him that Emily was his child? It was five years ago they'd parted. She'd had a check for an abortion in her hand. Connor was a common name in Boston with its large Irish population. And even if he saw her on television, would he recognize her? She'd seen her reflection. She'd been wearing her hair pulled away from her face. Her eyes were permanently swollen from crying every night in her sleep. She didn't have the heart to put on makeup. She had no resemblance to the hot babe he'd taken to bed five years ago.

Thea caught Tim's expression. She sat up straight. "Oh, now I'm the one under the microscope. So, am I telling the truth? Do you think I lied about John Warren? Picked someone with big bucks to hit up for child support?" Her voice was rising. She knew she was fast heading to another loss of control. She pressed two fingers to her lips, hard.

"Hey. No. I don't think you're lying," Tim said with his arms extended in front of him, palms outward, like a cop stopping traffic. He lowered his deep-timbered voice. "I think you are a mother whose daughter is missing, and you're living on the edge."

He was patronizing her. She had to make him see her logic. "It's just that . . . I never expected this kind of reaction. I mean, if someone you were so close to—" She shook her head. "Never mind. But where does this leave Emily? Right now, it would almost be better if he had taken her. At least we'd have a suspect."

"We'll be doing a thorough investigation on him. Check him out,

---

and the people close to him. But I don't want to give you false hope."

"Okay." Thea looked down at her hands while an uncomfortable silence filled the room.

"I got the polygraph report. You didn't exactly pass it."

"Oh, no. I told you I probably didn't pass it. I wanted to take the test as soon as I could. I knew you suspected me, and I'd hoped it would help. Will suggested I cancel the test after he told me about John being missing, but I thought I could put it out of my mind."

"You should have listened to your lawyer."

She stood up, looming over him. "I'm not guilty of anything." She felt like smoke must be coming out of her ears. "Stop worrying about me and find my daughter."

Tim shook his head. "I'd like you to repeat the test." He stood up, clearly planning to leave. Thea felt conflicted. He always seemed to make her angry, yet she also never failed to feel hopeful when seeing him because she knew he was working on finding Emily.

"Wait, what now? What are you going to do to find her?"

"We will follow up every tip, we will investigate even the remotest possibilities, and we will work tirelessly until we find your daughter. And anytime, day or night, you want to talk to me, call." Tim pulled out his wallet and handed her a card. "It has all of my numbers on it. Okay?"

"You've already given me several cards," Thea said and looked up at him.

"Thought you might have lost them. Make use of it."

CHAPTER SIXTEEN

"Dee, someone's at the door. Can you hear me? I'm going to open the door. All right?" Katherine called from the top of the stairs.

Katherine loved her big house. She'd bought it after her divorce. Moved back into Boston and started over. It had six bedrooms, seven with the maid's quarters where Emily was now locked up. There was a living room, dining room, library, kitchen, conservatory, and eight bathrooms. That's not counting smaller areas like the butler's pantry, the walk-in food pantry, the garden room, the nursery attached to the master bedroom. It was a mansion you could get lost in. In fact, Madison loved to play hide and seek in the house.

A distant 'go ahead' reached her, and Katherine descended the stairs to open the front door. Without a greeting, John Warren stepped past her, went through the foyer and into the living room, where he stopped and turned.

"John?" she questioned with a frown. "Madison's not here, she has morning kindergarten, remember? Anyway, you're supposed to call first if you want to see your daughter."

"I know she's not here. I need to talk to you. How is she?" John moved to the fireplace and leaned against the mantle, facing her. Katherine wasn't fooled by the nonchalant pose. He was electric, sizzling with taut nerves.

"What's wrong?" she said, then covered her mouth with her hands. Could the doctor have alerted him to Madison's worsening condition?

It had been easy to lie to John. She'd told him the same lie she'd told her parents: Maddy's treatments for the anemia were maintaining her health. She was not in any immediate danger. Even if she reached the stage of aplastic anemia, there were other treatments they could employ. In the very remote possibility Madison might, some day in the future, need a bone marrow transplant, they would cross that bridge if they came to it. Everyone close to her had been tested for a donor match, but only in case.

Katherine had barely been able to face the truth herself. Acknowledge that the disease was incurable. It would evolve to aplastic anemia. Then worse.

John rarely asked questions. Though this worked well for Katherine, the doctor was concerned that she would become too stressed by handling the situation alone. She worried that one day he might take it upon himself to speak to John directly.

"No, no. It's not about Maddy. Sit down. There's something I need to tell you." He pushed off from the mantle and folded his arms across his chest.

Katherine moved backwards and dropped onto the couch. *Not about Maddy.* She sat back and tried to relax her tense muscles.

"There was a time when we were married that we were fighting a lot. You were completely absorbed with Madison, and I was confused about our future." He shrugged his shoulders. "Anyway, during my summer clinic, this woman—she'd been coming on to me for some time—seemed to sense my vulnerability and, well . . . she seduced me. It only happened once." He paused, the muscle in his jaw jumping. "Then she came and told me she was pregnant. I just handed over the money for the abortion she wanted, and that was that. It was the easiest way to end it, whether I was the father or not."

Katherine stared at her lying ex-husband, worrying where this confession from his past was going and trying not to show her concern. The air conditioner whispered on, and goose bumps rose on Katherine's arms. "So, you had sex with another woman during our marriage? Not a surprise, John."

He walked a few feet in a small circle then faced her again. "I'm telling you now because the police are going to be calling soon."

As if she were slammed by a huge wave, Katherine jumped up, sputtering, "The police? Why?" *Dear God. Do they suspect me?*

He was too absorbed with the telling of his story to notice her reaction. "Everything isn't about you, Katherine. This woman, I didn't even remember her name until the police told me, she's accusing me of being the father of her child. She never had the abortion, apparently."

So he hadn't known about his child. She'd been right. The woman was careful to keep her daughter's birth from him. Katherine should have expected that the woman would tell the police about John. Oh God, another factor she'd missed.

She couldn't let him know she was afraid, so she affected anger to cover her fear. "A paternity suit? I don't know why you're even telling me about it. I don't want to discuss your lurid past. I lived it, remember?"

John looked up at the ceiling. "Jeez, Katherine. It's impossible to talk to you. You're so bitter. I'm here in consideration for you and Madison. I didn't have to come. I wanted to explain this to you before you got hit with it by the police. Do you want to hear me out or not?" He moved his hands to his hips.

She did want to hear; she had to know. "I'm sorry. I guess this is just one more insult to our relationship. Go ahead and tell me the rest, I won't interrupt." Her voice sounded strong enough, she thought, but she hid her shaking hands.

"There's no paternity suit. It's about who this child is. She's the one in the news, the kidnapped four-year-old girl." John narrowed his eyes at her.

Did he suspect her? Her heart rate soared. "I—I've heard about her."

"Anyway, I've convinced the case detective that this woman never even told me she was pregnant, and I have no reason to believe I'm the father." His eyes darted to Katherine and away. "Besides, I was in New York, speaking at a conference in front of a hundred lawyers the day she was abducted. So I'm hoping this will blow over quickly. God damn, this is all I need. Just getting my career back on track with the Nelson win and this comes along. Great headlines: Rising star attorney embroiled in child abduction case." He belted the top of an upholstered chair with his fist.

Katherine experienced a relief so profound she felt dizzy. She bowed her head a few moments to regroup. She should have known. John was so lost in his own predicament he'd never think to point the finger at her. She watched him sit down; heard him sigh.

"Everything's not about you, John." Katherine threw his words back at him. "And her name is Emily. It's all over the news." His ego infuriated her as much as his lack of compassion for a child that, as far as he knew, could be his daughter.

"I know. I know." He ran a hand through his thick sandy hair.

"I still don't understand why the police would focus on me. It has nothing to do with our relationship."

"Because they'll complete their investigation of me, and they'll be talking to everyone I'm associated with. Shit, this could set me back years. Don't tell any of your country club gossipmongers a word of this, understand? I just wanted to let you know." John rubbed his hands together and sighed again. "You don't think much of me, I know, but I really didn't want you to be blindsided and embarrassed any more than you have to be." He rose to leave.

The police are coming. Katherine got up and walked behind him to the door, trying to sound normal. "Thank you for letting me know."

John opened the door then turned back to her. "Look, I'm sorry about this mess. You didn't do anything to deserve this." He stepped out and loped toward his car in the driveway.

Katherine closed the door and leaned against it. Little did he know how much she deserved this 'mess.'

From the beginning, she had always been able to tell when John was having an affair. Even the first time. When she became suspicious and went through John's bank statements, she'd found a large check with Thea Connor's name on it. She'd hired a private investigator. He told her the woman was pregnant, and had moved away. He'd sent her a copy of the hospital record when the child was born. John never knew any of this.

At that time, it wasn't a consideration for her to divorce her husband. She'd never let on that she knew about his affair. But she did something so totally out of character; she was still ashamed when she thought about it. She'd called Thea Connor, demeaning and debasing her. Even threatening her future as a lawyer. Katherine's only defense was that she was out of her head over the possibility of losing the man she loved with all her heart. And that they had a new baby, Madison. If he left her for someone else, she thought she would die.

Later, the investigator told her the woman had kept the baby. Katherine was worried sick that she would contact John, and he would find out that she had known about the woman and her child all along. She was surprised that Thea Connor never made any attempt to contact him. Now Katherine regretted calling her and being so ugly. Why would Thea agree to help her child after that?

The day after Katherine had seen the bruises on Madison's body, in her desperation that the disease was taking the next step, she'd called Hannah Connor, Thea's mother. Hannah had left a forwarding number on her phone. Katherine called it and reached her at a nursing care facility. She'd been sympathetic to having Emily tested. She'd told Katherine, in her fragile, low voice, that her daughter still harbored an unhealthy anger for both John and Katherine, but promised to do her best. She thought having Emily help Katherine's daughter might be healing for Thea, too.

Katherine's optimism had soared. She'd been sure Emily would be a match. Hannah was going to see Thea the next weekend.

But Hannah had died before they spoke.

This was the time Katherine hit her lowest point. Unless a match came in the eleventh hour, there were no other options left. If she'd asked Thea to have her daughter tested, and she'd said no, she would have known immediately who kidnapped her child. Katherine had made the bold decision not to risk her daughter's life on a chance.

Katherine held her hands in front of her and watched their tremor. The police would be calling soon. Or would they just come to the house? What if they already suspected her? John's innocence in the matter was obvious in his self-preservation obsession. She didn't have that advantage; she would have to convince the police she never had knowledge of the child at all.

She stumbled back into the living room and collapsed into a chair. How could she do this? She'd never fool the police. Emily would have to go back home. But she couldn't give her back, she wouldn't. Maybe she could hide her somewhere else? No. Too risky to move her. Someone might see them. Emily had to stay upstairs. They would have to keep her quiet at all times in case the police came. Would they want to search the house? Not without a reason. But what if they asked?

She went to the bottom of the stairs and called up to Dee.

"What did he say? You look like you're going to faint," was Dee's response.

Katherine related the conversation to her as they walked back to the couch and sat down.

"We'd be fooling ourselves if we thought the police wouldn't want to interview you, once the woman told them your ex-husband was the father. They'd have to. They're going to check out everyone around him, like he said."

"How could I not have thought about that?" She pressed her hands to the sides of her face. "This is a huge mistake. Is there anything else I'm missing? I have to review everything. Be absolutely ready when the police come." Katherine looked at her housekeeper, holding a duster loosely in her lap. "Aren't you worried?"

"Of course I'm worried." She spoke in a soothing voice, and Katherine realized she'd nearly been yelling. Dee continued, "We have to be ready. But we're already doing what we should. Emmie stays locked in her room. She doesn't cry anymore. She's always asking for her mommy, but I have her convinced it won't be long before she goes home. She's having fun learning to speak Portuguese. Smart as a whip, that one."

"All right. We'll continue with our plan. And consider what we can do better. We also need a plan B in case they want to search the house. You could take her down the fire ladder—"

"They won't search unless they find cause. And then they need a warrant. I've seen that on *Law & Order.* Anyway, it sounds to me like they're coming to make sure your *ex-husband* didn't do it. How about you let them think maybe he did? Then, if you act nervous or afraid, the police might assume it's because you think he might be guilty."

"No. What I'm doing is bad, but it's not meant to hurt anyone." She looked up in time to see the frown on Dee's face. "I know. Don't think I don't realize how many people I'm already hurting."

"There's a reason, don't forget. It's a very small undertaking for the child. Then it's over for her and you'll get her back to her mother. It'll be worth it to save the little missy."

Katherine, calmer now, said, "Why do you always call her that?"

"Since I read her the rhyme, Little Miss Muffet. She loved that. I must have read it to her a hundred times," Dee answered.

Katherine smiled wider.

"That's better. You've got to try to relax. Your nerves could get us in real trouble." Dee patted Katherine's hand. "Now, what do you want me to do when they come?"

Katherine stood and paced while she thought. "I think you should do something she's used to. Do you read to her? Or, you could do her Portuguese lessons."

"What if the police come when I'm not here? What will you do?"

What would she do? What if Emily called out as she still did some-times, when Dee wasn't there? She clicked her fingers. "I'll warn her. I'll tell her there's a bad man who might—she's already afraid of Artie. I'll tell her if she ever hears a man's voice in the house to hide under the bed and be quiet as a mouse." She sat beside Dee.

"I don't know. She's been scared enough. Most likely they'll come in the daytime. I'll stay with her the whole time. Just in case, how about I come earlier and stay till later at night? Just until they arrive, then we'll go back to normal."

"Of course. That's a good plan. I'll pay you extra. Yes, that will work." Katherine stood and turned to fluff the chair cushions. "We'll devise a signal. Something I could call out to you when they're here."

"Then I'll go up and stay with her. Keep her busy. Make sure she's quiet."

"Yes," Katherine said, moving the lamp on the end table slightly to the left. "I'm so glad you're here with me, Dee."

"It works out all around, doesn't it? You know how I love the little missy. That's what we have to remember. We're doing this for her." She wiped her hands on her apron, looked down at her feet. "So, I'll be here longer and you'll pay me extra. We can work out how much later on." Dee took her duster and headed for the kitchen.

Of course it was also about the money. Dee had never been shy about asking for a raise. She'd had other offers so Katherine had never hesitated to give her what she asked. She was worth every penny. As she aged, she'd talked more about the money Artie had blown at Wonderland Park in Revere, betting on the greyhounds. By the time the state closed down the park for good in 2010, their retirement fund had been nearly depleted. Artie was seventy-three, and had recently been laid off by Sears. Probably, Dee had told her, because he told anyone who would listen that he couldn't bear to stand around. He'd been active all his life in construction, and he still played in a summer softball league. His bad habits and bad luck had given Katherine the courage to approach Dee for her part in this.

It was obvious Dee was worried that Katherine's nerves could bring the whole thing crashing down when the police were there. But this was better. She could handle this; she was a good actress. She'd had experience keeping secrets before. If only she was sure they were only coming to talk about John.

She climbed the stairs, stepped into Madison's room. She sat on the bed, freshly made up with ironed lavender-scented sheets. The room was full of imported dolls, a miniature kitchen, a princess castle, a computer and TV. Expensive clothes filled her bureau and closet. The room was lovingly put together by Katherine and a much-in-demand interior decorator from Boston. Everything the privilege of wealth could provide. But none of it could keep her daughter alive. And Katherine would sell her soul for that if she could. Maybe she already had.

CHAPTER SEVENTEEN

She parked illegally in a resident-permit area on Tamerind Street. The street was so short, Thea was sure she would be able to see a meter maid or police car in time to plead her case. She didn't even care if she got a ticket, her job here was more important.

Looking down the street, she suffered an instant replay of Emily's abduction. She leaned over and placed a hand on the car's front fender. Acid was swirling in her stomach, making her nauseous. It didn't help that she hadn't eaten more than a couple of power bars all day. Thea stood and gulped air. In a few minutes, she felt better. She had to look at what she was doing as positive, something done for Emily. Maybe someone who lived here would remember the one bit of information that could help locate her daughter. Thea had come to realize the intuitive kindness of people. So many had reached out to help her. She was confident the residents of Tamerind Street would answer her questions, take home a photo of Emily, and keep a vigil for her.

It was nearly four when the first car pulled in and parked in the townhouse lot. Thea ran over and startled a young woman who was pulling a baby out of its car seat. She jumped with the baby in her arms when she turned and saw Thea.

"I'm sorry; I didn't mean to frighten you." Thea held out one of her papers. "This is my daughter Emily. She was kidnapped on this street on May twenty-seventh." Thea watched the woman shift her child closer to her chest then wiggle the fingers on one of her hands. Thea put the paper into the woman's clasp.

"I wonder if you're familiar with the kidnapping case? Maybe you saw something? She was taken in a black Mercury Marquis. Have you seen such a car around here?" Thea clamped her lips together realizing the woman couldn't get a word in if she tried.

"I'm sorry. I haven't. I moved in recently so I didn't see it happen but I saw you on the news. I'm really sorry." She began to move past Thea, the paper fluttering in her fingers.

"Will you please read the information and keep an eye out?"

"I promise and I'm sorry, really." Her car lock beeped and she pocketed her keys as she rushed up the walk.

She won't do a thing. She just wants to escape. As Thea fought off a sinking feeling building in the pit of her stomach, the woman turned and called out, "Is there a number to call if I see anything?"

Thea smiled. "Yes, it's there. Thanks so much!"

People were, for the most part, interested. Most hadn't seen the abduction but a few had seen something. A couple in their forties carrying briefcases stopped when Thea approached and questioned them.

"Yes, we were home that morning. We heard your cries for help and went to the window, but we didn't get much of a look at the car. My wife called 911, and I ran down to help. Someone was already with you so I got into my car and drove around. I wish I could tell you I saw something. We've already told the police this." He rubbed the back of his neck like it pained him. "I can't tell you how sorry we are."

One man was downright creepy. "This is her?" he'd said, not raising his head from Emily's picture. "She's a pretty one. You can see why somebody would take her." Thea had snatched back the paper, which surprised the man. "Hey, what's the matter with you?" he said as Thea hurried away from him.

She'd passed out eighteen of the photos. Back at her car, Thea removed the ticket from under the windshield wiper, gasping at the amount. "Oh, crap." She got behind the steering wheel and tossed the ticket onto the dashboard. So much for keeping an eye out. What else could go wrong?

A police car pulled up, blocking her way out. The female officer got out and walked to the driver's window. "Step out of the vehicle, please."

Thea groaned but complied. "What's the matter, officer?"

"We've had a complaint. Are you the one passing out flyers on the street?"

"Is that illegal?"

"You've apparently bothered some of the residents here."

"Bothered, how? By asking them to look for my kidnapped daughter?" Thea's voice rose with her anger. "Tell me, officer, is that a crime? Don't I have enough trouble in my life that I have to be arrested for *bothering* people?" The tea kettle was about to whistle.

"Okay, settle down. Show me what you're passing out."

Thea took a breath then leaned into the car and grabbed a bunch of flyers. She stood up and handed them to the officer, who read every word then handed them back to Thea. She removed her hat, tucked back some loose tendrils of hair that escaped her French braid then replaced her cap. "Ms. Connor, I didn't realize it was you. The jerk that called in the complaint made it sound like you were hustling out here. I do apologize but I had to check it out."

Thea took stock of the woman. She was of average height and weight, yet she wore a heavy bullet-resistant vest under her thick shirt, a belt around her waist loaded with pepper spray, flashlight, gun and holster, a radio and more. She was out risking her life to assist people and maintain the law.

"I'm the one who should apologize. I know you're doing your job and I appreciate that, I really do. If it weren't for the police, I might never have the hope of getting my daughter back."

"We'll do everything we can. Stay strong." The officer leaned into the car and picked up the parking ticket. "I'll take care of this for you." She smiled then turned and walked back to her car.

It was after eight when Thea pulled into her driveway. She never fell asleep behind the wheel but when she put her feet on the ground and stood up, her legs were wobbly. Her body felt weighted down with the disappointment of not one thing gained by passing out Emily's flyers.

The next afternoon, a volunteer named Janice, small and pale with light brown hair, sat quietly beside Thea. "I know how you're suffering, Thea. My boy, Justin, was gone for a year before they found him. You have to stay strong. It's the hardest thing you'll ever have to do."

"They found your son?"

"They sure did. His father took him to Minnesota. He was home-schooling him in a cabin in the middle of a forest. The police never gave up, and they finally located him. I'm just telling you, you have to keep yourself well and never give up. It could take some time, and you need to be an intricate part of the team."

"How did you hear about Emily?"

"I'm a volunteer for Team H.O.P.E. It's a group of folks who've also had a child abducted. It stands for Help Offering Parents Empowerment. The police get us involved when there's an Amber Alert. We'll do absolutely anything we can to help you through this. Tell me, when did you eat last?"

When had she eaten? "I'm not hungry, but thanks." Thea rubbed her forehead, which felt like it was about to split open.

"I know you're not, but you should eat. How about I go into the kitchen and fix something for you? I'll make you an ice pack for that headache, too."

Another week of promising leads and devastating letdowns had passed. Thea was exhausted. She worried that the window of opportunity to find Emily had slammed shut, and she fell into a sense of hopelessness so deep, she couldn't eat or sleep.

Detective McIntyre sent over a social worker who tried to rally her. They had a long talk, but its effect faded in a day. Today he'd sent Janice. And meeting someone who had suffered what Thea was suffering, someone who had lived through it and gotten her child back was real encouragement. And Janice was right; she was feeling better after the food and ice pack. She left Thea, squeezing her hand and promising to return in two days.

First she took some aspirin, followed by a long shower, which cleared her head. Back in her bedroom, she looked at the stack of mail Annie had brought from the cottage. She separated out the junk mail and tossed it into the trash. There were two threatening notes, which she set aside for the police. She read every card from friends who wished her well. Feeling uplifted, she tackled the bills. Most were relatively small and doable, until she opened the tax bill from the town of Orleans. It was high enough to make her focus on her financial situation. She stood up and circled the small area around her mattress. Everyone warned her it might take a while to find Emily. She hoped desperately it wouldn't. But, in case it did, she had to make some decisions on the best course of action. Re-lease her Boston apartment? Go home to the Cape?

She called and made an appointment for a short meeting with Will, then went to find Star. She knew right where to look. Star had taken to lying across the threshold of the front door during the day, making visitors step over her. No one seemed to mind. Her sad eyes showed her broken heart, and people took time to pet her and talk to her. Every night, she lay beside Emily's bed.

"I think you and I need some exercise to clear our minds." Star raised her head, listening for a word she knew. Thea gave her one, "Want to go for a *walk?*" Star jumped up with a hint of her old enthusiasm.

It was after six when Annie came back to the apartment.

"You drove all the way to the Cape and back again today, didn't you?"

"Guilty, but hey, it was worth it, I sold a house." She pulled a bottle of pinot noir from her overstuffed tote bag. "To celebrate?"

They sat on opposite ends of the couch, Thea with her feet up on what she now thought of as the cop chair. The wine took the sharp edge off her pain and worry. She could understand the social worker's warning about the danger of developing an alcohol and drug dependence in her situation. For a little while, though, she would enjoy the wine as it made happy endings more believable.

"Annie, I'm moving back to the Cape." Thea heard the satisfaction in her voice and suddenly realized how much she hated this apartment. How hard it was to be close to the spot where Emily was stolen from her. She couldn't find solace in the smells and sounds here, the ubiquitous sirens heralding someone else's serious trouble. She needed the peace of Knoll Cottage.

"What? Why? Is it the right move for you to leave Boston?" Annie asked, sitting up straighter.

"I talked to Will and Tim today. They both agreed it won't make much difference where I am."

Annie rolled her bottom lip between her teeth at the thought. "What exactly did the police say? I mean, what if Emily came back here? What if someone dropped her off and you weren't here?"

Thea reacted to Annie's supposition. "Do you really think someone will just bring her back? They would never let her go near the crime scene. They'd drop her somewhere far away. Even if they were stupid enough to drop her off in the Boston area, she's four, Annie, she wouldn't be able to find her way back to this apartment. Someone would call the police, and Em would tell them my cell phone number, which she knows by heart."

"I still think you should stay right here." Annie folded her arms across her chest. "Tell me why the police thought it wouldn't make a difference. Did they just say, 'go ahead?' "

"They didn't put up any resistance. They made it clear I'm still a suspect, but they have no reason to hold me here. My calls and emails are being monitored at the station anyway. I doubt they think it's likely anyone's going to come to the door and ask for a ransom."

Annie studied the street through the window, as if she were looking for Emily. "No. I guess you're right." She turned back. "You're sure you want to go?"

"I'm sure." Thea took a sip of her wine. "And even though I am sure, it still breaks my heart to leave. In spite of what I said, I feel like I'm abandoning her." The wine weakened her resolve and tears rolled down her cheeks. "She's only been gone three weeks. This is where we were when she was taken."

"I know. Either way it's painful. But if it doesn't matter where you are to Will or Tim, why don't you just stay here?"

"I gave notice on the apartment. It's probably already rented to someone else. And it would be easier for me to be paying bills for one place instead of two. I told them I'd find a way to do it if it helped, though." She shook her head. "They said they'd keep me informed."

"Maybe you will feel better at home then," Annie said, with the strain of trying to sound like she meant it clear in her voice.

"I don't know what feeling better is. Wait, yes I do, a little." Thea raised her glass of wine a few inches and smiled. "I think it's best. And since I can't get you to go home any other way, some good will come of this. You'll get back into your routine."

"Will you be all right alone in the cottage?"

"I'm going to have to get used to it. Everyone tells me I have to lead a normal life, and I accept that, even though nothing will ever be normal again. I'll keep busy working and maintaining Emily's website. At least I'll be doing something constructive."

"What kind of work are you going to do?" Annie asked, then drained her glass and reached for the bottle.

"When I went to see Will today about all this, he was great. He said the office couldn't get along without my paralegal skills." She chuckled a little. "He told me I could work remotely, as long as I could come in about once a week." She flashed back on the tight hug Will had given her when she couldn't stop thanking him for all he'd done to help her. "It's going to work out fine. I'll see Tim when I come in to Boston, too, so he can keep me updated on the case."

"What about your graduation ceremony? You're not going, are you?"

"No, it's just a formality, I'm official."

"And the bar exam, when's that?"

Thea set her glass down, and Annie poured another inch of wine into it. "So, you can still take the bar, right?" Annie repeated when Thea didn't answer.

"I can't. Not now. I'll worry about it when Emily's home." She sighed, picked up her glass and stared into the deep-garnet liquid.

"Since you'll be in Orleans, you could pass the board and take the offer you got from Patricia Sullivan's law firm."

"I'd never pass the board in this mental state. My career will have to wait. I don't know what to do about Patricia's offer. When she heard about Emily, she called and said she'd hold the position open for me."

"Good. This is all working out. Your mother would say the spirits are looking out for you. Or would she say that the stars are in alignment?" She smiled. "So, when's this move going to take place?"

"As soon as I can rent a van."

"How much could there be to move?" Annie said. "It looks practically empty now. Except for this icky furniture, which, thankfully, stays here."

Thea looked around. "Hmmm. Maybe we could squeeze the rest into our two cars."

"Absolutely. You'll be home by tomorrow night."

Thea took another sip of her wine. She felt pleasantly sleepy. Maybe the arrival of the tax bill was synchronicity, pushing her to make the decision to move home. She felt at peace about it now. Of course, the wine and talking it out with a good friend helped. She thought about being back in the home her mother had left her. The cottage Thea was raised in. Emily would be coming home to live there, too. Tonight, she was certain of that.

Thea held a cup of fragrant brewed coffee near Annie's nose and waited until her eyes opened. "How about some breakfast in bed?"

Annie looked around. "Where's the breakfast part?"

"Oh, this is it. I haven't done much food shopping."

Annie let out a soft groan and pulled herself to a sitting position. "I will surely not miss this couch." She held her hands out for the coffee.

Thea had been up since dawn finishing the packing. Some boxes wouldn't close, they were so full. Once Annie was awake, together they shagged the boxes and filled both cars, with a nervous Star shadowing their every move.

"Don't worry, puppy, you're coming," Thea told her as she laid a blanket down for the dog in the only free spot left in the SUV.

Annie took her shower and left for a final visit with her grandmother. Thea cleaned the apartment, walked the key to the landlord, and was showered and dressed by the time Annie came back through the door.

Thea stomped out of the bedroom. "I can't find my purse. I must have packed it, and the car keys are in it. Damn!" She sat on the couch, dropped her head into her hands and wept.

Annie sat beside her. "It's right by the door, hon."

Thea looked up. "Oh, shit." She cried harder.

"It's not the purse, is it?" Annie said.

Thea looked at her friend, wiped the tears from her cheeks. "Part of her is here," she said in an almost inaudible voice. "We spent three years together in this apartment. She learned to talk here, do a somersault, take her own bath, match her clothes. I feel like I'm ripping apart inside." She crossed her arms over her chest and dropped her head. "I don't know how to leave those precious memories behind. I'm afraid I'll lose them forever. And her."

CHAPTER EIGHTEEN

Dee was staying overnight at Katherine's house. She'd stayed before, after working a party or a late dinner, or when the weather was bad. Tonight she was babysitting. Katherine was meeting with another man at two a.m. in a seedy part of Roxbury. Dirk had set up the meeting. She was to go to the back of a twenty-four hour convenience store and take out two gallon containers of milk. She would set the milk on the floor and wait to be contacted.

Katherine was petrified as she walked down the street with muscles that were so tense she was taking odd baby steps. Most of the shops were closed up with heavy metal bars and large padlocks. In some doorways, bodies that looked like piles of old clothes reclined. The reek of filth had her holding her breath. One man called softly to her, and sent her running to the end of the block. A low, dark car came slowly down the street. She could see shadowy white faces stare at her from behind the windows, but the car moved on.

She stopped at the front of the convenience store. It was a small shop, called EZ Mart. An Asian man sat behind a brightly lit counter, reading a newspaper. Katherine opened the door. She jumped when a bell rang over her head. The clerk looked up then turned his attention back to his paper.

Her legs were rubbery as she walked down the middle aisle. The back of the store was lined with refrigeration cases. No one was there. She stood still, checking across the back wall for the case that held containers of milk. It was to her right, about three-quarters of the way down. She proceeded toward it slowly. What would she do if no one came? She was sure she wouldn't find the courage to attempt this again.

She set two gallons of milk on the floor. Loud voices from the front of the store came back to her. Two lanky African-American teenagers, their banter preceding them, came out from the same aisle she had. They looked her over and made some low comments to each other. She froze as one of them approached her, but he only nodded, reached into the case and pulled out a two-liter bottle of orange soda.

It seemed like twenty minutes later when a man stepped through the back door marked EMPLOYEES ONLY. This confused her because she expected her contact to come from the front. Another man and a woman walked in behind him. The first man sauntered up to her. He pointedly looked at the two gallons of milk at her feet.

"You the lady that needs help?"

"Yes."

"Follow me."

He went back to the employees' door. Katherine didn't want to be enclosed in a room, or worse, be led outside to some dark alley. She hesitated. The woman said, "It's now or never, babe."

Katherine swallowed and continued forward. They passed rusty file cabinets, a time clock, and a scratched wooden desk and chair. A ratty gray cardigan hung on a hook beside the back door. The first man opened the door, indicating Katherine should go out. In the dark alley was a light-colored, very large SUV, its lights off. When the back door opened the overhead light did not go on. She could just make out a person in the back seat, and she hesitated. "Get in. Hurry up," the woman behind her said, her hand at Katherine's back, pushing her into the car.

"Did you bring the ring?" the man in the car asked.

Katherine pulled the small box from her jeans pocket. She handed it to him.

He turned on a map light and took out a loupe. He slid the ring on his little finger and examined the diamond, then put the loupe back in his pocket. "Let me see the photos."

Katherine dug into her jacket pocket. She took out the camera, which had been mailed to the house in a large box without a return address. Along with the rolled-up blue paper background, she'd found terse instructions on how to take the photo, ending with: DESTROY BACK-GROUND AFTER USE, BUT HOLD CAMERA UNTIL FURTHER NOTICE.

She handed the man the camera, and the pictures of Emily she had taken with it. He examined the pictures under the map light. Katherine studied his face under the circle of illumination. He didn't look like a thug at all. He looked like someone you might see having dinner in a more elegant restaurant. His fingernails were clean and short; the skin on the back of his hands was smooth. He turned and looked at her, and she quickly looked down at the floor.

"These are pretty good." He slid them into his breast pocket. "I have to tell you, this ring is worth about what you said, but it won't be enough. The government has become pretty sophisticated with passports now. Used to be, we could arrange to get some blanks and just fill them in. Now they've embedded a chip with digital pictures and biometrics in the cover. Things that aren't cost-effective to copy. So, we have to use a real one and alter it. Hopefully, we can find a child with a short lifespan, which wouldn't mean school records and all. Much more risk. Match up race, age, coloring. Then we have to produce a birth certificate to back up the information. A lot of detail work. Being paid in jewelry is a higher risk for me, too. There's no guarantee I'll be able to get the full value. So, I'll let you know, through Dirk, how much more we'll need."

Katherine took the long walk back to her car without fear. She was almost hoping someone would jump out and kill her. End this terrible hell she'd made for herself.

When the phone call came, it was a relief—the bad kind, like when you worry you're dying of a terminal disease and the doctor finally confirms that you are. The police were coming. A Detective McIntyre politely asked if he could visit to ask a few questions. He seemed to assume Katherine knew what the questions were concerning, so she mentioned that John had told her about the child. When she hung up, she ran upstairs to tell Dee, who was on her knees cleaning Maddy's bathroom floor.

"The police are coming. A detective will be here at one-thirty. He didn't say anything about a warrant. Does he have to? Should I have asked him?" She answered her own question. "No, of course not. He's coming about John. About *John*."

Dee leaned one hand on the rim of the bathtub and stood up with a small groan. "You'll never pull this off. You're acting guilty. You need to settle down. All you have to do is answer a few questions," she said, massaging the small of her back with a liver-spotted hand.

Katherine took some deep breaths and nodded. *I can do this.*

"That's better," Dee said.

She saw the worry in Dee's eyes, and wanted to change her expression. "I can do this," she said, this time aloud.

"Just remember our plan." Dee looked at her watch. "It's eleven-thirty now, time to pick up little missy from school. I'm going to get some lunch." When Katherine didn't move, Dee said, "I'm afraid that you can't calm yourself down enough to get through this without doing something about it." She put her hand on Katherine's shoulder. "Look, go get Maddy, then come home and take one of those nerve pills. You can't let the detective see your jitters. He's trained to pick up on that."

When Katherine picked Madison up at school, the little girl had skipped to the car holding her mother's hand, while telling her in great detail about the child who brought a rabbit into class. Katherine couldn't believe how happy and energetic her daughter was, as if she weren't ill at all. Seeing her so much like her old self filled Katherine with hope.

Half of a peanut butter sandwich and a whole glass of milk had disappeared, and Maddy was still talking about the rabbit. She even took a few bites of her apple and ate the whole cookie. Katherine thought about giving Maddy a pet. Dee always said she was allergic, and she couldn't work for anyone with a cat or dog. But she would be gone when this was all over. Katherine smiled as she imagined Maddy's joy over the surprise of a kitten or a puppy. Or a rabbit.

Maddy was not tired enough to nap, so Katherine let her daughter watch a Shrek DVD before she started her piano lesson.

Katherine took Dee's advice and swallowed a Xanax after her own light lunch. She tried to read until she went into the living room for Madison's piano lesson. She realized she needed to keep up a normal schedule. While Madison practiced her scales, Katherine went to warn Dee it was a quarter past one.

"You look better. Are you going to be okay?"

"Yes, I'm fine." And she was.

The detective was prompt. She heard the knock on the door but didn't answer, just continued to play the piano song she was teaching Madison, hoping the detective would hear the music and think how normal the household was. When the door bell rang, she got up and answered it.

As Detective McIntyre entered the living room, he stopped and stared. Katherine followed his gaze. He was looking at Madison, and suddenly Katherine could see why. Her daughter, even with her blond hair and lighter blue eyes, still resembled Emily. If you didn't know better, you might mistake her for the kidnapped child.

"Detective, this is Madison, my daughter," Katherine said.

Madison left the piano bench and came to stand by her mother, leaning close to her, one hand holding onto the fabric of Katherine's slacks. Katherine laid her hand on Madison's head. "She's a little bashful.

Don't be shy, Maddy. Say hello to the nice man."

Maddy turned her face against her mother's leg.

"Don't worry," Detective McIntyre said. "She doesn't have to talk to me." He smiled at Katherine. "I won't keep you long. Just have a few questions."

Maddy went back to the piano and plunked on an occasional key in between peeks at the detective.

"You mentioned your ex-husband told you why I was interested in speaking with you."

"Yes, he came by and explained the situation. It was quite a shock. I mean—to hear he might be the father of the kidnapped child that's all over the news." She shook her head.

"You had no idea?"

"Of course not. Although it shouldn't have surprised me. I mean, John is a handsome man. Women are attracted to him."

"You didn't know about his involvement with Emily Connor's mother?"

Katherine had to think. Did he doubt her? Would he know about the private detective? No, of course he wouldn't. "Maddy," she said to cover her unease, "why don't you go up and play in your room? Mommy will come get you when the adults are finished talking."

Maddy walked a few steps then seemed to hesitate to continue past the detective, who was now staring at her. It made Katherine nervous to have him focused on her daughter. She got up. "Be right back," she said, placing a hand on Madison's shoulder, ushering her past the foyer.

At the bottom of the steps, she listened. All was quiet upstairs. Dee was with Emily. Not that Katherine expected noise, but the silence was comforting.

"Maddy, go up and play in your room. Mommy will call you when it's time to finish your lesson."

Maddy climbed halfway up the stairs then plopped down hard on the middle step. Katherine went to her in a panic. "What's wrong, Maddy?" she whispered.

"I feel sick." Her daughter's voice was feeble.

Oh no! She couldn't call Dee, but she couldn't allow the detective to think of her daughter as ill. She scooped Madison into her arms, rushed her up the stairs and into her room as quietly as she could, and laid her on her daughter's bed. She touched her cheek, her neck, but she didn't feel warm.

"Stay in your bed and rest," Katherine said. "Do not come back downstairs until mommy calls you. Do you understand?" Maddy pouted, unaccustomed to such stern words from her mother. There was rebellion in her eyes. Katherine held up her finger. "I mean it." She grabbed a few books and handed them to the child. She had to get back. The detective would be wondering what was wrong.

She closed the bedroom door and moved to the top of the stairs. She was sick with worry, but she couldn't show it. She must act as composed as possible. She took several deep breaths and went back down the stairs, noting with comfort that they were plush with thick carpet that absorbed any sound. In the foyer, she forced a smile to her face and took another breath before entering the living room.

"I'm sorry to keep you waiting," she said, hearing her strong voice and thanking God for Xanax. The detective was standing in the middle of the room. Had he been out in the foyer? Had he heard? But he just nodded at her, didn't seem to be suspicious at all. She could tell by the relaxation of his face when she returned, he'd been impatient. He must have been pacing. No need to worry.

"Madison can sometimes be a little princess. I just don't know how she got so spoiled." Katherine affected her best doting-mother smile for the detective. "I had to bribe her to play quietly in her room so we could talk in peace. Tantrum avoided." She raised her hands in a helpless gesture and smiled again.

They sat on Bergere chairs, set slightly sideways to face each other. She looked directly into Detective McIntyre's eyes. Her beauty always gave her confidence around men. She was in control; she knew she could pull this off. For Madison. She would convince him there was no reason to ever cross her threshold again.

"Now, you asked me about the missing child's mother. John kept his secret well. I never suspected him. The first time I heard the woman's name was on the local news, and then again when John came to tell me."

"How often does Mr. Warren see his daughter?"

"Rarely," Katherine said, not having to feign her disdain. "He's too busy with his new life."

"But he has custody every other weekend. Correct?"

A flurry of thoughts flew through her mind. John didn't say whether he and the detective had talked about Madison. Did John tell him she'd been ill? Had Katherine convinced John well enough that Maddy had recovered, so that he wouldn't think to mention it? She hoped her angst looked like anger. "He only manages to make a few of them. It's hard for Maddy, but she's become used to his disappointments. Her grandparents and I adore her, though. She's doing just fine."

"Tell me, what was your ex-husband's attitude when he came to tell you about the child?"

Katherine frowned. "Guilty. He was adamant about convincing me it was a one-night stand. As if it mattered now."

"Guilty?"

"Oh, not because he had anything to do with the child's disappearance. For cheating. Then it was all about John. How the whole situation would affect *him*. His precious career. His new wife. Another daughter to ignore. No, he wasn't happy. He did say he was planning to spend more time with Madison. An olive branch. But I've heard it before."

The detective looked down at his notebook. "Do you know where your ex-husband was on May twenty-seventh?"

Katherine cocked her head in thought. "He told me when he came that he'd been out of town on business when Emily was abducted." Saying the words made her quiver inside. "I can't say if it was true. We don't communicate."

The detective smiled and thanked her for her time. She walked him to the door, listening for a sound from upstairs. When the door was closed behind him, she leaned against it, staring at the business card he had handed her. She had a strong urge to laugh, loud and long. She was confident that Detective McIntyre had left without any qualms about checking her off his list. She'd done it.

Then she started to worry. What if Maddy was beginning another crisis? The day could have ended in disaster if she hadn't walked Maddy to the stairs when she had. What if she'd collapsed again as she had in ballet class? But she hadn't.

Katherine went up to Maddy's room, and opened the door. Her little princess was fast asleep, her face smooth and relaxed.

The inevitable reaction set in, and her knees began to wobble. She reached out a hand to steady herself as she watched her daughter sleep. It didn't happen. It *didn't* happen. They were safe, and they could proceed with the plan.

Two days ago, she had withdrawn funds from three sources.

Tomorrow, she'd meet with her contact to pick up the passport and birth certificate, and to pay the additional costs.

For his part, Dirk had done an impeccable job with Emily's medical records, doctors' letters, laboratory findings, changing her name, birth date, and dates of service. All of her HLA testing was included. He had electronically sent the records to Maddy's oncologist, through a contact in Brazil, after Katherine had reviewed her own copy.

She smiled and stood straighter. She was doing this to save her daughter's life. What could be more important?

She closed the door quietly, went down the hall, and climbed the attic stairs. She knocked softly on the door. "Dee, he's gone."

When Dee opened the door, Katherine motioned for her to lock it and follow her. She waited until Dee was inside her bedroom suite before she closed the door.

"How did it go?" Dee asked.

Katherine saw that her housekeeper's face was drawn, showing her age. She realized what a toll this was taking on the older woman, despite her outward calm. "It went well. How was Emily?"

"She never knew anything was going on. I read to her."

Katherine nodded. "You can go home early. Nothing more to do here today. We got through it. Come to work early tomorrow. I don't have a time yet for the meeting, but it could be in the morning."

The next morning, Maddy was wan and listless. When Dee arrived, Katherine felt as if her insides were tied in knots. "I have to bring her in. She's going to need an infusion. This is how she gets, and I don't want to put it off. But if he calls for the meeting while I'm in the hospital, I won't be able to take the call on the cell he gave me. I don't know what to do."

"What if I come and sit with her?"

"No. No one should see you with Madison. That won't work. I have to think." Katherine began to neaten the kitchen counter, pushing the pepper grinder closer to the backsplash, and the jade plant toward the corner.

When the phone rang, the problem was solved. He made the appointment for eight o'clock that night. "Thank God. Now I can take Maddy to the hospital."

Katherine played checkers with Madison while her infusion of packed red blood cells dripped in. The oncologist came in to see them.

"We forwarded both Madison's and Emma's health records to the oncologist you chose in Brazil, Doctor Rodrigo Cabral. He called, and we discussed Madison's case. He told me the transplant center has agreed to go forward with the BMT, even though the match isn't as good as they'd like. He understands that Madison's case presents a difficult challenge, and that the five out of six HLA matches have a good chance of succeeding."

Katherine nearly choked on the bile that flushed up her throat. Doctor Cabral thought the donor child was in an offshore, floating frontier oil town in Northeast Brazil. Maddy's oncologist, Doctor Thompson, was under the same impression: that Emma was an American child living in Brazil. If any mistake led either doctor to find out Emma would arrive in Brazil from the US with Katherine and Madison, everything would come crashing down around them.

"I know," Doctor Thompson said, in response, it seemed, to the pallor and cold sweat that had broken out on Katherine's face. "You've been through so much. But it's good news. We'll finalize the arrangements with the transplant center now. Then you can make your travel plans." He turned to Maddy. "You're going on a trip. I'll miss you. Will you come see me when you get back home?"

Maddy looked confused, but nodded her head. "I will."

Katherine found her voice. "Thank you so much, doctor, for every-thing you've done."

"My pleasure. Keep in touch. Maddy is one of my favorite patients." He smiled at her then turned to Katherine. "This infusion should suffice until the transplant. You'll be in good shape, but if anything comes up before then, you let me know. I'll have my nurse call you with all the details." He turned and shook Maddy's free hand. "You be a good little patient for your new doctor, just like you have been for me."

Katherine fought back tears. It had worked. The oncologist was totally onboard, without a hint of suspicion. Now she had to get the passport and birth certificate, and the other documents they needed to go through American and Brazilian Customs. She was going to pick them up tonight. Then, they had to be authenticated at the Brazilian Consulate in Boston. A huge step. But weren't they all?

The memory of the last meeting with the forger sent a shiver of fear through her. Overwhelmed by a swirling mix of emotions, Katherine realized that she never really thought she would get away with it.

CHAPTER NINETEEN

The closer she got to the Orleans exit off Route 6, the tighter her shoulders became. When she pulled the RAV 4 up the driveway and looked at the cottage, the pain hit her. She rested her head on her arms, holding tight to the steering wheel, and cried until Star began to whine. She opened the door and let out the dog.

Star romped around the yard after Thea released her. When her joy was expended, she nosed around the bushes and trees checking out who might have visited. Thea left her loose—Star never went off her property.

Annie pulled up into the driveway. Thea stood facing the front of her home. She could smell the sweetness of the blooming wild roses, hear the birds' evening calls, feel the soft breeze on her skin. But all she could see was Emily running to her garden the last time they came to the cottage. The contrast of that joyful image, to the heartbreak of her loss, bent her over.

"I know," Annie said, placing her hand on Thea's arm. "Take all the time you need. I'll start unpacking."

Thea straightened and walked to the back door. She took a breath, opened the door, and went in. She had to dispel the ghosts in every room before she could unpack. In the kitchen, rays of the setting sun highlighted a greenish patch on the white porcelain sink, left by a slow drip from the faucet. She automatically tightened the tap then moved to the hall. She walked through the bedroom, living room, and dining room. There she saw evidence of the police search everywhere. Will Hebert had been there while they searched. He'd warned her of what to expect.

She went upstairs and stood crying at the open door of Emily's room. She couldn't go in. It was obvious this room was the focus of the most thorough search. In her own bedroom, she opened the windows and stared down at the lilac tree. The tree was about thirty feet high, and wide enough to provide shade in the summer. It was a breathtaking sight to see the tree bloom in early spring, one she would always associate with the miracle of Emily's birth. She'd never seen her mother as happy as she was the morning Emily was born.

"Hi, sweetie," Hannah had said, flowing into the birthing room, her arms filled with fragrant white lilacs in a large vase that she placed on the side table, then turned and embraced her daughter.

Perhaps because Thea had been studying Emily's face, her mother suddenly seemed older to her. For the first time, Thea noticed that Hannah's face had relaxed into soft wrinkles, her long wavy hair was more gray than auburn, the veins on her hands were more pronounced. Maybe Hannah's long watch over her labor had caused the pull of fatigue around her eyes.

"Oh, look at how beautiful she is now." Hannah caressed the baby's cheek with her index finger. "Even from the moment she was born you could see it."

"Mom, did you get any sleep? You weren't gone very long."

"I can sleep anytime. Besides, I feel wonderful." Hannah studied Thea with cornflower-blue eyes. "I see you've made your decision," she said, then seemed to hold her breath.

Thea gave her a joyful smile. "Her name is Emily."

Hannah leaned over and kissed Thea's cheek, then Emily's. "I knew it. I'm so happy."

Thea handed Emily to her mother, watching with delight as she swept gracefully around the room, crooning to the sleeping baby, her long, flowered skirt flaring around her ankles.

"What about Emily's father, are you going to contact him?"

"He made it clear he didn't want her. So, no."

Hannah moved closer to Thea's bed, lowering Emily in her arms so Thea could see her face. "Look at this new soul. She is the product of the love between two people. Her father should share in the joy of her being."

Thea raised a finger to stroke her daughter's cheek. "Mom, her father is a creep. He called her an *accident*. He didn't want me or his baby. He made that abundantly clear. I can raise her myself. I'll be able to support her. It might be difficult right now, but I can do it."

"Thea, there are no accidents in this world. There is only synchronicity, which occurs in a perfectly balanced universe. This baby was meant to be. She deserves every good chance in life and that includes having a father."

"But Mom, from the time I was two, you raised me alone," Thea said, tilting her head up toward Hannah.

"It wasn't easy either. I'm not saying you couldn't do it, too. I'm saying you don't have to. And you should consider giving him the option of being in her life."

"I don't want him there. Do I want Emily to have a father who completely deceived me? A liar I was madly in love with? A man who still didn't mention he was married when he found out I was pregnant? Emily doesn't need a father like that."

"Every child is an angel from heaven. Maybe you didn't give him the chance to explain himself. I think you should let her father make the choice of whether or not he'll accept her into some part of his life. I think he will."

"What? Did you already do this little angel's astrological chart?"

Hannah only smiled. "Not yet. Just think about it, sweetie. I understand your anger at her father, but you have to think about your child. You don't realize it yet, but raising her alone will be a huge challenge. What about finishing law school? How will you manage that? Are you ready to give it up if necessary?"

"No, of course not. Other single moms get law degrees, go to work and provide for their children. Things are different now, not like when you were raising me." She knew the words were futile; her mother would not give up. Not for the first time, Thea wished she could push a button to end the discussion.

"We'll give it time. Your spiritual guides will move you in the right direction. Meanwhile, it will be my joy to help raise my granddaughter." She began to sway from foot to foot, rocking Emily. "Everything will be fine once you're home."

Emily opened her eyes and Hannah began to speak to her. Watching them, Thea felt an overwhelming warmth flow through her that brought happy tears to her eyes. She turned and leaned her face into the bouquet of lilacs, inhaling their fragrance.

"The flowers are beautiful, Mom, but I'm going home this afternoon."

"I know, but you saw the number of blooms this year, and just look at the size of these flowers. I think the lilac tree is celebrating Emily's birth," Hannah had said.

Thea stared down at the tree. It was ancient, gnarled, but with deep sturdy roots. Years ago, her mother had planned to surround the aging tree with ivy when her digging uncovered a flat piece of field stone buried in the dirt. It bore a rough carving of a rabbit on it, along with the words: Lizzie's Lilacs. It had become a mission for Hannah to keep the tree alive and healthy. Since then, it continued to weather Cape Cod's tough storms, harsh winters, summers with too little or too much rain. And every spring its branches were heavy with blooms.

Thea smiled. Her mother had seen the world through a mystic veil that softened all the sharp edges. Everything had the potential for a happy ending.

For a few moments, she let herself wonder again who Lizzie was. Had the tree been planted as a memorial for a child who had died? Thea shook herself. Why was she thinking of dead children? Anger filled her as she turned from the window and headed back downstairs.

She should go out and help Annie unpack.

Instead, Thea walked down the hall and looked into the sacred space—she could never think of the sun porch in any other way. She wished for some of the magic her mother had found in this place, but what she found instead only seemed hollow to Thea. Nothing she had ever learned, no faith, no beliefs could help her, nothing except finding Emily. She tightened her fists, felt an overwhelming urge to run out of the house, far away, run for hours until she was finally ahead of the horrible moment Emily was kidnapped. But she couldn't turn back time, so she had to find a way to live day to day. For now. And she would start with unpacking the cars.

"Is there anything to drink in the house? Wine or something?" Annie sat on the metal porch glider. The blond hair around her face was plastered to her sweaty skin; her cheeks were cherry red from exertion.

Thea dropped the last box onto the porch. She went to sit beside Annie. The glider bumped from side to side until Thea steadied it with her feet. The labor of unpacking had loosened her tense muscles, and had dissipated some of the shock of coming home without Em.

"Alcohol is the only spirit my mother never believed in," Thea said with a lopsided grin.

"Want to clean up and go to the Yardarm for drinks and dinner."

They were rocking the glider in unison. "I'm dead. I've spent every ounce of energy I had. I bet there are frozen dinners in the freezer."

"I guess I don't feel like going either. I think I'll head home," Annie said, then planted her feet on the wooden planks of the farmer's porch to stop the glider's motion.

The sound of the car engine faded as Annie drove away. Thea stood with her arms crossed over her chest, listening to the silence, a silence she craved before she lost Emily. But now it amplified the void of companionship. It was representative of her aloneness, and it was so cold.

With Annie gone, sadness filled her again. Thea was on her way to bed, but her steps drew her back to the sacred space. The H.O.P.E. volunteer had told her to choose a quiet place to cry when grief overcame her.

She stood staring into the sacred space, while memories assailed her. Flashes of Emily and Hannah ran like a movie in her mind. Good memories of their shared joy and the bond they'd had. She saw the pile of seashells, and knew Emily could name each one of them. She remembered trying to read her less than the three books she'd pulled from the shelf, books Emily could almost read herself. Hannah had passed so much knowledge on to her granddaughter. Emily was smart—bright enough to hold on, to keep herself safe. Thea believed that to be true at this moment, and it gave her strength.

Emily's tiny wicker chair still sat beside Hannah's rocker. In spite of the warm evening, the porch felt cold. A sweet lilac scent infused the air. Thea's quick scan of the shelves didn't turn up the potpourri her mother must have made of last spring's blooms. She sat down in the rocker and reached her hand over to hold the arm of Emily's chair. *Emily, my baby, where are you?* She was fully prepared to weep. Instead, a feeling of peace washed over her, easing the rigid grip of grief ever floating just below the surface of her emotions.

Hours later, unable to sleep, Thea got out of bed and padded in bare feet across the bedroom she'd had since she was a child. Even in the dark, she knew every inch of the room. She went past the stairs in the hall and into Emily's room. She felt a heavy pressure on her chest as she crossed the threshold. As she made her way through the room toward the chair by the front window, she rammed her shin onto what must have been the corner of Emily's toy box. She grabbed her leg and hopped to the chair, rubbing the pain, feeling wetness that must be blood. She began to cry. Why didn't she know Emily's room as well as her own? Why didn't she know right where the toy box was? Because it was Hannah who knelt in front of it with Emily. It was Hannah who read to her in the big chair. And often, it was Hannah who tucked her in because Thea was busy studying. How many moments of joy had Thea missed?

For a long while, she obsessed about what she could have done differently. But in her heart, Thea knew she'd been working hard for *both* of them. Maybe too hard. But at least Emily had the best grandmother possible loving her while Thea struggled to realize her dream of becoming a lawyer.

Some felon had taken that dream away from both of them. She wanted to *kill* him; rip him to shreds. But first she had to find him. No time to waste looking backward with regret.

She slowly rose from the chair and made her way to Emily's bed. She dropped to her knees and put her hands together. "God," she whispered, "there's a little girl who needs you. Someone evil took her from me. Will you help me find her? Will you please let me have her again? She's the sweetest little girl you ever made. Don't let anyone hurt her, God. Please help us be a family again." She lowered her face into her hands and waited. For what? Vibrations? Thunder claps?

Slowly, she became aware of a feeling of warmth spreading through her, and for the second time that day, she was filled with a sense of hope.

On the way back to her room, she stopped in the bathroom and turned on the light. Her leg was gouged and bleeding. When she stood up to open the medicine cabinet, she saw her reflection. It wasn't her pale complexion, her red swollen eyes, or the shock of her tangled hair, it was the handprint of blood on the right side of her face that made her catch her breath. She trembled as she ran the water full force and began to scrub away the blood. As if she could scrub off all the bad that had happened and start anew.

Four days later, she was set in her routine of work, exercise, and keeping up Emily's website. This morning, as she did every morning the weather permitted, she and Star went for their daily walk. If it weren't for the slashes of short fur that had been shaved for suturing her wounds— carved out like seawater running through the marsh grass—there would be no indication that Star was ever hurt. She pranced beside Thea, the love of the walk in every step. Thea's house was three down from the bay. They went in a loop, starting with the beach, across the sand for a half mile, then down a street of vacation homes, with signs of their returning occupants. These were just the beginning. Most summer residents would be returning in droves—regular as migrating birds—when their children's schools closed, the unofficial beginning of summer. Thea saw bedding airing on the clotheslines, kayaks and canoes dragged back out of the garage, along with patio tables and chairs, and the real give-away, the American flag raised on poles and masts.

She'd always thought of summer as the happiest of times, never wondering about other people's sorrow, fear, or horror. Her own suffering had opened her eyes to a different world.

CHAPTER TWENTY

This time, Katherine had to meet the same man from the black SUV at Whole Foods Market. Having once considered this to be a fun shopping experience, she now wondered if she would ever consider this store again. She was to pick up several items, buy a Whole Foods reusable bag to put them in, pay and leave the store. She would head down the street toward Finagle a Bagel. He would pass her at some point along the sidewalk, and they would stop to chat. She would set her bag down next to his. After they talked, he would pick up her bag. She would take his and continue to the bagel shop.

It was after five p.m. and many people were rushing up and down Cambridge Street. Katherine tried to walk normally, as two or three people passed her. She could feel the bag handles crumpling in her tight grip.

"Is that you, Jane?" he said, turning back after he'd passed her. "How are you?" He walked closer, gave her a hug. She felt herself stiffen, as rigid as a post. In the daylight, she could see his pock-marked face clearly. He was shorter than she was.

"I'm fine. I haven't seen you in ages. What's new?" She almost laughed, felt hysteria bubbling up. As he began to say things that had no meaning whatsoever, she set her bag down on the sidewalk. People passed them without apparent interest.

"Hey." He moved his head closer to hers. "I said, did you bring the extra cash?"

She blinked. "I missed that. Sorry. Yes. It's in the bag."

"Stop looking so scared. Smile."

She did, but she could feel her lips trembling. "Did you get everything on the list?"

"It's all there," he said, then hugged her again. "Great seeing you."

And then he walked off, crossed the street, and disappeared into the parking garage. She took two small steps closer to his bag, and then just allowed herself to breathe. A few seconds later, she picked up the bag and went on to Finagle a Bagel. She bought a mocha latte to go, then went back to her car in the Whole Foods lot.

She was loaded down with passports, birth certificates, vaccination records, permission letters, bank account statements, a death certificate for

Emma's mother, and even a gas bill to prove residence for Emma's father.

Katherine compared Emma's passport to hers and Madison's. To her eye, they looked exactly the same. The other documents all seemed official. Emma's vaccination record was even scrunched with a few dog-eared pages.

Now they had to hustle. Dirk was sending a "plumber" to the house, who would take a photograph of Emmie for her visa. Katherine had to pick up a court-certified copy of her divorce custody information. The visa application forms were filled out online and forwarded to the consulate. She needed to obtain a US Postal Office money order to pay the fees the consulate would charge. The airline tickets she'd purchased were printed out.

It worried Katherine that the consulate required proof that she could afford to be in Brazil for the ninety days of the visa. Her bank account statements showed some heavy withdrawals. She hoped they wouldn't question her.

It was past time to contact John and let him know they were leaving. She'd intentionally waited until there was some pressure of time. She would appeal to him by explaining she didn't realize she had to have his notarized permission letter to take Madison out of the country. He knew she'd been working on her PhD before Maddy became ill. She would tell him what she was telling everyone close to her—that there was an opportunity for her to study in Brazil, which would contribute to her thesis on multi-cultural globalization and its effect on education. She didn't expect him to put up a struggle, but it was one more worry to consider.

It took John two days to answer her calls. By then, she didn't have to fake the pressure she felt.

"Why didn't you tell me about this earlier?" John demanded.

Katherine could discern he had her on speaker. "This opportunity came up suddenly. Another person was scheduled to go, but he's sick and can't make it. He then offered it to me."

"Are you sure you don't want to leave Madison with Sondra and me?"

For a second, she couldn't catch her breath. "Really, John? You'd do that?"

There was a moment's pause. "Well, how about your parents? Wouldn't they keep her?"

Yes! Thank God. She knew him so well. "They're travelling this summer, too. It'll be fine, John. Maddy's looking forward to it, and I'd miss her too much to leave her behind."

"If you're sure about this. Give me what I need to sign. I can have it notarized in the office."

Katherine walked into the Brazilian Consulate at 20 Park Plaza with her forged documents. She wore a plain natural linen sleeveless dress with brown ballet flats. It was nine-seventeen when she approached the man at the visa desk. She took a seat and fumbled the documents out of the plastic document envelope, then handed them to him. She felt as if she were breathing through a thin straw. The man sorted the documents, checking them against his computer screen. While he worked, she said a rosary's worth of Hail Marys. Finally, he nodded and extended his hand for the money order she was still holding. Katherine gave it to him. When the man handed her a receipt, he was smiling. He told her the hours when she could pick up the authenticated documents the next day.

She left the consulate on stiff legs that felt as if they were lugging ankle weights.

In twenty-four hours, she'd either be set to go to Brazil, or to prison.

Katherine returned home with the envelope of authenticated documents. She carried it up to her bedroom, calling Dee as she climbed the stairs.

"Is it all set? Did they approve the records?" Dee asked, coming down the hall.

"All done." Katherine sat down in her bedroom. The envelope was still in her hand that now dangled over the arm of the chair. "Nothing else to do."

"That's it then. You'll be leaving in a few days."

"You're all set, Dee. The retirement annuity has been created. You can get ready to go."

"There's the house to sell and all. I might still be here when you get back," Dee said.

"Don't wait. Go when you're ready."

"But how will I know if the transplant works? You said you can't call and mention it. Can we set up a code? I have to know about the little missy."

Katherine stood and walked over to Dee, who was in the doorway, and put an arm around her shoulders. "I'll find a way after we're safely back to let you know how it went."

Dee wiped her eyes. "Maybe I'll still be here. The real estate market stinks."

CHAPTER TWENTY ONE

In the last two weeks, she'd done a radio and a television interview, and another press conference. She was exhausted from the yoyo of anticipation every time she got out there, then despair when nothing resulted from the effort. She was beginning to lose hope. It was sinking away like a pebble to the bottom of a deep pond. Thea knew the unspoken dictum of the police: The longer the child was missing, the more likely the child was already dead. She gasped at her own betrayal with the thought. This was something she had to control. She would never be able to go on if she believed Emily might be dead.

Thea was leaning against the kitchen counter eating breakfast. She straightened and turned to dump the crumbs from her toast into the sink, shaking the dish with such vigor she bumped it against the porcelain and it shattered into sharp little pieces.

Emily is alive, damn it!

She gathered the broken dish pieces with her bare hands and threw them into the trash. She realized she was backsliding into despair. She had to push forward, find a purposeful life. Otherwise, she'd never make it until she had her daughter back. And Emily would come back. She would. She would.

Everyone encouraged her to settle into everyday life. Her everyday life had been entwined with her daughter's, and her absence left a gaping black hole in Thea's new daily grind. It was a constant struggle to fill the vacuum. Emily was everywhere in the cottage, with bits of memories of her placing her shells in the sacred space; standing on a kitchen chair, helping Hannah make her oatmeal; running up and down the hall, making Star bark and chase her; sitting on the big blue living room chair, coloring in her book. What was she doing now? Where was she? Thea clasped her hands under her chin and searched the kitchen walls for answers.

"Star, come on, girl, let's go to work." The tapping of the dog's paws on the hallway hardwood followed Thea into the living room. Star circled three times, then flopped down beside Thea's desk with a half sigh, half groan. She was happier in the cottage, but she still slept by Emily's bed every night, and patrolled the property every day.

Thea spent hours on the computer, holding tears at bay while blogging on Emily's website, perusing lost children sites, and keeping up her Facebook page. Every day she added an item about Emily: her favorite book, something funny she said, what plants were growing in her garden. She received uplifting responses: *Your daughter will come home. Believe!* And, *May God hold you in his arms until you're holding Emily in yours.* She deleted the few cranks' notes and threats that she'd learned to ignore; and responded to everyone else who wrote, with a note of thanks.

After lunch, Thea decided to clean Emily's room as a positive act confirming her belief in Emily's return. She gathered her cleaning supplies and headed upstairs.

The cottage had two spacious bedrooms on the second story, both with slanted walls on either side following the roof line. Thea had always taken the room facing the backyard and Lizzie's lilac tree. The day she came home from the hospital with Emily, Hannah took Thea upstairs to see the pink and purple princess bower she'd created for her granddaughter. She'd been secretly working on refinishing the furniture at her friend Alice's house. Hannah and Alice then painted the room—with non-toxic paint, of course—and set it all up during the time Thea was in the hospital. "But how did you know I would keep her, Mom?" Thea had asked. Hannah smiled and simply said, "I knew."

"The same way you knew she would be a girl?"

Hannah had the grace to look sheepish. "No. That information came from the tech who did the sonogram. You didn't want to know the sex, but I did."

Now, Thea looked around the room. A white iron daybed, which had replaced the crib as Emily had grown, stood along the side wall. A princess crown, suspended from the ceiling, held sheer curtains that tented the bed like purple mosquito netting. Thea trailed her fingers over a spray of pink rosebuds Hannah had hand-painted on the top of a white pine bureau on the opposite wall. The toy box Thea had run into sat next to it. Between the two front windows was a mirrored vanity table and bench, each with a skirt composed of layers of pink tulle. A stuffed chair sat in the corner, slip-covered in crisp purple and white-striped chintz. Thea remembered her daughter sitting on Hannah's lap in that chair as she listened, enthralled, to a story her grandmother read to her. How lovingly Hannah had worked on the room. She'd been rewarded as Emily grew old enough to express her pure delight with her princess bower.

Hannah had almost four years of loving Emily before she died. Why hadn't Thea understood the serendipity of Emily's birth before? She knew it was partly because she'd allowed Hannah to take on some of the mother role, so Thea could concentrate on her textbooks. But that wasn't all of it. Hadn't her anger at John's rejection also blinded her to the pure joy Emily's presence brought to their lives?

Thea sat down in the chair, her dust cloth and mop forgotten.

Emily was a nature girl. She loved her garden, discovering bugs, and finding seashells. She had a rock collection so big she couldn't lift the canvas bag she kept them in. Emily could lure a butterfly to perch on her tiny finger. But Emily wasn't a princess. This was Hannah's room for her. It was Thea's turn to create a new room for Emily.

Thea took the Route 6 exit ramp and drove down Iyannough Road to the Cape Cod Mall. She parked the car, leaving all the windows halfway open. No one would come near it with Star sitting on guard.

"I'll be back soon," she promised.

It took over an hour, but it was worth it. Back at the car, she chuckled to see Star sitting in the driver's seat, her ears up and her eyes alert. When she saw Thea, she jumped over the front and back seats and stood in the way-back.

"You did a great job, Star. What a good girl," Thea said. Under the dog's supervision, she stowed her load of packages in the back seat then got behind the wheel. As she pulled out of the parking lot, Star snorted while lying down, her watchdog job successfully completed.

Thea brought in all the packages and surveyed the haul she'd made. For a moment she doubted her instincts. But then she began to drag the bags up to Emily's bedroom, piling them in the middle of the large space. Emily would have a new room to come home to.

Thea stripped the bed, removed the netting, the princess crown, and then detached the pink fluff from the vanity table. She pulled the slipcover off the chair and checked the moss-green upholstery. It would do just fine. She folded and packed all the items into cardboard boxes left over from her move home. She rolled up the throw rug and slid it into one of the plastic bags that had held her purchases.

Thea opened the half door to the storage space along one wall of Emily's room. She peered inside with a flashlight to check for bugs or animals. It was empty of both the living and the inanimate; nice and dry. She moved the old room decorations into the space. She would keep them for a while, just in case this was a mistake.

"Whew," she said aloud, dusting off her hands. "Now for the good stuff."

Sitting cross-legged on the floor, she opened all the bags, tamping down her buyer's remorse at seeing the extravagance she couldn't afford. She removed the price tags and sorted the items into piles. The items that she would wash first, she tossed down the stairs. She draped everything else with paint cloths.

Next, Thea dumped all the toys from the sharp-cornered toy box then dragged it into the hall. Later she would organize Emily's toys by placing them into the two large woven baskets she'd purchased. She pulled the rest of the furniture away from the walls, put down more paint cloths, and began to blue-tape the woodwork.

When everything was ready, she opened the windows, pried off the lid to the yellow paint and got to work.

"Come on, Tim, you promised. Think of it as my birthday present. I'm sure you didn't get me one. You never leave work before the stores close," Tim's brother, Sean, said.

"I'll get you anything you want. Name it. But please, let me off the hook. I'm not in the mood."

"When you see her, you'll get in the mood. She's a babe. Just what you need."

Tim's family was always setting him up, or trying to. Once in a while, they broke him down, and he ended up enjoying himself. But he still hadn't met a woman he cared enough about to see her more than once or twice.

He stood in front of the mirror and worked his tie into a neat knot. He watched himself grimacing. If he could just get through this night, he swore he'd never say yes to a blind date again. Tim didn't care how beautiful the woman might be—he wasn't interested. His mind was on his work. His mind was on Thea Connor. He glowered again.

Tim had made detective after five years in the Boston Police Department. He had a high rate of case closings and was well respected at the station. Time on his job had replaced his social life, except for occasions out with family and a few close friends. But most of those people wouldn't be satisfied until Tim found love again.

The woman was a babe. Sean had introduced them, and they were sipping drinks at a table in No. 9 Park, a restaurant in Boston. She was almost as tall as Tim. Her hair was sleek, pulled back in some sort of clip. She had nice brown eyes and full lips.

"So, tell me about some of your cases. I think police work is fascinating," Lacey said in a voice so deep the table rumbled. It annoyed the hell out of him.

"How about you tell me about yourself instead? I don't get away from work often enough to enjoy talking about it in my free time. What sort of career do you have?"

It worked every time. Lacey launched into her life as a sports reporter, mildly interesting; that is, when his thoughts didn't keep returning to Thea and Emily.

Katherine tipped the skycap who carried her luggage—not too much, not too little. Nothing for him to remember as unusual. When she extended the bills to him, they stuck to her damp fingers, shooting a rush of adrenaline through her. But the man was already on his way to another traveler when the red flush hit her face.

"Mommy, I'm tired. How come she gets to ride?"

Katherine looked at her daughter who was almost ashen. *Oh God. Hold it together, Katherine.* She could not make a scene anyone would remember.

"Here you go, sweetie." Katherine lifted Madison onto her hip and wrapped her right arm around her, while she pushed the stroller with the left. She also had a carry-on bag whose strap was digging a rut into her left shoulder. But she held her head high, pasting a small smile on her face when she wasn't talking to her daughter. Anyone watching would see she was completely in control. No one would offer to help, or wonder how she could manage. It was only for a little while, she told herself. Through security, through customs, and then she could relax. But not yet. Sweat ran down her neck and trickled between her breasts.

"Mommy, why is Emmie sleeping all the time?"

"Emmie's just very tired, honey. Remember, I told you she has a cold. You know how icky you feel when you have a cold and you have to take medicine, right?"

Katherine prayed Madison would not bring up any further objections to bringing Emily along on their *vacation.* She had handled everything badly, tripping over the story she'd told Maddy about Emma being her cousin. Fortunately, Maddy was so excited about the trip she'd accepted her mother's assurance that 'Emmie' was going to be fun, someone with whom she could play. Even though she was only four.

She glanced down at her daughter's sweet face. She dreaded the thought of telling her the vacation would be spent in a hospital.

"I don't have a cold but I'm sick," Maddy said with such nonchalance Katherine wanted to bawl. Instead, she pushed her face into her daughter's shoulder for a few seconds in a make-shift hug.

"You are going to be all better soon, Maddy. Don't you worry about that. Mommy is taking care of it. Okay?"

Maddy turned in her arms and placed her small hands on each side of Katherine's face, her gaze focused on her mother. "Okay, Mommy."

Katherine stopped, let go of the stroller, and gave Maddy a full-press hug. Her darling daughter, how could this happen to her? "Everything's going to be fine, my little princess. Mommy loves you so much."

Before they got to security, Katherine moved to the side of the hall. "Okay, Maddy, your turn to ride." She lifted Emily to her shoulder, noticing with a pang of worry how much more solid and heavy she felt than her daughter.

With help from a female TSA agent, they sailed through security. Katherine told her the same thing she'd told Maddy. "This one has a cold. The antihistamine just knocks the socks off her." The girls looked related. Emily was taller, and even though she'd lost weight since she was taken, she was still heavier, making her look a year or so older than petite Madison.

Almost there. She continued to hold Emily as the line crept closer and closer to the customs agent sitting in a booth ten feet ahead of them.

She watched the people in front of her pass through customs. The agent's expression was unfriendly, and Katherine told herself she had to play her role accordingly. He wouldn't be charmed. She could feel herself breathing too fast and tried to relax. It had been a month since the kidnapping. It had faded from the news. But if she showed any signs of nervousness, he would suspect something was wrong. The thought made Katherine even more nervous. She wasn't sure she could hold it together any longer. It was all becoming too much, and she was yielding to the pressure. *Please, please, God, help me.*

Two more people in front of them. Katherine was trembling from head to foot. Her hand holding the three passports was visibly shaking. She felt as if they were crossing a huge chasm on a rotten rope bridge and the ropes were fraying, about to break.

Then Emily began to cry.

It started as a small whine then grew in volume. She opened her eyes and looked around, but it was clear she was not fully awake. Was she having a nightmare? She was sufficiently drugged with antihistamine; she should have been asleep. Emily dropped her head back on Katherine's shoulder, but continued to weep.

"Passports," the agent demanded.

"Oh, yes—here they are," Katherine said, juggling a noisy Emily, the stroller, and the carry-on, as she placed the passports in his hand. Emily turned to look at him, and then wailed louder. Her eyes were squeezed shut and the tip of her nose was red. The agent studied her face, holding up her passport, ignoring the crying.

They had tried their best to make Emily look different from her poster photos, but there was only so much they could do. Her short hair was now blond, like Maddy's. Her face was thinner than a month ago, enhancing her resemblance to Maddy. The girls had different last names, but that was not uncommon in families. Katherine had dressed them in matching pink sweats to reinforce the relationship.

The customs agent turned to his computer. Katherine watched with a new jolt of adrenaline as pictures scrolled in front of him.

She felt faint. Had he recognized Emily? Would armed TSA officers surround them, take the children away? Arrest Katherine? *God, God, God, God.*

He looked at Madison, then back at Emily. Emily's passport had cost a fortune. Thank God she was wealthy. She would never take one penny of her money for granted again. The agent set down Emily's passport and picked up Madison's. He leaned over, staring at her face the same way he had Emily's. Katherine began to hope. Emily's cries became weaker as she slipped back into sleep.

"Do you have permission to take these children out of the country?"

Though it wasn't required, Katherine knew she might be asked this. "Yes, I do. Hold on." She pulled the clipped papers from her carry-on and handed them to him. He read through each one. It seemed like the earth had stopped spinning and time was suspended.

"You have your hands full," the agent said to her, returning all three passports and the folded documents in a stack. "Enjoy your trip."

Katherine didn't look back. She was light-headed, weak-kneed as she continued toward the departure gate. Emily was again fast asleep. She had cried just in time. Katherine realized God had answered her plea for help. If the child had not started crying so loud, the agent would have wondered why Katherine was so nervous. Instead, her anxiety conformed to the norm for a lone mom with two little children, one cranky, trying to get on a plane. It was all meant to be. Now she was sure she was doing the right thing. Her heart filled with gratitude.

The rest would be easy. Before they boarded, she would give Emily another full dose of antihistamine, so she would sleep on the long trip. Madison would fall asleep easily, as she did after any exertion now. Katherine didn't anticipate any issues going through Brazil's customs, since all the necessary paperwork was authenticated by the consulate. And some of the documents had already passed the scrutiny of the US customs.

She chose seats in the waiting area at the end of a row, and pushed the stroller backwards next to her chair. "Maddy, come sit in this chair next to mommy. Emmie is not feeling well and she'll sleep better in the stroller." When they were settled, Katherine took out snacks and a coloring book and crayons for Madison. From time to time she glanced down the long hall leading toward the customs booths, but no one came looking for her. She felt better, more relaxed, but she wouldn't be completely at ease until the plane landed in Brazil.

CHAPTER TWENTY THREE

Natives only considered driving to the Cape on a Friday or *from* the Cape on a Sunday when there was no other choice. Thea was driving from the Cape on the Friday after the Fourth of July. Having finished her meetings at Hebert & Massey and completed a few errands, she now walked along a residential street, deep in thought about a case on which she was doing paralegal work. If it wasn't for the noise of children at play, she would have missed it.

She turned at the happy sound. A large play area with swings and monkey bars was fenced for the safety of the pre-schoolers. As she stood and watched them play, sorrow filled her. Emily should have been there or someplace like it, climbing the monkey bars.

Several young children were jumping on a trampoline close to the front door of the pre-school. The trampoline was surrounded by high netting, but Thea could make out a little girl with bouncing red-blond curls inside. She gasped. She was looking right at her daughter! She was a distance away, but was certain it could be Emily tumbling with the other children.

Thea jogged around the fenced area, in search of an opening, while keeping her eyes on the child. There was a small gate, but it was locked. She walked around the building until she found an entrance door.

It was also locked. She rang the bell and waited, swaying from foot to foot. It had to be her. Oh God, she was sure it was Emily.

The door was opened by a young blond woman with rimless glasses and a harried look. "Can I help you?"

"There's a child in the playground out front. I think she may be my daughter."

The woman looked at her as if Thea had just told her the moon really was made of cheese. She mentally kicked herself. "No. Wait. Please, listen. My daughter was kidnapped in May. She's four years old. There's a child out there who could be her. Please let me see her."

"I'm the administrator, Susan Blackwell. Come with me to the office."

Thea followed the woman down the hall. Her heart was pounding in her chest, nearly bursting with hope.

"I can't allow you to disturb the children. You must understand that their security is our responsibility."

"Yes. I understand. Would you let me call the lead detective on the case? You must have heard about Emily's kidnapping. It's been all over the news. He'll tell you it's all right to let me see the child."

"That's fine. The police can come here and we'll work this out." The administrator led Thea into a small office and indicated a chair for her to take while she waited.

She sat and called Tim. He didn't answer, but Thea left breathless messages on all three numbers, begging him to call her back.

A bell rang and Thea froze. "What time is school over?"

"Not for another hour," Ms. Blackwell said, standing by the door.

Twenty minutes later Tim got back to her and she gave him her location. He was about a half hour away.

Thea felt like she could shoot electricity out through her fingers. Her whole body was poised to react if the bell rang again. Her eyes were glued to the large round clock over Susan Blackwell's head. The administrator finally perched on the edge of the seat behind her desk. It was clear she thought at any moment, Thea might bolt outside in an attempt to see the child she knew was her daughter.

Another bell rang. Tim was still not there.

"Oh my God. Please. You have to wait for him," Thea said, jumping up from her chair.

"That's a ten-minute warning bell for the teachers. But I must tell you, I cannot hold the children here," Ms. Blackwell returned, also standing now.

"Please, look at the picture again." Thea pulled her phone from her pocket, and brought up a picture of Emily. "You know every child here. I saw a little girl out there that looks just like my Emily."

A young woman stuck her head in the door. "The police are here."

A second later, Tim filled the doorway. His coat was open with his gold badge evident on his belt. Thea thought she'd never seen a more beautiful sight. "This is Detective McIntyre. Susan Blackwell, the administrator," she introduced.

Susan came around, clear relief on her face, and shook Tim's hand. Her left hand still held Thea's phone with the picture of Emily.

"You understand, detective. I couldn't take this woman's word and allow her near the children."

"You did exactly right. I'm sure Ms. Connor mentioned her daughter Emily's abduction. She would be the right age for your school. Could we take Ms. Connor to the children's area so she can get a better look at the child she saw outside?" Tim watched Susan return the phone back to Thea. "Thea showed you her picture? Do you recognize the child?"

"I can't be sure from the photo. We have two little redheads." She turned to Thea. "I'm sorry about your daughter. It's terrible what happened to her, but I hope you understand why I couldn't let you near the children until the police were here."

"Susan, you run your school exactly the way I would want you to for Emily."

Susan took them to the first room, where the children were collecting their belongings before they left. She introduced Tim and Thea to the teacher then gathered the rest of the children in the other classroom.

Thea handed the teacher her phone. She studied Emily's photo, then looked up with sad eyes. "I have one little girl you might have seen, but I don't think it's her. Come, take a look."

They crossed the room full of elf-size tables and chairs. The children's art lined the walls. Thea scanned every child in the room.

"Samantha, could you come here for a minute?" the teacher said.

Thea could hear the thud as her heart dropped to her feet when she saw the child was not Emily. They thanked the teacher and went out of the class. Susan Blackwell was standing in the hall at the door of another room, which was Thea's last hope.

She recognized at once the child she'd spotted in the playground. She was wearing a purple shirt with short puffed sleeves. It wasn't Emily.

"I'm sorry," Tim said as he led her out of the school. She couldn't manage an answer, but she refused to dissolve into tears.

"Where's your car? I'll walk you to it."

Thea turned down the offer. She needed to walk off the deep visceral disappointment. She'd been so sure this would end with Emily in her arms. Her body ached with longing.

By the time she got to her car, she was feeling a little better. Every day carried a disappointment of its own, threatening to eat away a tiny piece of her, and each time she withstood it, she grew stronger. One of these times, it *would* be Emily.

But then she wept in spite of herself.

Back home, she wandered around the cottage at a loss of what to do. Her steps drew her down the hall to the sacred space. She sat in the rocker and closed her eyes. A wave of lilac scent filled her nostrils. As always in this place, she felt her mother's love. Thea's tense muscles relaxed. She breathed in deeply. "Emily is alive!" she said aloud. Hearing her own words reassured her. She kept her eyes closed, but she could feel her eyelids trembling as the three words continued to echo in her mind. She sat quietly until she was utterly calm and then slowly opened her eyes. She felt peaceful and comforted.

Later, as she lay in bed trying to sleep, it occurred to her that if someone in Boston had taken Emily, it was possible they'd enroll her in preschool. She didn't expect they would use her true name, but they might keep her first name. She smiled when she thought of her headstrong daughter. It would be tough for anyone to convince her that her name was not Emily.

She would check other preschools in various communities around the Boston area. Maybe they had websites where she could leave information about Emily. Possibly send a picture and contact information. With the comfort of having something else to do in the search to find her daughter, she drifted off to sleep.

CHAPTER TWENTY FOUR

The months of anguish, the risks she'd taken, the lies she'd told, the harrowing ordeal of the flight to Brazil were finally over. If earlier, Katherine had been able to dwell on what came next during this process, she wondered if she would ever have gone through with it. But she had only one real choice.

The day after they arrived in Brazil, Madison had been admitted to the transplant center hospital to begin the preparative regimen of four days of chemotherapy and radiation. She'd vomited and had diarrhea throughout the treatment. She had to be coaxed to eat. She became weak and lifeless. Every time she fell asleep, Katherine cried.

It was July seventh, day zero, the day the bone marrow transplant would take place from Emily to Madison. Doctor Thompson had told her how infrequently extended family members' HLA, Human Leukocyte Antigen, turned out to be a close enough match to be a safe donor. From her research, Katherine knew half-siblings were in that group. Madison was one of those patients whose HLA variation had made it difficult to find a perfect match to anyone. The fact that Emily had the same variation and was a close match was a small miracle. It was meant to be.

The taxi was at the curb waiting when they exited the hotel.

Bruna, a local woman who was hired to care for Emily, carried her into the taxi. The doctor had prescribed a medication to be given to Emily two hours before they left the hotel, so she was mildly sedated. She woke momentarily when she was moved, then fell back to sleep. Bruna cuddled the little girl in her arms. Katherine slid onto the back seat beside them. She handed the driver the name and address of the transplant hospital. She hadn't been able to sleep until four a.m., and then only for a short while. She had some coffee this morning, but nothing to eat. She stared out the window during the short drive. Looking at Emily was too painful.

Katherine was so filled with fear she felt her sanity slipping. If she could only get through the next few hours without anyone discovering her crimes, her daughter would have a good chance of living. Most of the hospital personnel spoke some English. Even though Emily was pre-medicated, what if she said something suspicious? And after her procedure was finished, would they have completed the marrow infusion into Madison before Emily was awake enough to talk? What if she said she wanted her mommy, as she had continued to do? Katherine would simply tell them she'd recently lost her mother. What if she said she was living in a house that wasn't her mommy's house? Katherine would say she meant the hotel suite. Could she say her aunt wouldn't let her go home? Easy answer. But what if she said her door was always locked? Harder. But reasonable, in a strange country.

Stop! She was driving herself crazy. She had all the answers ready. *Relax.* She could appear nervous, but not hysterical—that might make them take a closer look.

In the preoperative suite, Bruna helped a drowsy Emily out of her clothes and into a hospital gown, printed with frolicking lambs. She lifted her onto the bed and pointed to one of the lambs. She said, "Cordiero."

Emily looked down at her lap. With a tiny smile, in a soft voice, she said, "Muitos cordieros." Bruna laughed and gave her another hug. When a nurse entered the cubicle, Bruna moved to a chair next to Katherine's alongside the wall.

The nurse introduced herself to Emily first, then to Katherine and Bruna. She helped Emily lie down on the bed and covered her with a soft blanket. "I'm going to start an IV and place some electrodes on her chest for the heart monitor. Perhaps you could go on the other side of the bed and comfort Emma while I work?" She directed her statement to Katherine. She stood up, momentarily light headed, and then took her place beside Emily. When she took Emily's hand in her own, it felt cold.

When the nurse put a tourniquet around Emily's arm, her eyes opened wide.

"It's the nurse, sweetie," Katherine said. "She's getting you ready to help your cousin. Remember?" Emily frowned, blinking her eyes. When the nurse wiped an area on her arm with an alcohol pad, Emily cried out in fear.

"It's just for a minute, Emmie. It's to keep you safe when you go to sleep. It will—"

Emily screamed and tried to pull back her arm as the needle went in. "No! It hurts me!"

Katherine tried to console her, but her voice couldn't carry over Emily's.

"I've injected a numbing agent," the nurse said to Katherine. "She'll be all right. She won't feel anything more in a few moments."

Katherine held her breath as she watched the nurse push a slim plastic tube into Emily's arm. She continued to cry but she was beginning to give in to her sedation as the pain disappeared.

"The anesthesiologist will be in shortly," the nurse said, taping the tubing to Emily's arm. "He will give her medication and then we will move her to the operating suite." The nurse's expression turned to concern. "You've become very pale. Why don't you sit down?"

Bruna moved to stand beside Emily when Katherine returned to her seat.

"There's nothing to worry about. The procedure is very easy. Shall I explain?" the nurse asked Katherine.

She didn't want to hear it again, but she didn't want the nurse to misinterpret her reaction, so she nodded her assent.

"The child will be placed on her stomach. In the operating suite, she will be put more deeply under anesthesia. She will not wake. She will not feel pain. The surgeon will make a few small slits over the back of her hip. Then he will withdraw some marrow from each area with a needle and syringe. That's it. Emma's part is over. She won't even have stitches. Maybe some soreness for a week or two, at most."

"Thank you," Katherine said. She did feel better listening to the procedural details again. It wasn't too much to ask of Emily. Katherine would make it up to her.

A half hour later, the anesthesiologist and another member of the transplant team wheeled a sleeping Emily out of the pre-op room.

Because she still felt lightheaded, Katherine went to the hospital coffee shop and ordered juice and a roll. She knew it would take some time to withdraw Emily's marrow. Then the marrow would be treated to prevent clotting. Emily's T cells would be removed to help prevent the dreaded Graft versus Host Disease, GVHD, which could make the process fail. Finally, the marrow would be delivered to Madison's room for infusion.

When Katherine arrived at Madison's new room, she entered though an anteroom where she donned a mask, gown, and gloves. From now on, these precautions would be taken by everyone entering Maddy's room. Her immune system had been brought down by chemotherapy and radiation. She would have no defense against infections until the marrow began to produce new white cells.

The transplant *had* to work after all this time and effort. She was determined to think positive. It *would* work. But Katherine knew the emotional cost would be devastating. She'd done terrible things to others:

abducted a child, corrupted her housekeeper, lied to Maddy's father and others about the purpose of their trip, broken the heart of Emily's mother. She'd dragged two little girls to Brazil because she couldn't risk bringing Emily to a US hospital. Her only defense for what she had done was the fact that her daughter's illness had sent her into a senseless, desperate madness.

She pushed open the inner door to Maddy's room. "Good morning, my sweet darling," Katherine said. "Guess who I am?"

It broke her heart to see Maddy's weak attempt to smile. "Mommy." Her little face was white and there were arcs of purple shading under her eyes. She'd lost weight quickly; her arms and legs were thinner. She wore a colorful head wrap to hide her hair loss. When Katherine had sobbed while holding a golden tress of Maddy's fallen hair, the doctor had been kind. "Her hair will grow back, don't worry." But she knew it was punishment for the trauma Emily suffered when they cut off her pretty hair.

She grasped Maddy's hand and held on.

Nurses were already in the room preparing her for the transplant. Her central venous line and ports were exposed and disinfected. An IV was flowing through one of the ports.

A half hour later, the marrow had still not been delivered. Katherine began to fear the worst. Something had gone wrong. Was Emily awake and able to tell them about her kidnapping?

"It's taking so long for the marrow to arrive. Do you think something went wrong? Can you go and check for me, please?" she asked one of the nurses.

"It sometimes takes a longer while. But I will go see," the smallest of the three nurses answered.

The nurse didn't come back. Katherine began to feel nauseated, certain the police were on the way. They would never proceed with the transplant if they suspected Katherine was a kidnapper.

She could see the nurse in the anteroom now, putting on a mask. Her face was serious as she looked through the glass at Katherine. When she stepped into the inner room, she said, "It will be here shortly."

Katherine did not feel relieved. Was it the police or the marrow that was coming? She could hardly breathe.

And then it came. The marrow looked like just another blood transfusion. She could hardly contain her emotion. Nothing had gone wrong. They were minutes from passing the healing cells into Madison's body.

The nurse hung the blood bag on the pole behind the bed and attached the end of the tubing to another port on Maddy's line. They took her vital signs as the first drips flowed down the tube and into her bloodstream.

Madison was also mildly sedated as the transfusion would take about an hour. Two of the nurses would stay with her until the bag was empty.

Katherine stared at the drops. *Drip. Drip. Drip.* She had come so far from the day the doctor had explained what the diagnosis of Fanconi's anemia involved.

She'd first tried to fight the system. The National Organ Transplant Act, NOTA, made it a felony to offer compensation to a donor of blood marrow, despite it being legal to pay for blood. What was bone marrow but young blood? It was so difficult to find a perfect match among the thin list of donors that had been tested. Money was plentiful, so she had even worked under the radar looking for donors. Then there'd been one choice left. And no time.

Today it would all come down to the transplant. *Please God, let it work.*

CHAPTER TWENTY FIVE

Emily's room in the new house was smaller than the other one, but it had another bedroom for Bruna, and a TV room. Auntie Kay had a room, too. This time the window in her bedroom wasn't painted black. She loved to look outside at all the people far below on the sidewalk. Some days, Bruna took her down the elevator and out to the stores or to the park.

Bruna was more fun than the other lady, Dee. She talked different, like the other people where they were now. Bruna said she had an *accent* when she spoke. She told Emily that she spoke Portuguese. Dee had taught her some Portuguese words and Bruna taught her more. She gave Emily noisy kisses, and then she would give her a big loud laugh that made Emily laugh, too.

When she told Bruna that she wanted to go home to her mommy, Bruna said, *"I know menima,"* with a sad face.

Sometimes, Emily forgot about her mommy. Then she would feel bad and Nana would come.

"Bruna, I want to play with my cousin today," Emily said as she finished her milk and slid off her chair.

"Your cousin cannot play with you, Emmie, she is still sick, doente, in the hospital. You know that."

"When will she come out?"

"Not for a while. You are stuck with me, little girl." Then Bruna gave her a hug and a big kiss on the cheek. She chuckled and Emily giggled with her.

Laughing made Emily feel sad sometimes. "Can I go home soon? I'm not sick in the hospital anymore."

"Not yet. You must wait for your cousin to be well. We will have fun, Emmie. Would you like to help Bruna make some cookies? We will have Maddy's mama take them to her in the hospital." She stooped down in front of Emily and put warm hands on her cheeks. "We will put good things in our cookies to make her better and then you can go home with your cousin."

Katherine was paying for her sins with this extreme stress. As she sat at Madison's bedside she felt the nagging ache in her right ear and the distant rumbling of nausea that heralded a bad migraine.

It seemed she and Madison were stuck in a circle of hell. Every day, a repeat of the day before. Madison didn't even cry anymore when she vomited or had diarrhea. Her brave baby. The staff continued to infuse her with blood, antibiotics, and medication to prevent rejection of Emily's marrow. Every day, they took samples of her blood to see if the transplanted marrow had engrafted. Katherine didn't allow herself to be hopeful any more. It was nearing the end of July, and she felt as if she and her beloved daughter were floating on a raft, rapidly approaching a huge waterfall. Worse, part of her thought it might be a relief to go over those falls. It was nearly impossible to keep up a happy face for Maddy, but she worked at it.

She hated to leave Madison alone in the hospital, but it was clear, the aspirin she'd swallowed wasn't working. She would have to take the strong prescription she'd brought and go to sleep. The private nurse she'd hired promised to call her if Madison showed any sign of distress, so Katherine walked back to the hotel.

It's going to work. It's going to take. She chanted the words like prayers as she went. The transplant was done, leaving only the interminable wait for signs of engraftment or rejection.

She arrived at the hotel suite and went right to the small kitchen. The smell of the baking cookies made her more nauseated.

"Bruna, I'm going to lie down." She took a few breaths through her mouth. "I'm not feeling well. I'm going to take some medicine and try to sleep. Wake me at four o'clock, please." She placed a hand on Emily's head as she moved gingerly to the refrigerator for an ice pack.

In the bathroom, she swallowed a pill with a mouthful of water then waited by the toilet in case she vomited. She should have left Maddy sooner, but she kept hoping the aspirin she'd taken would work.

Her head pounded as she curled up on the bed, still dressed. Katherine had suffered migraines since she was a child, but they'd become more common and more severe since Maddy's illness. An illness that even with a successful transplant would continue to pose a threat to Madison's life. Vigilance was the watchword, and would be forever. She rolled over, adjusting the ice on her neck. Every new migraine reminded her of the blackest day of her life. The day Madison hadn't awakened on her own.

Katherine hadn't been this nervous about a sleeping child since Madison was an infant. Back then she remembered waking during the night and listening for the sounds of breathing from the baby in a bassinet in their bedroom. Sometimes she would wake her husband and make him get up to feel her little chest.

But that black morning when Maddy didn't come downstairs, she was alone.

She had stepped into Maddy's sweetheart-pink room, and could see her daughter's small body snuggled under the pink and green puff. She tiptoed to her bed, so as not to startle Maddy, but ended up having to shake her to wake her up. A cold stone replaced her heart. But after a few minutes, Maddy rallied, asking for her breakfast.

Katherine adored her daughter. Madison was a beautiful child, with her father's even features, blond hair, and blue eyes. She was two and a half years old that morning and due for her yearly checkup. As Katherine had watched her daughter eat without enthusiasm, the coldness in her chest grew. Her daughter was almost white and by the time she finished breakfast, she seemed listless and lethargic. Katherine called the doctor and by the end of the day, her life had changed forever.

But Katherine was a good mother. She was determined to do everything she could to help Madison. She would do what she had to for Maddy. What good was it to have money and privilege if she couldn't use it to heal her sick child?

Now, with the throbbing in her head a smidgeon less harsh, she wondered what she would do with Emily when they were back in the States. The child was smart. She'd already learned many words and phrases in Portuguese. Could Katherine use that to her advantage? Could they take her to Portugal and leave her somewhere safe? She'd always thought she'd find a way to get the child back to her mother. But then they'd had to move too fast to think about anything other than kidnapping Emily.

She had to formulate a plan, a plan with the best chance that she and Dee would never be caught. Not that she didn't feel she deserved punishment, but no one could love Madison more than she did, or take care of her the way she would in the future.

Katherine raised a hand to cup her right eye. The migraine pain had moved up the side of her face. She couldn't concentrate, and so she gave up. Bruna would take care of Emily, who had already rebounded from her own hospital procedure. Katherine would be able to sleep while the medicine did its job. When she was asleep she wasn't worried sick, the only respite she'd found.

CHAPTER TWENTY SIX

A couple of cases had stayed with Tim. Cases of children who'd suffered a terrible death. Innocents some evil maniacs took for their twisted pleasure then murdered.

He thought about six-year-old Charlie Clark. Tim had had the address in his hand, which was gripping the steering wheel. The scream of the siren, flashes of the lights as he'd sped down the road were engraved on his mind. He'd raced faster and faster, marking miles, and more miles. He'd been so close. He was on his way minutes after finding the piece that solved Charlie's case. But it may as well have been years. He was too late.

Tim hadn't waited for back-up. He ran up rickety wooden stairs and kicked open the door. The house was deadly silent. Gun in hand, he rushed from room to room. Cigarette smoke stunk up the living room. He looked up the stairs. Listened. Dead silence. He took the steps two at a time. With his gun pointed in front of him, he checked the first room, the closet. As he passed the bathroom, he leaned in and pushed open the dirty shower curtain. One room to go.

In the last room, he found Charlie in a dog kennel. A kennel where his sadistic pedophile locked him up between sessions of abuse. The little boy was curled up, dead. He was naked, his white skin marked with bruises. Dried blood.

Tim had been the one to tell the boy's parents.

"God damn!" He forced the image from his mind. He ran his damp hand over his short hair. It wasn't the first time he'd relived the anguish of finding Charlie.

He raised an arm and wiped away the sweat that had beaded on his forehead. And he hadn't even started to work yet. It happened every time he remembered. He physically struggled, as if there was still hope of getting there in time to save Charlie.

Tim now gazed down at the pattern of the eco-cherry floorboards he'd arranged. The color of each pre-finished piece varied from light gold to deep brown-red. It was like assembling a jigsaw puzzle based on an abstract painting. It took all his concentration, which was what he loved about home improvement projects. His whole Boston Arts and Craft house was a project. He'd purchased it four years ago. Someday, it would be finished. Then maybe he'd buy a new old house. With the stress of police work, he needed periods of physical work demanding enough to give him complete mental rest. Making an old house shine fulfilled another deep need in him as well, something he couldn't put into words.

He nodded his final approval of the arrangement of the floorboards, and went to heft the pneumatic floor-nailer he'd rented. He tied a bandana around his forehead, put on his kneepads. He knelt down on one knee, knocked the first board tight against the wall with the rubber mallet. Next, he moved the nailer into place. The first blast of the machine sent a small shock through him; it'd been a while since he used one, and he'd forgotten the force in the tool. Then he settled into a pattern: pick up the board, align it, knock it into place, and force a dozen or so nails into it. He left the edges to finish later.

Instead of offering the peace of mind he sought, the work became rote. He found himself thinking about his case, thinking about Emily Connor, and her mother, Thea.

Yesterday the team had reviewed the case, brainstorming their next moves. Tim was frustrated with the results of the tedious work they had done so far. All of the Mercury Marquis sedans had passed muster; all the local pedophiles had an alibi. John Warren's alibi checked out. According to his ex-wife, their families, and other contacts, Warren had never indicated to anyone that he had a child by another woman. The number of family members on both sides was few, which was strange to Tim, whose own family was a large tribe of multiple generations. Most of them still living in the Boston area.

He hadn't ruled out Thea as a suspect. There was still something intangible that bothered him about her. Was he being overly careful? From the first time he saw her, sitting in the cruiser at the crime scene, he knew he would have to work to stay detached. Her shining chestnut hair, her pretty face, in spite of her distraught state, and her big blue eyes drew him in. But he'd been successful in suppressing his attraction to her.

He laid down the next board, checking along its length, before he knocked it in place, using more force than needed. There had to be a trace of Emily's disappearance somewhere. What was he missing? He dropped the mallet and picked up the nailer. The loud compressed air shots of the tool deadened his hearing and numbed his mind. But a few minutes later, his thoughts were back on the case. This one was driving him nuts.

Thea Connor. At first he assessed her as simply a devastated mother. Sincerely broken-hearted. But after interviewing her friends and colleagues, a glimmer of doubt began to appear.

Tim had been a detective for five years, and had a pretty good close-rate on his cases. He'd managed to rely on healthy habits like being with friends, regular exercise, and the kind of physical work he was doing today, to keep the pressures of his job at bay.

He stood up and shook out his arms and legs. He began to clean up the work area. What had he missed in Emily's case? Thea was a smart woman, straight-forward, who answered his questions directly, except for the delay in giving him the father's name. She didn't want to take the poly, but no one wanted to take the poly. Although she didn't pass the first time, she took it again with a normal reading. It didn't help much.

Tim's brow creased in confusion as he pictured her the last time he'd updated her. What was it? What about her bothered him? He always listened to his inner voice. He concentrated. After the ear-splitting sound of the nailer, the silence insulated him. Then he had it. In his mind, he saw Thea's face. It was something in her eyes. Guilt? He knew parents' reactions to abducted children took many forms, some of which looked like guilt. It was his job as investigator to determine if she was blaming herself in an expected way, or guilty for something she'd done that she was holding back from him.

She clearly harbored anger at the father. Tim figured it was a jilted lover scenario, which turned out to be the case. But the "something" was still in her eyes after the father issue went away. He hadn't focused on that fact until now.

He unplugged the nailer and removed his knee pads and bandana. He wondered if he should bring Thea Connor back in for questioning by another detective. Or maybe he'd ask her some pointed questions next time she came by for a case update. Shake her up a little.

His mind made up, he headed for the shower.

"What is the correct age of Emma Cruickshank? There is a discrepancy in the record." A heavyset doctor, one member of the transplant team, stood holding the door ajar. He was wearing scrubs and holding an untied mask over his nose and mouth.

"What?" Katherine said, feeling a tightness begin in her chest. "I . . .

I'm not sure." She was safe inside her cap and mask, sitting beside Madison's bed. The doctor could not see her panic.

"She is a cousin, correct? Do you have her exact birth date?"

Katherine drew a blank; she couldn't remember what date they'd made up for Emma Cruickshank when they altered Emily's records. "I'm sorry. I'm not sure. I'll call her mother and let you know later."

He stepped back and let the door close. She watched him through the glass as he shuffled the papers in his hands until he found what he wanted. Then he looked at her and furrowed his brows. He pushed the door back open with his shoulder, holding up his mask with his hand. "The records state the mother is dead. Permission is signed by the father."

Good Lord. She'd forgotten the mother was supposed to be dead. How could she forget something so important? And now the doctor was clearly suspicious. How many other people had skirted the law to save a life?

"Doctor, I didn't even know Madison had a cousin living in South America until we began to search for a match. We were so lucky to have found Emma. I've been sick with concern about my daughter. I didn't spend much time with Emma before she returned home to her father." Katherine let her eyes tear up. "I'm so embarrassed. Let me call him and get the correct date for you."

She burned when the doctor left. The amount of money the hacker had charged her and he'd still made a mistake. He'd obviously left Emily's true birth date somewhere in the records. How would she find out which date was the one set up for Emma? She had no doubt the doctor would not be satisfied until the inconsistency was resolved. She couldn't call Dirk; he'd taken back the phone she'd used to contact him when his work was finished, and warned her never to use his home number again.

"Mommy," Madison said, in the panicked voice she used when she had to throw up.

Katherine grabbed the basin and held it as her daughter gagged. She pushed the button for the nurse, but she knew there was nothing anyone could do at this point. Madison had to tough it out, part of the cost of the cure.

She rubbed Madison's back as she slipped into a light sleep. Was she cured? They still didn't know. So far, her tired little body had not rejected Emily's bone marrow; there was no sign of the Graft Vs Host Disease that had the doctors so worried. They should soon be able to tell if Emily's marrow had engrafted in Madison, and begun to produce the blood cells she needed to live. They were twenty-four days past the transplant.

Katherine was excessively protective of her daughter at this stage when Madison was so vulnerable to infections that could kill her. Her little girl endured all the medical ministrations without the strength even to cry. But Katherine cried. Inside she railed against the world, against God. She was half crazy with worry, with the pain of watching her five-year-old child suffer.

How would she find the birth date? She had skimmed her copy of Emily's records. She hadn't thought to bring them once the electronic records were confirmed as received. Now she had no idea how to retrieve the information.

She would have to gain access to Madison's records. Then pray they included Emma's correct information as the donor. The doctor had held a thick paper file, but she had also seen him review records on the computer outside Madison's room.

Wait! All she had to do was look at Emily's passport. Of course, she had not really gone *home;* she was right at the hotel. Along with her passport and birth certificate. God. She'd told so many lies her mind was muddled. She had to think clearly or she could make a serious mistake. If they discovered the crimes she'd committed, Madison might recover her health, but she would have to grow up without her mother.

Would her private hell ever end?

CHAPTER TWENTY SEVEN

The gardens were at their summer peak. Dark-blue spikes of delphinium contrasted with hot-pink cone flowers and blood-red tea roses. Delicate guara plants with their airy stems dotted with small pink blossoms rubbed shoulders with tall white phlox. The bounty of Hannah's labor of love was left for Thea to enjoy with very little work. She tried to absorb the beauty and joy but it was anathema to her wounded spirit. This morning she woke in a funk of hopelessness she couldn't shake, even in the midst of this soul-lifting gift of nature.

She stood in the downstairs bedroom, looking out over the front garden. She'd come in to open the window, but the contrast of the happy garden and her despair stopped her. As she stared out the window, she pulled on a lock of hair and wondered when she'd had her last cut. Her hair had grown to a few inches below her shoulder blades. She hadn't noticed until now because every day she shoved it into a pony-tail or a clip.

Summer was still in full swing. The tourists jammed the roads and beaches, which were covered by panoplies of brightly colored umbrellas. But Thea barely noticed the crowds; hadn't been to the beach. She'd turned down invitations from her friends and neighbors. Sometimes they wouldn't take no for an answer, so she'd spend a short time with them. Though she usually felt better afterwards, her inclination was to be alone. If it weren't for her walks, Thea could become a recluse. If only there was something, anything, to give her hope of finding her daughter. It was now early August and there wasn't one clue of her existence. In the ten weeks since her abduction, her posters, hanging on telephone poles or pasted in shop windows, had faded in the summer sun. Just like Thea's optimism for Emily's return, her child's image in the public eye threatened to slip away. Like a raft sinking under a shipwreck survivor, Thea faced drowning in her sorrows.

She needed coffee! Lots of it! Then a hot shower. She had to get out of the house. Away from the phone, computer, and her own inner voice. And, she needed a haircut.

The shower improved her outlook. She was looking for her keys and purse when, like the perfect friend that she was, Annie arrived.

"What's going on?"

"I was just on my way out," Thea said. "I'm going to see if Darlene can fit me in for a haircut."

"Do you have time for breakfast first?"

"Why not? I drank a lot of coffee and I'm starting to get caffeine shakes. Sure."

Between bites of scrambled eggs and home fries, Annie looked across the table at her friend. "Are you doing okay? I think about how hard it must be in the cottage alone. Waiting."

"Sometimes staying hopeful is almost impossible. This morning I had to practically kick myself out of a funk. But most of the time I know in my heart that Emily's coming home."

"I know she is, too. I've never doubted it."

Thea felt a spurt of joy—the first upbeat emotion she'd felt in a while—at hearing Annie's positive thoughts about Emily's return, too.

They sipped coffee after they ate. Annie looked vibrant in an electric-blue top over white capris. Her blond hair was loose, one side tucked behind her ear, exposing a delicate silver loop with a dangling starfish.

"So, do you have plans for tonight?" Thea asked.

"Yeah. I'm going to break up with Hugh."

"No! Not Hugh-hoo?" Thea said, grinning at the name they'd given Annie's latest flame. "Why?"

Annie screwed her face up. "It's hard to say. We're not, I don't know, it's sort of become a dull relationship, like flat soda. Remember, it started with such heat. That day on the steps to the beach—"

Thea raised her hand. "You don't have to remind me. I can't even think about going back to that beach since you told me about the sex-on-the-steps story."

"Well, it's not for lack of sex, it's lack of heart. At least on my part. There's no depth. And by now, I thought I'd want to spend every minute in Hugh's company—don't say it!" Annie said when Thea's lips formed the H shape to add the hoo. Thea put her hand over her mouth and grinned, nodding for Annie to go on.

"Anyway, I'm not getting any younger and I can't afford to waste time. I really don't think Hugh—don't say it—will be unhappy. I just have too much energy for him. He even looks tired." She giggled.

"I never thought Hugh-hoo was right for you. He's so, um, starched or something. Way too formal. You need someone with a sense of humor who's laid back and can appreciate your many gifts. And I'm not just talking physical gifts. I think Hugh-hoo appreciated them plenty. But, it's too bad. Are you okay with this?"

"A little down on myself for another failed relationship. But enough about me. I found out who was cutting your lawn before you came home."

Thea raised her eyebrows. Annie went on. "It was Jacob Etheridge. Remember him? He was in our high school class."

Thea thought for a minute. "I think I do. Quiet guy, tall?"

Annie brought her hand to her mouth as if to hold it closed. Then a smile began. "Yep. That's him. I guess high school is the last time you saw him?"

Thea detected something behind the expression on Annie's face that intrigued her. "I guess so. Have you seen him since then?"

"Let me put it this way, I have *known* him." It sounded like an attempt at a joke but it fell so hard it cracked.

Thea pretended she didn't notice. "Why would he cut my lawn?"

"Because he is a sweet, big-hearted guy. Anyway, I ran into him, and he asked me how you were doing. He has a landscape business, and he was working on a property I had listed. When I told him you were back, he mentioned he'd been cutting your lawn before you came home. He was going to ask you if he could keep cutting it. He never asked you?"

"No, probably because I go out there every week and mow the lawn like a madwoman chopping up a kidnapper. But I'll have to thank him. It's typical of who I've become, I'm momentarily touched by someone's kindness, but I crowd out gratitude with my problems." Thea reached over and broke off a piece of the donut on Annie's plate. "So, you and Jacob had a thing? When? Why don't I know about it?"

"It's old news, hon. Nothing you missed."

As Annie chatted about her latest real estate sales and listings, Thea continued to break off pieces of Annie's donut, nearly finishing the whole cruller while she listened. She'd eaten most of her eggs and potatoes, too, and was starting to feel sleepy. When Annie stopped talking, Thea said, "Tell me about you and Jacob." The second the words were out of Thea's mouth, Annie blushed. Thea looked back at her, surprised at the reaction. "Hey, are we not best friends? Don't I already know way too much about your sex life? What's so special about Jacob and you?"

Annie turned her eyes to the restaurant's counter, where every stool was taken, and everyone seemed to know each other. When she looked back at Thea, resignation was written all over her face. "I never told you. It was a bad time for you and it's long over."

"When?"

"The summer you didn't come home."

"Oh, the time I was busy making Emily." Thea laughed, and since the sound was rare as kiwis, it lifted her heavy spirits. "So what happened?"

"I was crazy about him. I really loved him, Thea. I thought I was going to surprise you and ask you to be my maid of honor. He met my parents and I met his. It all happened so fast. Too fast, I guess."

"Go on. What went wrong?" Thea saw tears sparkle in Annie's pine-green eyes.

"It wasn't my fault. He never let me explain. It was a stupid misunderstanding between two stubborn people who wouldn't listen to each other. I guess it just wasn't meant to be."

Thea didn't push further. Instead she changed the subject, and when she did, she realized *she* was helping Annie for a change. For once she wasn't accepting everyone's generosity in ways she'd never imagined, all to get through another day. The realization of how she'd been existing the last several weeks caused her to open her eyes wide as she stared into the past.

"What? Thea?"

Thea was filled with a warm, loving sensation that felt wonderful. "I am so amazed at what a good friend you are. How did you know I needed you today?"

Annie tapped her hand over her heart. And they smiled at each other.

Still basking in the glow of friendship, Thea stopped at the mailbox, pulling out a bunch of envelopes. She got as far as the porch and stopped. In the middle of the pile of mail, she saw a heavy bond, cream envelope. She dropped the rest of the mail onto the glider, moved her finger under the flap, and slid out the card inside. Enclosed by a narrow gold border was a short paragraph. Her mother's tombstone had been placed.

Thea had been in college when her mother shocked her with her burial plans. Hannah had told her she'd purchased a neat little plot in the cemetery of a small Protestant church in Eastham. The church was postcard-New England with its white clapboard siding and high narrow steeple. It had two black-painted doors with a gothic arch at the front entrance, doors through which Hannah had never passed, at least to Thea's

knowledge. Behind the church, gravestones dated as early as the 1700s
rose up a grassy hill dotted with oaks and maples. Hannah had made
rubbings of the oldest stones with their engraved angels and charming
poetry, and bound them in an album. It was a serene resting place for
Christians who embraced the faith and hoped to rest in peace.

When Hannah showed Thea the plot deed, she looked wide-eyed at
her mother.

"Mom, are you kidding me? I was afraid you'd ask to have your ashes
scattered on a mountain in Tibet. Maybe officiated by a lama. But a
church burial? How did you even convince them to let you buy this plot?
Don't you have to be a member of the church to be buried there?"

"Pastor Joe and I used to have long discussions about God. Joe was an
old soul with a loving heart. You know, Thea, every great religion teaches
the same message. That's no accident. There's a spirit working in the world
to bring us the truth. Everyone hears it differently, in their own way, and
in their own time. Pastor Joe believed in the tenets of his faith, but he
never thought it was the only way to God."

Thea shook her head. "But how did you convince him you should be
buried in this church graveyard when you've never attended services?"

"I told him I needed a holy spot to leave my body, so that my only
child could have a physical place to come visit me."

Thea had rolled her eyes and smiled. "You are one amazing woman,"
she'd said.

She had not been able to visit her mother's grave since Emily was
abducted. It would be too hard to focus on both losses, so she'd put it out
of her mind. She'd commissioned the headstone the week her mother died.
Thea looked down at the card. It was time.

She picked flowers from the garden to bring to the grave, but when the
bouquet was arranged in a vase, it didn't seem to be enough. She walked
around the house and added some of the herbs from Emily's garden. Still,
it didn't feel sufficient. Then she knew. She went into the sacred space and
scooped up a handful of Emily's seashells. She held them against her cheek
for a minute. Then she called Star, and they drove to the cemetery.

When her mother was buried, the current pastor of the church had
performed a short ceremony at the gravesite. A large group of people had
attended, some of whom Thea had never met. Others, friends she hadn't
seen since they were children, also showed up.

Thea's childhood friends had loved Hannah. There was always a group playing at their house. But once Thea started elementary school, she began to be embarrassed by how different her mother was from the other mothers. Hannah wore her auburn hair long and loose. She dressed in full-length, brightly colored skirts. In the summer, she made daisy chain wreaths to wear in her hair. She made them for Thea and the other children, too. She read them poetry in her lilting voice, and taught them to identify the seashells they collected from the beach.

How did Hannah do so much? She ran a business, the Natural Foods Market, put a wholesome if simple dinner on the table each night, kept up with the wash and gardens. And Hannah always found time to spend in her sacred space, even if it was late at night. She meditated—her form of prayer—and studied numerology and astrology.

Thea's second grade teacher once called Hannah the 'gypsy mother' and made Thea cry. When she told her mother, Hannah laughed and hugged her. "We're all gypsies, Thea. Gypsies are people who wander."

"But, Mommy, we don't wander. We live in Orleans."

"We're here on earth for a short while to dance among the flowers, to lighten each other's burdens, and to seek the Spirit."

"Then where do we go?"

"We're gypsies. We can go anywhere we want next."

At the age of seven, it was enough to satisfy her. She was a happy, secure child. But as she grew into her teens, her mother began to appear foolish to Thea. Lovable, but flighty. Thea earned good grades and excelled at subjects with facts and logic, like science and history. The gap between their philosophies widened as she went to college and on to law school, but the bridge of mutual love between them had kept them connected.

Thea, remembering the way, walked to the plot with Star on a short leash. The new granite headstone was shining in the sun like a beacon.

Hannah Mary Connor
My spirit rises with the rising wind

She read the Roethke quotation her mother had chosen to be engraved on her stone. Hannah had spent hours looking through her books of poetry and philosophy before she selected these few words that she felt most captured her belief of death.

Thea placed the flowers she brought to one side of the face of the stone. She took Emily's seashells from her pocket and held them in her hands as she sat down on her mother's grave. She closed her eyes, attempting to feel her mother's presence, hear her supportive words of encouragement. She desperately needed her mother's comfort. If any angel could wrap her wings around her as she sat by her mother's grave, it would be Hannah. Thea quieted her mind, and with every breath, tried to sense her mother's spirit.

But she felt nothing.

Star was sitting beside her, her head raised and her ears straight up, as if she was also trying to sense Hannah's spirit. Thea smiled, moved the shells into one hand, and reached out the other to pet her dog. Feeling a little foolish, she said, "Thanks for the great dog, Mom. She's been a big help." Then she leaned forward and placed Emily's seashells in an even line at the base of the headstone. A second later, she started to pick them up; overwhelmed with a confused fear that putting Emily's shells on a grave might hold a negative significance. She bent her head until the dark sensation passed. Not Emily. *Emily is alive.* The thought came from her own mind. No spirit on the wind. Thea was alone.

She put the shells back alongside the gravestone. "Find her for me, Mom." She paused. "I love you," she added. Just in case.

"ust wanted to ask you a few questions," Tim said once they were seated at the table in the interview room.

Thea knew right away it was an ambush. She'd stopped in for an update while she was in Boston. She stared at the other detective. He was looking down at the notebook, pencil ready in his hand. Because she'd never seen him before, his presence was intimidating.

"Detective Repucci and I have been reviewing Emily's case. We want to go over your statements. Talk a little more about your life as a single mom attending law school. I'd like you to fill in more background on the case. Maybe about Emily's father, your friends."

He kept at her for over two hours. Still, she couldn't understand what it was he wanted from her. She answered his questions honestly, but it didn't seem to satisfy him. Repucci mostly made notes on his pad, but he occasionally asked for clarification. Tim kept pushing and pushing her; for what, she didn't know. Finally, she'd had enough.

"Why won't you believe me? What are you thinking I did? Why don't you just come out and say it instead of being so angry?"

"Angry? Why do you think I'm angry?" Tim said.

"Take a look at yourself in the mirror. It's all over your face. What do you suspect? Why are you harassing me?"

He spoke slowly in a low voice. "Because there's something you're not telling me. Because whatever you're holding back could save your child's life."

Thea stood. "I'm not holding anything back. I have no idea why you continue to think I had something to do with Emily's abduction."

Tim rose also, and moved to stand in front of her. His voice was tight, in an attempt to rein in his temper that was clearly ready to explode. "Because it's in your eyes. And it makes me angry, because I hate it when children suffer. I hate it when I'm trying to save them, and there's something standing in my way. I look at you when you answer my questions, and I see more there. Maybe guilt."

"Take it easy, Big Mac," Repucci cautioned.

"Oh God," Thea whispered. Her eyes welled up when she looked back at him. "I had nothing to do with Emily's kidnapping. I know what you see." She sat back down and stared at the beige wall. "It's *regret*. I—I feel like I could have been a better mother to Emily. That I was so busy becoming a lawyer, I missed too much of her life. Now she's gone, and what if she doesn't come back?" Thea dropped her face into her hands and sobbed. She should have known something was wrong when she came to Police Headquarters. The expression on Tim's face, and the fact he'd brought along another detective to the interview room, should have warned her. She'd thought she was past this.

Tim sat and talked with her, settling her emotions before he let her go. Thea realized he had what he worked so hard to get. Something in her emotional confession satisfied him. She hated him for making her cry over his stupid interrogation when she had her own heartbreak to grieve. She hated him for making her expose her most personal conflict. And she hated him for betraying her. She thought he cared about her, but it was obviously only police technique.

It bothered her more than it should that this man still suspected her. It didn't matter. She would make it not matter. The important thing was she trusted him, enough to be questioned by him without Will being present. This deeply caring cop was exactly who she wanted to look for Emily. He was a man who would never give up on finding her daughter, and he'd run over anyone and anything standing in his way—including her—and keep looking.

The doorbell began ringing insistently. Thea crept into the guest room from where she could see the farmer's porch. John Warren stood stabbing the button.

Thea had been out in the garden with Star earlier. Along with her paralegal work, gardening was one of the activities that grounded and calmed her. But her serenity fled the moment she saw her visitor was John.

How could she face him? What did he want? She watched him stride off the porch back to his car. What if he knew something about Emily? Thea ran to the kitchen and threw open the door. "John."

He turned and looked at her. He was even more handsome than she remembered. He raised a hand, and then dropped it to his side. He began walking back. Suddenly, Thea knew she didn't want him in her house. She went outside and stood on the porch. He stepped up and hesitated, as if he didn't know why he was there or what to do next.

"Thea, I'm sorry."

His eyes supported his statement. "Sorry for what, John?"

"For all of it, but mostly because your daughter was kidnapped. Can we go in and talk?"

"I don't think so. And it's *our* daughter. You can sit on the glider. I'll listen."

He nodded, stepped to the glider and took a seat, crossing his legs. "Our daughter. Yes, so the police informed me. You should have told me, Thea. Why didn't you?"

She sat down on the top step of the porch and thought about her answer. "You made it clear you didn't want her," she answered, staring off to the wooded area beyond the garage. "You paid me to end the pregnancy, remember?"

"Of course. And I was kind of callous about it. I'm sorry."

"You were married when I told you I was pregnant." She turned to watch his reaction.

He shifted his body and the glider banged around until he planted both feet firmly on the ground. "My marriage was another mistake. I should have seen it. It didn't last more than three years. I always wondered what it would have been like if I'd married you."

"Bullshit, John. You would never have married me. Your daddy wouldn't have allowed it. I was not in your league. And you never loved me either. Please don't treat me like I'm stupid."

John rested his elbow on the arm of the glider, held his chin in his hand and looked at her. "Yeah," he said, mooning at her with puppy-dog eyes.

She stared at him. "John, what are you doing here?" What a fool she had been. She'd been awed by a character she had assigned him from her fabricated fantasy. Now she could see right through him. It was like looking through a sheet of plastic wrap—there was nothing to him beyond being handsome. "And why are you here now? It was months ago when the police talked to you."

"I've been thinking about it, and I need to know if she's really mine."

You creep. "There was only you. I couldn't be wrong about it. You're her father."

"If I was the father—of course, I would need a paternity test to prove it—but if I was, what would you want from me?"

"I've never wanted a damn thing from you except that you stay out of our lives. That hasn't changed."

"Come on, Thea." He extended his hand out to her, as if offering his help, tilting his head to one side. "Everybody wants child support."

"Really? Everybody? How many children do you have, John?"

He stood and walked to the end of the porch, held onto the corner post, and gazed out over the backyard. "Only one other," he said so quietly, Thea barely heard him. He turned and looked at her. "And that's all I can handle."

There was something in his face that stopped Thea from making the sarcastic remark she could still taste on her tongue. She instead waited.

"I had nothing to do with it, Thea."

"So the detective told me."

He ran his fingers through his sandy hair, leaving spikes that made him look silly. "The *Globe* recently came out with the story that I'd been questioned by the police. I don't know what it might to do to my career."

Right then, Thea knew she had the potential to murder, but he spoke before she could open her mouth.

"No, that didn't come out right. Don't blow up." He held his hands up, palms facing Thea. "I've had some issues at work, but I've overcome them. I just won a big case. I mean, my father is finally beginning to have faith in me. I've had a hard couple of years, let's say, but I'm back on track, have a new wife—who wants to remain childless—and my life is on the uptick. When the article came out, I asked McIntyre if we had to go public with my paternity—if, of course, it turns out I'm the father—and he told me the police wouldn't be putting it out there."

"So, you came to make sure I would keep your secret?"

"You don't think much of me, do you, Thea?"

"I don't think anything of you at all, John. And you can go home happy. As far as I'm concerned you are not Emily's father, not since the day you told me to abort her. You gave up any rights to her then forever, and I'm happy to hear you agree with that."

She watched his shoulders relax.

"Listen, I never meant to hurt you."

"I got over it a long time ago," Thea lied. "Go in peace, John."

She slid over on the step so he could go by. He walked to his car and opened the door, but he didn't get in. He faced her. "She looks a little like me in her picture."

Thea felt the bile rise in her throat. She stood up and started for the door. He called after her. "Wait." She heard his feet crunching on the driveway gravel as he made his way back to her. "I was just wondering. Has anyone put up a reward for Emily?"

She turned to him. He was framed by the large viburnum bush at the edge of the porch, its blossoms long past. He looked like a movie star on set with his handsome face and earnest expression. She could suddenly understand how such a face could have lured a young woman into bed, and she felt a crack form on the last bit of the hard surface that had sealed up her memories of that time.

"No. I don't think the police like the idea of a reward very much." She knew without a doubt, John had nothing to do with Emily's kidnapping. He was every name she'd been calling him: shallow, egocentric, selfish. But he wasn't Emily's kidnapper.

"I'll call McIntyre myself. If he can keep it anonymous, I'm going to offer it. Money's no object."

And this was the greatest irony: He'd used the exact words—"money's no object"—when he offered her a check to abort the same child he now wanted to help.

CHAPTER TWENTY NINE

A nurse in a protective gown and mask entered the room. "The doctor is at the nurses' station. He asks to speak with you."

Katherine couldn't see the expression on the nurse's face, but her voice was flat, and dread filled Katherine's soul. *The graft didn't take.* After all they'd been through. After all the crimes she had committed. She looked at her daughter's white face, watched as the nurse turned Madison over and began to rub her back.

Maddy opened her eyes and followed her mother's movements as she left the room. Katherine waved to her, a jaunty movement of her hand to hide her despair.

She walked down the hall with her head bent low. Her body leaned forward with the weight of four and a half weeks of isolation in the hospital and no good news. Today, on August eighth, she had no hope left. Katherine had been asking herself, if she had to do it over again, put her daughter through the horror of this treatment, watch her suffer, would she go through with it?

A counselor had tried to engage Katherine in a discussion but she'd refused. She was so depressed she worried that she would give in to a kind word, say something that would expose her crime. Instead, she'd been coping alone, trying to find hope. Failing in every aspect.

She approached the desk and saw the doctor. His back was turned to her. She tried to read his body language as he studied a patient's chart. A nurse told him in Portuguese that Katherine had arrived. He turned, smiling at her, then beckoned for her to follow him.

They went into a small office off the nurses' station. When she took the chair he indicated, Katherine couldn't say how she had arrived at the room. Her body was numb, and her brain had shut down in anticipation of what she was about to hear.

The doctor placed a sheet of paper before her, his big finger stabbing at a number. "This is her latest ANC, absolute neutrophil count. The graft is actively producing white cells."

Katherine stared at the paper. Slowly, his words re-formed in her brain. She looked up at him.

"You had no confidence. You see? You were wrong. Madison is recovering very well. She is building defense against infections very rapidly.

Soon you will take her back to the hotel with you. She will continue to be treated on an outpatient basis. Remember, our main concern, especially since her cousin was not a perfect match, is GVHD. We will continue her medicines to help prevent this complication. For now, she shows no signs."

Katherine was gulping in air. The first happy tears began rolling down her face, some sliding into her open mouth.

The doctor was nodding at her, smiling. "We'll see how long before you can return to the United States," he said. Then he handed her a clean white handkerchief to wipe the tears soaking her face.

CHAPTER THIRTY

Tim sat with his chair tipped back just far enough not to fall over. His big feet were propped on his cluttered desk, while his large hands massaged an official Red Sox baseball.

"I'm telling you, they're toast this year," Detective Darnell Jackson said to the group hanging out around Tim's desk. "There's not one guy at the top of his game on the whole team. Ortiz isn't swinging the bat, and the bull pen's full of losers who can only pitch a good game if the stars are properly aligned and the damn temperature is just right. Those power necklaces they all wear aren't working. I get suckered in every year, but by God, not next year. I'm going to be a Yankee fan next year."

Tim pulled his Red Sox cap farther down over his eyes. "Whine, whine. I don't want to hear it. What a bunch of girly-men work here. The Sox always screw up at this point of the season. It's strategy, man. Give them a break." He pushed his hand deep into his pants pocket and pulled out two tickets. He had season tickets with his brother, who couldn't make the game tomorrow. "Okay, let's hear it. Who's the fan now? Who would kiss my feet to go to the game with me tomorrow night? Who's going to be the highest bidder?"

All five law officers began to speak at the same time.

"Sorry guys, I only have one extra ticket," Tim said, waving the pair of tickets in the air. "You know I can't show favoritism, you'll have to work it out amongst yourselves."

All eyes went to the young officer approaching the group. The pretty brunette sergeant was the newest addition to the Unit.

"McIntyre, Haddon asked me to tell you he's ready for the wrap-up."

Tim groaned. "Your timing is perfect. The kids are fighting, and I'm getting a headache." He stood up, towering over the young woman, and shoved the tickets back into his pocket. He thanked the sergeant before he turned back to his colleagues. "Okay, my boys, play nice, and let me know who's coming to the game."

In the walk from his desk to Haddon's, Tim returned to the world of crime he faced every day, Emily's kidnapping at the top of the list.

"We went back over all the interviews from Tamerind Street at least twice. No help there. We're still getting a few tips a week." Haddon's expression was sour. "We're getting low in manpower. They pulled Bauman for a new case on Friday."

Tim didn't expect to hear any progress on Emily's case from the detective's update. And he didn't.

"Here you go, Haddon." A short officer, with facial features sharp enough to have been chiseled from stone, stepped up to Haddon's desk and handed him a list. "I finished this group." He raised his shoulders and shook his head. "Nothing. I'll help the others, or do you want me to do something else?"

"Yeah, Jockey." Haddon sifted through papers on his desk. "Follow up on this call. It sounds, I don't know, like it could pan out."

The officer walked off, reading the slip of paper Haddon had given him.

Tim felt a twinge of hope. "What's the tip you gave him to follow up on?"

"Just came in. A guy called from a body shop in Southie, saying a customer brought in a black Mercury Marquis for repair of the right rear fender. The shop owner said when the car came in he tried to look nonchalant, so as not to give away his noticing that the vehicle fit the Amber Alert description." Haddon broke a smile. "Just gave the customer a receipt and called the tip line."

"Maybe this is it. Give me a call the minute you hear back on this one," Tim said over his shoulder, on the way back to his office.

He knew better than to place too much hope on one of the hundreds of tips they received. There'd been Emily sightings all over the United States, and every one had been followed up by the local law enforcement or the FBI. People from coast to coast had called in saying they saw the Mercury Marquis. Every tip with any merit had been acted on, though recently the number of calls had dwindled. Crank calls continued, like the psychic who, while she was astral-projecting, saw an angel who looked just like Emily, flying in the clouds.

Tim shoved his chair away from his desk. His hands gripped the chair arms as he directed an exasperated stare at the folders and papers—all accumulated information on Emily's abduction—piled on his desktop. All worth spit. He was a man of patience, but he was rapidly running out of that commodity. It wouldn't be the first case that was never solved, but this one he couldn't accept. If he failed, it would be his nemesis.

He glanced at the framed picture of his son, wearing his baseball uniform. JT was a natural athlete. Like the rest of the family, he was a big fan of the Red Sox. Tim had started tossing him a Whiffle ball when he was two years old. Coaching his baseball team was one of Tim's greatest joys, even though his assistant coach was JT's stepfather. It was working out, though. Rick was a nice guy, who seemed to be a good role model for JT. But they'd always had a little competition as to who was the best father. Tim's ex-wife was fair. She talked to him first about any major decisions in their son's life. She often included him in their holiday gatherings. When he could come—and that had been the problem in the marriage—he usually couldn't. Tim's job had taken too big a chunk out of his family life.

The custody settlement was fifty-fifty, but he had unofficially agreed to make it every other weekend. It was one of the hardest things he'd ever had to do. But JT was only three when they were divorced. Making him split a week between parents would be tough. A boy so young needed his mother, not a nanny, so Tim had agreed to the arrangement. So far, it had worked well. As JT got older, their arrangement had become more flexible and amicable. He saw his son more often in soccer and baseball season.

He adored JT. He couldn't imagine how wrenching it would be if anything happened to him. The thought made him grit his teeth. He was never without the mental pictures of those kids who suffered a grisly end. Over and over, he had to actively remove them from his inner vision. But in truth, he could never forget.

He looked down at Emily's file on his desk. They only needed one piece of solid evidence. Something to tell them she was alive. He had to admit, he was beginning to doubt. But as he drove home, he could feel himself growing optimistic about the body shop call. Maybe the sensation was due to lack of nutrition. It was eight-thirty, and he hadn't eaten anything substantial since noon. But sometimes it was one tip, one person paying attention that closed a case.

He went into his house, took off his gun holster and locked up his weapon. He left his Bluetooth in place; he'd sleep with it tonight if necessary. The next ring could be the case breaker for Emily. He hoped with his whole being that Emily would be one of the children he could save.

When she entered the office, Will came around his desk and enveloped her in a big hug. "How are you doing, Thea? I'm so glad to see you. Sorry I missed you when you were in before. Come in. Have a seat."

She sat in one of the two butterscotch leather chairs facing Will's desk. "I'm doing better, thank you. When everyone told me to move on with my life, get back to work, prepare for the long run ahead, I didn't believe it would ever happen. But it has. There's still the heavy rock I carry around where my heart used to be, but I manage to get through the days."

"I'm glad to hear that, Thea. Maybe now you'll plan to take the bar exam? We need you here."

"I can't tell you how much I appreciate everything you've done for me. I'll never be able to repay you. You have the most generous heart."

Will jumped up and made a big deal of running over and closing his office door. "We can't let that get out, for heaven's sake. It'll ruin my attack-dog reputation."

Thea laughed out loud to see Will perform so out of character.

"That is the best sound I've heard in a long time. You laughing." Will nodded his head and smiled at her. "So, you didn't answer my question about the bar," he said, laser-focused in on her with the intuition that made him one of Boston's best defense lawyers.

She took a breath and looked him in the eye. "At this point, I don't know if I'll ever again pursue my career in law. I do know I won't even think about it until I have my daughter back. I hope you understand, Will. I'm grateful for the offer, but please don't hold a spot open for me. You need someone you can count on, and it's just not going to be me."

Will leaned his elbows on his desk and rested his chin on steepled fingers. For a few minutes he remained silent. Thea began to squirm before he spoke again.

"All right. I'll accept your decision. I understand. So what's next for you? Will you still do paralegal work for us? I hear you do a superior job."

"As long as you'll have me."

"Okay, that's settled," Will said, his words followed by a devilish smile. "For now."

Jeez!

Thea sat on a bench outside of Whole Foods market, where she'd stopped to buy a few items. She was amazed at the high cost of everything and that led to thinking about her money worries. She'd worked on organizing her bills all morning. On her spreadsheet, the expense column total was higher than the income. How had her mother managed all this and helped her pay for her education at the same time?

There must be another way she could make money. She'd waitressed in college. But if she moonlighted with another job, how would she have time to continue looking for Emily?

She checked her watch. It was nearly time for her appointment with Tim. When she stood up, she noticed a woman standing nearby staring at her.

"You're the one on the news. Emily's mother."

Most people had been kind to Thea, but there was clear accusation on this woman's face. It chilled her through and through, despite the fact that she was warm from the hot sun. She decided to move on without answering.

"Wait a minute. I—I mean, such a cute little thing. So God gave you this sweet little girl, and you—"

A man beside her touched her arm. "Judy, don't. It's none of your business."

"The world's going to hell in a hand-basket. It's everyone's business," she said, turning back to Thea. "You should help the police to save your daughter." She took a step closer, her finger pointed at Thea's face. "If you did anything to that child—"

The man took her arm and began to pull her away. But she kept her eyes on Thea as she was dragged off, eyes full of repugnance.

Thea couldn't breathe. How could a total stranger convict her without knowing a thing about her? Where did the woman even get the impression she might be guilty? Something she saw on television or in the newspapers? Thea felt like everyone was staring at her. She turned and hurried up the street.

She didn't relax until she reached the New Sudbury Street police station, where she waited for Tim, gratefully cooling down in the air-conditioned foyer. She was still stinging from the woman's accusation. Detective Haddon came and led her to an interview room. Tim, he explained, was finishing up with a meeting and would be in shortly.

Thea couldn't help but feel nervous. She'd revealed to Tim her innermost remorse about her inadequate mothering skills, a confidence she regretted. But he was good at his job, ferreting out information he needed. Would he show, in any way, that he thought less of her now? Why should she care what he thought? But she did. She cared a *lot* about what he thought of her.

Tim came in minutes later and sat across the table from her.

"I thought I'd check and see if there were any new leads you were working on," Thea said.

After a few seconds of hesitation, he said, "There is a new tip. It's from a body shop. The owner called to report a Mercury Marquis in for the repair of a sideswipe on the right rear fender. Remember the Honda at the crime scene that had been scratched by the kidnapper's car? We notified local body shops to report any jobs on black Mercury Marquis sedans, and we continue to send out reminders periodically. This is why we got the info."

Thea moved to the edge of her seat, hanging on his every word.

"It could be nothing, but sometimes it happens with one tip. You go through hundreds without a hit, and there it is." He leaned forward. "I repeat; this could be nothing. I only want you to know people are still paying attention out there, and we're working every day to find Emily."

She looked around the room to hide the welling of tears in her eyes.

"Don't give up if nothing comes of it. I've been at this a long time. The good news is there's no bad news after the months of searching and investigating we've done."

"Is there anything more I can do? Hold another press conference?"

"It's difficult to excite the press when there's no new information. Maybe you could call around to the radio and TV stations, see if you can interest them in doing a follow-up story."

He walked her out and opened the door. He promised to call when he heard back about the body shop, giving her a rare smile.

Why did she have to have a handsome detective on the case? The kind of man a woman in different circumstances could fall in love with. It only made her feel more aware of her loneliness. But why was she even thinking about that? There was no room in her life for romance. It was all about Emily. Still, it felt like salt on the wound.

On the way back to her car, she thought about Annie's theory on holding open houses in a slow market: They're a pain to do, and no one buys during them. Public appearances at this point seemed similar. But Thea would take Tim's advice and contact the media. Maybe the body shop would be the break they'd been waiting for, the one that would lead them to Emily. Then Thea would never have to think about going public again. She ached with her longing for good news, and couldn't stave off the hope Tim had warned her against having. There was no use trying. She was going to crash anyway if this turned out to lead nowhere. She would just fall from a higher point back to the crushing despair she'd come to accept in her life.

CHAPTER THIRTY ONE

The call didn't come until late the next afternoon. Tim noted the caller ID on his phone and headed out of his office without answering. This would be the break they needed. He could sense it. His steps on the way to Haddon's desk were light and quick.

"What do you have?" he asked. Before the words were out, he read the bad news on Haddon's face.

"Sorry, Big Mac. It was a sideswipe all right, but it was done by a 1994 red Ford four by four. Not the silver Honda Civic. The grooves were filled with oxidized red paint. The owner of the Merc said he found it that way, hit and run, when it was parked in a Stop & Shop lot. He's one of those finance guys who make a fortune with your money even when your 401(k) is tanking. Checks out okay."

"Shit!" Tim's fist hit the desk hard enough to make Haddon's coffee cup wobble. "We can't catch a fucking break!"

Haddon sat still, waiting for the storm to pass.

"Keep me informed." Tim began to walk away, but came back. "It's not you or the team. I know you're all knocking yourselves out and doing a hell of a job." He didn't wait for a response.

He wanted to kick his butt all the way back to his office. Why had he weakened and given Thea hope? Now he had to hit her with the bad news.

He sat in his chair, staring at the phone. What was he missing? Something kept nagging at him, but he couldn't quite grasp it. He knew he was letting this case get to him, which could muddy his instincts. He had never been anything but professional on the job. He was almost too focused on every case he was assigned. But had he ever before been affected the way he was by Thea and Emily?

When Tim told her the Mercury was not the Mercury, he apologized for bringing it to her attention before they had it checked. "We'll keep looking," he'd said. With those few words, Thea figured she was back at the top of the suspect list.

She hung up and stomped around the kitchen, blinking her eyes, which kept refilling with tears. When she saw the mail stacked on the counter, she yelled in frustration and catapulted it into the air. Star flew out of the kitchen and down the hall to cower. Thea crumpled into a chair, dropped her head on the table, and cried. Emily had been gone for nearly three months. Where was she? Was she with someone who was taking care of her?

Thea was exhausted from the long emotional wait for Tim's answer, followed by the huge disappointment. The hard run she'd taken with Star after he called had added to her fatigue. She decided to fix a quick meal then go to bed.

While a grilled cheese sandwich cooked in the electric frying pan, and soup warmed on the stove, she picked up the scattered mail she'd sent flying in her temper, dumping the junk. She ate her food without enjoying it.

Tomorrow had to be better. She wouldn't start it with dirty dishes in the sink. As the dishpan was filling with hot soapy water, she stared out the window. Because it was dark outside, she was seeing her reflection.

She noted the shadows under her eyes, which felt too heavy to hold open. Who was this strange woman? Not pretty, really quite nasty looking. *So what?*

Not quite settled enough to sleep, she wandered into the sacred space and sat in the rocker. She read some of titles of the books on her mother's shelves. Some titles she remembered from her childhood; others were newer hard-covers or trade paperbacks. Except for a shelf filled with Emily's books, all the others were related to her mother's spiritual beliefs.

Since Emily's kidnapping, the most difficult times for Thea were the hollow spaces between tasks, when dark, frightening thoughts began to parade through her mind. She had taken to filling the voids and counteracting the fear by perusing books from her mother's eclectic, numinous library. Over time, Thea noticed her dependency on logic and proof was softening. Somehow, the arcane beliefs of her mother's comforted her more than facts could.

mily peeked into the room and stared at Madison. "Is it Halloween?"

"No, silly."

"Why are you wearing a Halloween mask, then?"

"It's not a Halloween mask. It's because I'm sick. But now I'm getting better."

"I'm better, too."

"No, you're not. You weren't sick, so you can't get better."

Emily frowned. She knew she was sick, because she went to the hospital. "Why didn't I wear a sick mask?"

"Because you weren't sick. You can come into my room now. But you have to ask me first every time."

Emily took a few steps into the room. She wondered what Auntie would say if she saw her in Madison's room. She took a few more steps, and then stopped.

"Don't be afraid of her," Madison said, when Emily noticed the woman sitting near the window, reading a book. "She's my nurse."

When the nurse only smiled at her, Emily walked over to Madison's bed. "If you're better now, can we go home?"

"Not for a while." Madison stared at Emily. "Why don't you have a mother?"

"I have a mother," Emily said, frowning again.

"Where do you live?"

It was strange talking to Maddy with only her eyes showing. "In Nana's cottage. I'm supposed to go home. My mommy wants me home."

"Then why doesn't she come and take you home?"

"I don't know. Nana says I have to wait."

"Your nana's here?"

"Sometimes she comes."

Madison's eyes widened, so Emily determined she didn't believe her. She looked around the room. It was all white, the walls, the bed covers. There were a few toys, some books and a teddy bear.

"Want to color with me?"

Emily nodded.

"Go get the books and crayons. See them over there?" She pointed. "And pull that chair over here."

At the bottom of her driveway, now having arrived home from their walk, Thea detached Star's leash then watched her race up the hill. As Star galloped across the front of the house, Thea gasped. What was left of the chimney stuck up like a broken tooth. She walked around the side of the house to see the bricks, mortar still clinging to them, scattered over the grass. The chimney cap had rolled farther away to the edge of the tree line.

She squeezed her fists in frustration. Why did bad things keep happening to her? Didn't she deserve a damn break? Where would she get the money to fix this? And it was just a matter of time before the refrigerator stopped working. It had begun to sigh and groan, as if it were in pain.

After a few minutes of nurturing her ire and self-pity, she went to stack the bricks against the house. Then she picked up the cap and set it atop the bricks. She would have to do something about this situation. Find ways to cut her bills. But where? She could give up the land line and save a little each month. Emily only knew Thea's cell phone number, because she kept that with her at all times. It wouldn't be enough, though. She would have to find something else to cut, too. As she shagged across the lawn to the side door, an answer became clear.

She knew what she had to do.

In the living room, Thea began to pull books off the shelves, coughing from the dust kicked up. After she washed down the shelves, she pulled her law books from the unpacked boxes lined up against the wall, and arranged them in the empty spaces. She sorted the removed books into a keep pile and a give-away pile. She carried the give-away books to the car to bring to the library. Then she packed up the remaining books for storage in the basement closet. She made room near her desk for the one remaining box, which contained her files. The last thing she did was open her Massachusetts Bar Examination Information folder.

Ten days later, on the second day of the predicted five August "dog days," Thea thought she and Annie must be crazy to be out weeding the garden. The temperature was only in the mid-eighties, but the humidity made it feel ten degrees higher. Still, the weeds were out of control, so she couldn't turn down Annie's offer of help.

She looked over at Annie, who was ruthlessly yanking out long vines with tough roots, some with sharp thorns. What a friend. She'd come for coffee, and finding Thea working in the garden, offered to lend a hand. Tendrils of Annie's blond hair were sweat-glued around her face, which was red with exertion. Thea knew she must look the same. She wondered for the thousandth time how her mother had accomplished everything she did. The un-planted areas of the front garden invited weeds of every stripe: violets, dandelions, buttercups and other mystery weeds, in spite of how much mulch Thea had dumped on them.

"Annie, do you know what this is?" she said, holding her gloved fingers gently around a tall stalk. "I hate to pull it in case it's going to turn into some exotic flower like that Asian poppy."

"You're asking me? I was just wondering how I ended up with dirt ground into my knees and sweat running down between my boobs. I'm only focused on trying to get this done. I'm pulling out anything willing to be pulled." She swiped her face with the back of her glove, leaving a streak of dirt that ran from one eye, across her nose, all the way to the opposite ear.

Thea opened her mouth to reply, when a horn honked as a truck pulled into the driveway.

"Oh my God, Thea, it's Jacob. How do I look?" Annie asked.

She was making matters worse, using the same dirty glove to push the sticky hairs off her face. She looked like she was decked out in war paint. It was all Thea could do not to burst out laughing. "You look beautiful, Annie," she said, as sincerely as she could.

A tall man got out of the truck and walked over to them. He was nice-looking with a tanned face, gray eyes, and an aquiline nose. He had the heavily muscled arms and legs of a man who did physical work for a living. With his long brown hair tied in a pony tail, and his two-day growth of beard, he reminded Thea of a modern-day pirate. He wore olive green shorts and a black t-shirt that read: Ethridge Landscaping.

"Want some help?" Jacob said. He looked as hot and sweaty as they did. He was grinning as he looked from Annie to Thea.

"Jacob, I don't think I've seen you since high school." Thea rose, stiff from squatting for so long. "So, you're the one who cut the lawn before I came home? I should have thanked you long ago." She pulled off her gloves then extended her hand. "I'm so grateful." His grip was strong. She could feel the calloused surface of his palm.

"No, no. Don't apologize. I didn't want the place to look empty. I knew you had enough on your plate." His expression turned sober. "I hope you don't mind if I say how sorry I was to hear about your daughter's abduction. I know they haven't found her yet. How're you holding up?"

"Some days are better than others. But thanks for asking."

Thea was distracted by the expression on Annie's face. It was an open book of yearning, as she stared at Jacob's back. "Uh, you remember Annie, Jacob?"

"Of course." He turned, and his voice seemed to drop an octave as he said, "Hi, Annie." They stared at each other in silence, like a movie film that froze in the middle of a scene. *Oh my God. Their romance is perennial. It's blooming again right in my own garden.*

Finally, the spell broke. Jacob repeated his offer to help.

"Now that we've stopped for a minute, I realize how sore my legs are. Maybe we're done for the day. What do you think, Annie?" Thea said, bending forward and knocking the dirt clumps off her sneakers.

Jacob made a point of inspecting their work. "Really? That's all you did and you're hurting? You two need to get more exercise." He looked at the cleared patches. "I'll give you this, the parts you worked on," he pointed, "that tiny part there, and there, you both did a solid job." He turned back to Annie. "Are you a regular here?"

"I foolishly offered to help, but I'm not stupid, I learn from my mistakes. If I were you, Thea, I'd be tempted to poison the whole area with weed killer and grow grass instead." Then she gave Jacob a smile so sweet, she could have wilted the flowers around her. Thea suppressed a giggle. She'd rarely seen Annie so vulnerable.

Jacob stepped in front of Annie, his arms spread wide, protecting the garden behind him. "Bite your tongue! This is one of the best gardens in Orleans. Some of the most unusual flowers pop up here."

When Jacob left, Annie and Thea dropped their gloves and tools in the garage. They went into the kitchen for a cold drink. Annie had just walked into the bathroom when she shrieked. "Thea! How could you not tell me about this dirt all over my face? In front of Jacob, too? Oh, no."

Thea broke out in hysterical laughter as Annie came marching out of the bathroom, wiping her face with a wet cloth. "I'm sorry, Annie, I was going to tell you, but Jacob was already pulling in. And girl, we have to talk. You skipped a lot of important pieces of your story. That man is still in love with you."

Later, Thea sat on the living room couch waiting for Annie. She stared at the neat row of her law books on the shelves, and let her thoughts drift. The law had always lifted her to another place, an enthusiastic, stimulating, happy place. When her mind was engaged in a legal issue, it had no room for anything else. The law wasn't just her chosen career path, she realized, it was her first love, a home for her future. It was the glue that held all her parts firmly in order. She missed exercising her brain with legal drills.

Financial circumstances were bringing her back to her career. Her mother would have called the fallen chimney a sign. Thea didn't know if that was true, but she was going back to the work she loved. She wasn't just studying for the bar exam, she was embracing her law career. And she now understood that it could never diminish her love for Emily. The usual heartache stabbed her at the thought. *Emily.*

She was still deep in thought when Annie came in, wearing knee-length gray sweats and a long white t-shirt with an athletic logo. She padded over to the couch in her flip-flops, holding a large bowl of popcorn in her hands.

"Ready to watch the movie?"

Thea folded her arms across her chest. "Annie, I think I'll make a good lawyer."

Annie set down the bowl. "Huh? Of course you will."

"I sort of gave up on the idea for a while. As you know. I thought I could've been a better mom to Emily if I wasn't so focused on my career. But now I don't think that's true. I was working hard to give Emily a good life, too."

"Exactly. I'm not planning to give up my career if I ever find the right person and we have a family." She blushed, but Thea pretended she didn't notice. "Besides, how else would you support yourself and Emily?"

She stared at Annie for a few beats, and then replied, "I didn't give that question much thought until lately. I'm not making enough money doing what I'm doing now."

"You've wanted to be a lawyer for years. You've worked so hard to get there," Annie said.

Thea leaned over and grabbed a handful of popcorn. She chewed while she thought. "I think I'd decided, somehow, that if I hadn't worked so hard, none of this would have happened."

"And now you realize that isn't true?"

Thea nodded. "Now I know I can be a good mother and still be a lawyer. But I would balance it differently. Maybe work on real estate closings and wills until Emily's in school."

Annie smiled. "I love this new plan. I can see you've been doing a lot of soul-searching."

"Yeah. It bothered me when I realized I'd been so busy with law school that Emily's first years were a blur. My mom had more quality time with Emily than I did."

Annie spoke quietly, affirmation in her words. "She needed her time with Emily. She filled in when you couldn't be there. It was a perfect setup for Hannah, too."

"And just when I was ready to take over—"

"I know." Annie reached over and squeezed Thea's shoulder.

"I love the law, but somehow now I don't think being a defense lawyer will work for me. I could instead spend my days putting away evil creeps who prey on kids. Oh, yeah."

Annie raised her hand up high enough that Thea had to stretch to high-five her. "Welcome back, Madame Attorney."

"And Emily will come back!"

"Yes, sweetie, she will. Now, let's watch the movie. It might be the last one you see for a while, since you're going back to hitting the books."

Thea picked up the remote. "You're right about that."

CHAPTER THIRTY THREE

Tim looked up when Haddon dropped new reports in his inbox. Haddon was a man who didn't speak unless he had something worthwhile to say. It was difficult to read his dark brooding eyes. He was known to work diligently without fanfare.

"Sit down, Haddon." He waited until the detective was settled. "Tell me again why we do this damn job?" He pressed his lips into a straight line.

"Case getting to you, huh?"

"Son of a bitch. We can't catch a break. Not a trace of Emily Connor."

"Come on, Big Mac, you lose some, you win some." When Tim gave Haddon a hard look, he quickly added, "I'm not saying this one's lost. But we've got nothing to go on. The fact is she may already be dead. You know that."

Tim took a breath, let his muscles relax.

"Look, ask yourself what's eating you about this one," Haddon continued. "You know, maybe a couple days away from it would help. Work on your other cases. I'll let you know if anything comes up."

It was one of the longest string of words he had ever heard Haddon piece together. And he was probably right. But goddamn, Tim couldn't stop, wouldn't let anyone else take over his responsibility. He couldn't admit Emily was dead. He didn't believe it. And *when* he found her, he would have a few private moments with the man who took her.

He checked his watch after Haddon left. Thea would be here soon.

When she'd asked to look over her daughter's file, Tim immediately wanted to know why. He didn't actually say 'no,' so that he could watch her face when he talked to her.

She was usually prompt; he went out to see if she was already there.

She was sitting in the waiting area right below a poster of her daughter. Tim made sure the poster was changed from time to time, to keep Emily fresh in the minds of the officers who passed it.

He led Thea back to the interrogation room. He set up the recording device.

Tim noticed her face had filled out some. Her hair was shorter. She looked . . . he shoved the thought from his mind. "You made a request to read Emily's official police file. Tell me why."

"What if there's some information with a significance only I would know?"

"Thea, that's not a reason. What's going on?"

"Nothing. And that's the problem. Nothing's happening. I'm sure you're doing everything you can. But there isn't much to do when there's no evidence."

She leaned forward with her hands flat on the table. When he sat back quietly in response, she also sat back, leaving damp palm prints on the shiny oak surface.

"What sort of information do you think you'd find in the file that we wouldn't see?"

"It's not about you. I don't know." She dropped her head. "I've got to do something. It's all I can focus on."

"I want you to tell me what this is really about. You're a lawyer. Do you expect me to believe you don't know about the confidentiality of police reports?"

"I know. I just thought there might be something that would jump out at me." She waved her hand dismissively. "Forget it."

He sat quietly a full two minutes to shake her up, but she didn't break. "Were you thinking of anything in particular?" he asked next.

"No! There's nothing suspicious in my asking. Some days I just wake up desperate!"

He waited until she stopped crying. "I know it's discouraging. I wish I had something promising to tell you. It bothers me that we can't find the kidnap vehicle you identified."

"Not just me. Other people saw it." She felt defensive, like he'd accused her of lying.

"Not as close up as you did."

"What do you want me to say? I made it up?"

"Of course not. It's just strange. There's no evidence on this case." He paused but Thea remained silent. "But as I keep reminding you, it could all come together with the next tip."

She leaned forward again, her eyes piercing his. Her voice was barely above a whisper. "Do you think she's dead?"

"No." Tim was surprised how confident the single word sounded, even to him. He *didn't* feel she was dead. "No, I don't think she's dead."

Thea let out a breath. "I don't either. Sometimes I hear her voice." She put a hand over her chest. "I feel her here."

He studied her a moment. "We'll keep looking for her."

She stood up, extending her hand to him. He shook it. "I know," she said. When she was gone, he still felt the warmth of her hand in his.

CHAPTER THIRTY FOUR

Katherine and Madison were being treated like celebrities. The hospital employees threw a goodbye party for Madison. They had balloons and cake, chocolates and ice cream. Many of the medical staff, all of those who had worked in any capacity for Madison, attended.

The doctor who had questioned Emily's date of birth did not. Another hurdle Katherine had barely cleared, satisfying everyone but him with a confirmation email sent by Emily's "father." The email was entered into the official record, and Katherine had heard no more about it. Still, either because of her own guilt or the doctor's suspicion, he'd never seemed to treat her the same.

They took a private limousine to the airport, two days before their visas expired. Madison, wearing a mask, and Emily were hustled through security and customs, and given a private room to wait to board their flight. People reacted to Madison with sympathetic expressions. No one complained when they boarded first.

The girls slept on the plane. Katherine sipped her second vodka with a twist. The numbing effect was welcome. It was over. She couldn't feel either elation or joy. But she finally had no anxiety. She knew her skin was the only thing holding together the slush that used to be her. The emotional cost to save her daughter had destroyed her. She gulped down the rest of her drink. Would she ever recover? If not, how would she go on?

Hours later, the limousine she'd ordered smoothly conveyed them from the airport to Katherine's Boston home, a little after three a.m. She settled the girls in their beds, and was asleep herself minutes after she laid her head on her pillow.

The doorbell was ringing. Katherine opened her eyes to bright sunlight. She threw on a bathrobe and rushed down the stairs. The girls were still sleeping. Katherine had made plans for Dee to come after noon, but a glance at the hall clock told her it was only ten. Was she early?

She looked out the peephole, expecting to see her housekeeper. When she saw the police officer, she jumped back and covered her face with her hands.

They're here. They know. Oh God, no. She was going to prison. She grabbed fistfuls of her hair to keep from running off, screaming.

She shouldn't let them in. Did they bring a warrant? She should call John's law firm.

The officer rapped hard, on the door this time. Did he know she was standing there?

"Police. Anybody home?"

Katherine pressed a hand over her too-fast beating heart. Why would he ask that? His voice was not threatening. She finger-combed her hair. Only one officer. It had to be about something else. An accident? As she opened the door, she felt a lump forming in her throat.

"Ma'am, we had a call from a neighbor to check on this house. Can you give me your name, please?" the officer said.

She swallowed. "Katherine Anderson. I own this home. What's this about?" She pushed her shaking hands into her bathrobe pockets.

"Your neighbor was concerned and called us. She told us the house has been empty for some time, and she noticed the lights were on around four a.m."

"Oh, yes. We've been away. We just got in early this morning."

"Okay. Welcome home." He smiled. "For my report, do you mind showing me a picture ID?"

"Um, sure. Please come in."

"I'll just wait here."

Katherine's mind went blank on where she'd left her pocketbook. She ran in bare feet through the living room, then back upstairs to her room. Her insides were jelly. Was this a ploy? Would he arrest her once he had her ID?

Her purse was on her bureau. She grabbed her license, and was heading downstairs when Madison opened her door. "Stay there, Maddy. I'll be right back." She took the stairs slowly, composing herself.

She opened the front door. The officer was standing with his back to her. She offered him her license.

He checked the picture then copied the license information into a small notebook. "All set. Thank you."

"Thanks for checking," she said, beginning to feel relieved, that everything was all right.

She closed the door and jumped when she saw that Madison was standing right behind her.

"What did the policeman want, Mommy?"

"Madison, you know you can't be near strangers yet. Stay away from the door."

Maddy pouted.

"Come into the kitchen. Mommy will make you breakfast."

She'd dodged another bullet. She felt like singing.

When Dee arrived, Katherine hugged her. All the time she was in Brazil, she'd had no one to confide in. She thought she would burst with all the good news she wanted to tell Dee. They drank coffee and talked. Katherine told her everything that went on at the hospital.

"You look terrible. Your face has thinned out. I can see how hard it's been on you. I should have come with you," Dee responded.

"I couldn't have you involved in that part. You've done more than your share."

"We both survived, and more important, little missy is cured. It's over. My God; it was all worth it."

Katherine only nodded. She knew it would never be all over. But for now, her baby was on the mend. Maybe Maddy would be one of the lucky ones from here on out.

"Did you get your house sold?" Katherine asked with a small smile.

"Cross your fingers. They're having the house inspection in two days. Artie's been working like a madman."

"When is the closing?" Katherine asked, dreading the answer.

"Next week—if all goes well—October fifth." Dee was tapping the table with her fingers.

"I'll miss you, and so will Maddy."

Dee's eyes watered. "I'll miss you both, too. And all of my family that's here."

"You should be able to come visit. Don't give up hope. If I can pull it off, Emily will be returned to her mother, and we'll never get caught. Once you're safely away in Cape Verde, I'll find a way to get her home," she said with more confidence than hope.

"I'm glad you're still here, Dee. It's better if both of us talk to Emily about going home. From now on, we'll tell her if she wants to go back to her mommy, she must never say our names. We'll stress that if she tells anyone our names, we will come and take her away again."

"That's your plan?" Dee said.

"Think about it. She has no idea she's in Boston. No sense of how far away she is from her home. I'll drop her off somewhere hours from here. She's been to Brazil. She speaks some Portuguese. I think we can count on the fact that she couldn't bring anyone back here. All she knows that could point to us are our names, Auntie K, Dee, and Madison. I think over the next week we can have her so scared about coming back, she will never say a word on who we are."

"I hope you're right."

"You'll be here for the next week, won't you, Dee? I need your help."

"For another week or so."

Dee came to wake her up. Emily opened her eyes and looked around. She remembered she was back in her dark room. She glanced at the items she had piled up in the corner to take home with her. Auntie said when they came back, she could go home. But they didn't take her yet. She promised she would never tell their names, but they still didn't take her home.

She didn't want to be in this room any longer. She wasn't allowed to play with Maddy, either.

She wanted to go home, but she was so tired. She closed her eyes.

"Why are you sleeping all the time? I hope you aren't getting sick, Emmie," Dee said. "Let me take a look at you."

Emily rubbed her eyes with her fists. Dee helped her sit up with her legs dangling over the side of the bed, then leaned down and looked into Emily's eyes. She put a hand on her forehead, her cheek. Then she tousled her hair, which made Emily pull back. "Don't."

"You're all right. You're just a sleepy girl. Let me wash your face and brush your hair. Then, guess what? I'm going to take you down to see Madison," Dee said, smiling.

Emily insisted on washing herself. She brushed her hair, but it was so short, it didn't tangle. She brushed her teeth and dressed. While Dee waited, she stressed to Emily that she couldn't tell anyone their names. "Or else, we will come and bring you back here, and you will never be able to see your mommy again."

Emily wanted to cry, but she didn't. When she was finished washing up, and after again promising not to tell, Dee took her downstairs and opened a door for her.

She peered in and saw Maddy sitting in a grown-up pink chair—except it was little. She looked around the big room, its many colors made Emily think of Nana's favorite candy, Necco Wafers. Nana used the candy to teach Emily her colors. She was allowed to eat every piece that she got right: green, yellow, lavender, white, gray, and pink. Pink was Emily's favorite. It must be Maddy's, too.

Maddy looked up and beckoned her with, "Emmie, come in."

Dee gently nudged her, and she walked across the soft carpet to Maddy's chair. She was dressed, and she wore a hat with puppies on it. Emily knew that Maddy had her hair cut, too. She couldn't have ponytails anymore.

"You're not wearing your mask," Emily said.

"No, Doctor Bob says I'm getting so much better. I only have to wear it if I go out where people are."

"You made her better, Emmie," Auntie Kay said from across the room, where Emily had not noticed her.

She didn't want to think about the bad time when she made Maddy better. "Now, I can go see my mommy?" she asked Auntie Kay.

"Well, Emmie, Maddy and I were just talking about that." Maddy giggled, and Auntie Kay beamed her special smile at her. "You see, Maddy would like you to stay with us. You could be just like her sister."

"Forever and ever," Maddy said, clapping her hands.

Auntie's eyes scared her. She wasn't crying, but her eyes were big and sparkly, like Emily's dolls' eyes.

"Wouldn't you like to be Maddy's sister?" Auntie said.

Emily turned and stared at Maddy's smiling face, but she couldn't speak because her words were stuck. She was so sad, she couldn't help it when a big sob came out and made Maddy jump. Then she couldn't stop, and she began to wail. Auntie Kay rushed over to her; she was waving her hands and calling for Dee, who came running in from the hall.

"Settle down, Emmie. Quiet, now," Dee said, reaching down to turn Emily to face her.

Emily shook her off and turned back to Auntie. "No! You said! You said I can go home." She grabbed Maddy's leg, and held on while Dee tried to peel away her fingers. Maddy began to cry, too.

"Stop it now, you're upsetting Maddy," Auntie said, moving to Maddy's bed and hugging her. "Emmie, it's going to be all right. Please stop crying."

Emily was still crying, but she let go of Maddy's leg.

Auntie was sobbing now, too. "Take her back up to her room, Dee. I don't know what I'm going to do. What am I going to do?"

Dee carried her up the stairs and laid her on the bed. "Hush now, little one. We'll get you home. Don't worry."

But Emily wept until she had no voice left and it was too hard to force out the sounds. She didn't believe Dee. She lay still on the bed, staring at the black window. She didn't turn her head when the door lock clicked.

They would never let her go back to her mommy. She didn't want to be Maddy's sister. She didn't want to be Emmie. Her name was Emily!

She wiped her face. They wouldn't ever take her home. They were lying to her, and people shouldn't lie. She got up and walked over to the window. She looked out the little hole in the paint that she had scratched out with a spoon.

She would have to go home by herself. She would have to find a policeman. Policemen helped little children. But how would she get out of her locked room?

"Are you all right? You scared me," Dee said when she found Katherine standing at the window in her bedroom. "What nonsense were you saying to her? Maddy's *sister?*"

"I'm afraid to give Emily back. What if Maddy needs another transplant?"

"But I thought this one took? Isn't she better?" Dee's voice was shrill.

Katherine didn't turn. She knew she was acting crazy. Knew Dee was watching every move she made now. "You're right. I don't know what I was thinking."

Dee crossed the room to stand beside her. "You've already done the hard work. No one's the wiser. All you have to do is leave her somewhere. Don't lose it at this point." Dee patted her shoulder. "You were acting pretty strange in there."

Katherine finally turned to look at her housekeeper. "I'm all right now. I'll be fine. God. What was I thinking?" She shook her head from side to side as if to shake out the fear.

"Let me get you one of your nerve pills. You're just not settled in yet. It'll take a while before you stop worrying about the little missy. It's understandable. You'll be fine. Just one more thing to do—get Emily on her way. She's ready. We have her all set now."

She heard worry in Dee's voice. But she was right. Emily had to go.

"I'll be here a few more days. Take the child away before I leave. I'll stay with the little missy. If Maddy needs anything, I'll call Mimi. You don't have to worry. Just get Emmie back. That was our agreement, right?"

"Yes. We agreed."

"If you don't come to your senses and take her away, we could all go to jail. You can't lose your grip now," Dee said, a clear warning in her voice.

"I don't know what I'll do without you, Dee."

CHAPTER THIRTY FIVE

Today began a new month without her daughter, October first. But every day she became more certain her daughter was alive.

Annie had invited her and a group of friends for dinner. Thea had to force herself to go, but she knew being with her friends always made her feel happier.

Annie was waiting in the front yard when Thea pulled up.

"You're here!" she said, taking the bowl of macaroni salad Thea had brought.

"What?" she asked, looking at Annie's face, seeing her friend was dying to share some news.

"Guess who else is here?"

Annie owned a small ranch house on a quiet street in Eastham. Her deck overlooked thick woods of tall oaks and pines, climbing up a steep hill behind her house. There was no grass around the property. Annie used layers of pine needles as mulch, a "Cape Cod lawn," much encouraged by local environmentalists.

Thea saw Jacob coming around the house. He greeted her then walked off to take the macaroni salad into the kitchen. She watched a building wind pull and tug at his shirt, but at least the sun was shining for the cookout, and it was a comfortable seventy degrees.

She noted Annie's glowing face. "Okay, tell me. What's going on with you two?" When Annie practically blinded her with a smile, Thea said, "I am so happy for you both."

"Two days after we saw each other at your house, Jacob asked me to meet him at the Beachcomber in Wellfleet for a drink. Sit down," Annie said, dropping onto the pine needle lawn and patting the spot beside her. "This can't be rushed and it's for your ears only."

"Are you kidding? I saw the way you looked at each other. Nobody's going to miss what's going on between you two."

"Well, it's not a secret, except we don't want people to think we're rushing into it. But we are. There's no need to wait. I mean, we just picked up where we left off. That night, we sat at the noisy bar and talked for hours. It seemed like no one else was there. We exorcised the misunderstanding we had. We both fought to take the blame, and we ended up laughing about it. Then Jacob kissed me and I about melted off the bar stool."

Thea clapped her hands. "I saw your face that day he came to my house. I knew you loved him then. I also told you, if you remember, Jacob was still in love with you, too."

"Those words were magic. I felt so good when you said that. I was trying to work up the courage to call and ask him out when he called me." Annie's fingers were digging into a mound of pine needles as she spoke.

"And?" Thea said, knowing her friend was struggling with sharing something else.

Annie brushed her hands together and sighed. "Jacob is going back to school. He wants to get a degree in landscape architecture. He's been accepted into a work/study program in Boston. By the end of our Beach-comber date, he told me about it. He was already considering not going."

"Uh-oh. A dilemma."

Annie gave off a radioactive smile again. "We worked out a simple solution. He's going, and so am I."

Thea pressed back hard against threatening tears. What would she do without Annie? She had lost her mother and her daughter. She had no other family. What would this further loss do to her?

Annie read her thoughts. "I hated to tell you this now."

"I really am happy for you. You belong with Jacob. I'll be fine. I promise. And look how often I'm in Boston. I'll see you every time I come in." She tried to sound like she meant it, but she was struggling with an ocean of emotion threatening to overwhelm her.

It was going to be a long afternoon. Thea had never felt so alone.

Two maroon chairs were square-on facing each other with a round, brown rug under them. Circling the small setting on the stage were cameras, klieg lights, and the technicians who operated them. Others walked around carrying meters and electronic equipment Thea couldn't name. Below them, an audience was receiving instructions from a young man wearing a microphone and holding a clipboard in his hands. The people laughed from time to time during his talk.

Thea had agreed to be interviewed for a television news special about parents of missing children. Her interview would be only a few minutes long. Other participants would be filmed separately.

She was shocked by the tone of the journalist's first real questions to her, after the introductory back and forth. The woman launched into an onslaught of questions bent to demonstrate Thea's possible collusion in her daughter's abduction. Thea tried to maintain her composure as a sheen of nervous sweat covered her face.

"Are you saying the police no longer consider you a suspect?" the journalist asked, blinking her false eyelashes.

She stared at the woman's shoes as she swung her leg back and forth, waiting for Thea's answer. The shoes were patent leather platforms with at least a four-inch heel. Thea raised her eyes to the woman. "Parents are always considered suspects when their child is abducted, but there has never been any evidence against me."

The reporter wore a helmet of hard, short black hair. Thea wondered what kind of hairspray could turn tresses into wood. She wore heavy orangey make-up, and her lips were outlined in a darker shade than her lipstick. It helped Thea to critique the woman's looks; otherwise, she might be tempted to cry.

"Yes, I'm aware of that. But you didn't pass the lie detector test."

"No—I mean, not the first time." She locked her lips between her teeth to regroup. Speaking more slowly, she went on. "When your child is ripped right from your hands, your emotions go crazy. I took the polygraph willingly, but they couldn't get a good reading. They called it 'inconclusive.' Later, I was retested and passed it without any indication of guilt."

The next line of questioning caught her off guard.

"You applied to take the bar exam recently. You're able to move on now?"

How could she explain the machinations that had brought her back to pursue her career? That she now knew being happy in her career wasn't anathema to being a loving mother. In fact, she was sure it would only enhance their lives. And, she needed the money. But the interviewer had already put a negative slant on the fact that she planned to take the bar exam.

If Thea voiced the angry thoughts swirling through her mind, her interview would be cut and serve no one.

As sweetly as she could, she answered the question. "Yes. I had just finished law school when the kidnapping occurred. I was offered an associate position in a law firm as a defense attorney. When my daughter was taken, I gave up on everything. I felt like an eaten-out bug carcass on a spider's web, hollow and drifting in the breeze." Thea leaned forward, bringer her face closer and looked into the journalist's eyes. "You lose your inner compass, but you have to live through each day. Lately, I realized that I should get back to my career."

"It's so sad. You don't feel like you'll ever see your daughter Emily again?"

"On the contrary. I feel like Emily is close to coming home. I've never given up hope and I won't. So, I'm going to pass the bar and go to work. When Emily's home, I'll be able to support her, send her to school, and provide the good and happy life I've always planned for us." Thea smiled.

"That's commendable. I know how difficult it must be for you to maintain hope after all this time." The journalist looked into the camera with an expression of deep understanding for a moment, then back to Thea. "You'll be working as a defense lawyer?"

Thea hoped Will Hebert would see the show. She raised her head. "No. I've changed my mind. I think I can do more good in the world by putting away kidnappers, pedophiles, and anyone else who preys on children." The audience broke out in spontaneous applause.

When they walked off the stage together, the interviewer took Thea's arm. "I just want to say, sorry for some of those questions. I don't have control over the direction of the show. And I want you to know, I'm doing this program because I have two children of my own, and I can't imagine what it would be like to live without them. I hope the show spurs more interest in the public to help look for Emily and the other missing kids."

She had redeemed herself. The warm, sensitive mom beneath all the make-up was a nice surprise. And Thea hoped she was right, because she'd given it everything she had. She prayed, this time, for something wonderful to happen.

CHAPTER THIRTY SIX

Katherine feared she was on the edge of madness. How else could she account for her strange thoughts, reaching into the realm of the ridiculous? She couldn't stop worrying about Maddy. Ten days since they'd come back, and she still couldn't decide on where to take Emily.

Her parents, whom she'd managed to fend off the first few days by stating the danger of Maddy's exposure to colds or other illnesses, now wanted to come visit every day. Katherine didn't think for one moment her mother had bought the story of Madison's sudden need for the transplant after the lies she'd been told. She did not probe. She was just elated that her granddaughter was well.

On top of all that, John had a sudden change of heart. He insisted he would have Maddy every other weekend. And of course he couldn't.

Since she'd asked Emily to be Maddy's sister days ago, the child had become more resistant to Dee's attempts to exert control over her, one minute a rag doll, the next minute screaming. Dee had managed to keep her quiet that first month, before they left for Brazil, but no more. If she chose to cry out when Mimi and Gramps were in Maddy's room, they might hear her. How would she explain it? And yet, Katherine couldn't seem to figure out how to get rid of Emily.

Dee had grown more nervous with every passing day. She and Artie had closed on their house. She didn't tell Katherine the day they would fly out, but she knew it was too soon for her employer. Dee had begun to leave after lunch, stressing the need to pack, now that time was running out.

Katherine was snapping at all of them. The only thing holding her together was Xanax. But it made her sleepy and fogged her brain, so she couldn't think clearly. And she must. All she knew was what she couldn't do: leave Madison alone now. Katherine was the only one who understood what signs to watch for if her body began to reject the transplant. Or who could detect early symptoms of an illness that would require immediate treatment by a doctor. And Maddy remained weak and thin from enduring all the treatments. Dee had lovingly cooked only her favorite foods to encourage her to eat.

There was just no way Katherine could leave her alone while she took Emily far away. Dee was the only one who could do it. And she was leaving for good.

"Ouch, Mommy," Madison said with her old vigor.

Katherine realized she was using too much pressure when forcing a narrow-necked t-shirt over Maddy's bald head. "Sorry, darling. All done. What would you like to do now?"

"I want to go to ballet class."

"Sweetie, the doctor said you have to wait awhile before you can be around the other children. Remember? We discussed this."

"But I want to!" Madison stamped her foot like the spoiled child she'd become. Then she calmed and demanded instead, "I want to play with Emmie."

"Honey, I explained to you. You can't play with Emmie right now." Katherine felt her lips tremble. Madison continually brought up the subject of Emmie. It had been a mistake to allow them to bond in Brazil, but the scenario they played out there was that Emmie was a cousin, so she would naturally be a part of the family. Coming home and suddenly keeping them apart again did not sit well with Madison.

"Why can't she come to play with me? She wouldn't cry so much then."

Katherine didn't think; the answer just came out. "Because she's going to go home soon." Then she knew the decision was made. She had to convince Dee to help her one last time.

"No. I told you, Mommy. I want her to stay. Mimi *said* she should stay with me."

Katherine felt instant knots form in her shoulder muscles. Her mother knew about Emily? "Madison, did you forget Emmie is a secret? What did you tell Mimi?"

Maddy scowled at her mother.

"Madison, tell me right now what you told Mimi about Emmie."

Unaccustomed to the harsh tone Katherine couldn't contain, Maddy raised her voice. "I want to play with Emmie. I want to!" Then she threw herself on her bed and wept crocodile tears.

"What's all this?" Dee asked, walking into the room.

Katherine flinched, even though she was used to her housekeeper lurking around the rooms. "Dee, I have to talk to you." She turned on Madison's TV and inserted a DVD. She pointed a finger at Madison. "You lie on your bed and watch the movie. Mommy will be back in a few minutes." Madison turned and climbed farther onto her bed.

Katherine was by now used to the worried expression that never seemed to leave Dee's face. She took her arm and led her out, closing the door behind them. "It's nothing to worry about. Just a snit. Let's go downstairs, where we can talk."

"I heard what you said about Maddy telling her grandmother about Emmie," Dee said when they reached the living room.

"I think Madison mentioned Emily," Katherine affirmed, nodding.

Dee's mouth dropped open. Katherine watched her grow pale.

"What do we do now? I was afraid something like this would happen," Dee said. "You can't ask a little kid to keep a secret."

"Listen, Dee. There's no need to worry. If my mother thought anything about it she would have said something to me. She probably thought Maddy had an imaginary friend. Come to think of it, she mentioned how lonely Madison must be. That's it!" Katherine gave Dee a broad smile. The look Dee gave her made her realize she was acting nutty again.

"I'm going to have to leave now. I can't take a chance this will blow up."

"Wait. I need you to do one more thing. I can't leave Madison. She's still too sick. Can't you and Artie drive Emily to California or somewhere else far away? You could take a plane to Cape Verde from there. Please, Dee. I'm desperate." She held her hands palms up.

"No, Katherine. I'm sorry. That wasn't the deal. You have to take the risk now. I've done my part."

"Please, Dee. I'll pay you. You deserve more."

"Listen to me. Artie and I are leaving in a couple of days. All our plans are made. Don't ruin everything now. Your daughter is well. Be grateful. It was amazing what we did. But now you have to finish it. Have Madison stay at your mother's. She'll be fine. You don't have to take Emmie more than half a day away. When someone finds her, what a story she'll be telling them. They'll never figure it out. Just drive to Pennsylvania or Vermont. That's all you need to do." She went into the kitchen and came back with her purse. "I have to go now."

"Dee! You can't leave me. I need your help. I don't know what to do."

Madison opened her door. "Mommy?"

Katherine went to the bottom of the steps. "Get back in your room!" she yelled. Madison's eyes grew big. She began to cry again, this time real tears. Katherine remained focused on the stairs, listening for Maddy's door to close.

When she turned around, Dee was gone.

Katherine paced the living room, bumping heedless into tables and chairs. "I can't do this alone," she said aloud. How could she convince Dee to return? Wasn't it just as important to her to have Emily safely away? If Maddy telling her grandmother about Emmie brought out the truth wasn't Dee in as much trouble as she was? Of course, and she had to see that. Katherine needed to give her enough time to think about it. She would see Katherine couldn't handle it alone.

She would call her later. Dee would do it. She and Artie would take Emily away. Tomorrow. Yes. Tomorrow. Why wait?

For a moment, she felt good about her decision, picturing Thea Connor's face when her daughter was returned to her. Just like Katherine's daughter had been returned to her.

But what if Madison needed Emily again? "Oh, please. No." She bent her head into her hands. *God, I am going crazy.*

There was only one thing to do. Emily must be gone, and soon. She raised her head. She would call Dee. She should be home by now. Artie could come with her and they could drive Emily far away. Wasn't that their plan? Weren't they leaving soon? They could just drop Emily off on their way. There. It was decided.

Katherine looked around the living room, then began to straighten the pieces she'd set askew. She felt better. She knew she could make it work. Hadn't she masterminded it all? And wasn't Madison now far from the horrible disease that almost took her life? All that terror was in the past now. Look how far Katherine had come. Maddy was well again, and though the process had left Katherine a shadow of herself, it was done. Just one more part of the plan was left to do. Emily must go.

She stood up, fluffed her linen skirt, and walked to the kitchen and the telephone.

The next morning, Saturday, Madison woke up sick. She was weak and tearful and her temperature was above normal. Katherine called the doctor in a panic. Doctor Thompson wasn't on call, but she begged the answering service to have him call her. By the time he did, she was beside herself.

"Katherine, calm down. You can take her to the emergency room now, or wait until later this afternoon, and I'll meet you there myself."

"I'll wait for you. Will she be all right?"

"She's on antibiotics already. I'll meet you at the hospital at four. If she spikes a fever or anything else particularly worries you, take her right to the ER."

How could she take Maddy to the ER? She no longer had Dee to stay with Emily. She couldn't leave her alone in the house while she took Maddy to the hospital. Katherine pulled at her hair again.

She would call Dee again, beg her to come. Oh, why had she set up her retirement annuity before this was finished? Her eyes widened. She could offer her more money. A bonus.

But Dee wasn't answering. Katherine left her a tearful message.

CHAPTER THIRTY SEVEN

Four members of the team were standing around Tim's office on Saturday morning at eleven a.m. They'd all been assigned additional cases, but Tim didn't want them to overlook Emily Connor. These were the four, along with Tim, who had pulled weekend duty. But he was a man who loved his job. Ever since the crossing guard put his hand on his shoulder in elementary school, he knew he wanted to be a cop.

Tim raised a hand. "I know your case loads are heavy, but we're going to push forward on Emily Connor. We picked up a few tips from Thea Connor's television interview this week. I know you've done some initial work on the leads we have. Devote as much time as you can to running the rest of them down," he told the team. "While you do that, I'm going to review the file, see if anything merits a second look. If you find something substantial, let me know immediately."

It was past time to replace the faded Emily posters in Boston. On Saturday morning, Thea took Star and drove to the city, knowing traffic would be light—heading for Boston. She drove to a parking garage on Hanover Street, deciding the large fee was worth not having to face the aggravation of finding a parking spot.

On Cambridge Street, she went from shop to shop, handing out new posters. Some of the proprietors were just as warm as when she'd brought them the original posters. Others were reluctant to talk to her, or couldn't maintain eye contact. Those, she knew, had given up hope for her. She refused to let them bring her spirits down.

Star maintained a strong, steady gait toward the corner where they would cross. Thea was deep into her thoughts, until she tripped on the uneven sidewalk and fought to stay upright. Just as she regained her footing, Star began to bark and growl. Thea almost dropped the leash handle as the dog jerked her forward. Star pulled her along the sidewalk with such strength, Thea could hardly hold her back. When she looked up and saw where Star was headed, her mouth fell open.

"Heel!" Thea tugged on the leash, but Star didn't slow down. "Star! Heel." This time, the dog obeyed, but she whined her frustration. With Star under control, Thea moved up the sidewalk at a slower pace.

A black car was parked in front of the hardware store. As soon as she saw it, she knew it was the same make and model of car as the kidnapper's. Was that what upset Star? Or could it be the exact same car?

Her heart was pounding so hard she thought the people passing by would hear it. When she was about thirty feet behind the Mercury Marquis, she pulled Star into the recessed entrance of a stationery store. "Sit." Star sat, but her eyes were glued to the car, her ears straight up and twitching.

Thea could see that the car was empty. She sloughed off her backpack. She unzipped it with one hand, reluctant to release her grip on Star's leash, knowing if any person approached the car it would be a struggle to hold the dog back. She pulled out a scrap of paper and a pen. Wrapping the leash twice around her wrist, she carefully wrote down the license plate number. Then she took out her cell phone and hit the speed dial for Tim's cell. People leaving the stationery store glared at her for blocking the doorway. She pushed Star closer to one side then ignored them.

"Tim! I see the black car! Oh my God, it's right in front of us. I'm with Star. She saw it first and started going crazy," she said when Tim answered.

"Where are you?"

"On Cambridge Street. I have the license plate, Tim." She read off the letters and numbers.

"Okay," he said. "I've got it. Move away from the car. Right now. Hold on." After a minute he said, "A patrol car is on its way. What are you doing in Boston?"

"Passing out new posters. Tim, I think it's the car."

"Keep walking away."

"I just finished replacing posters on one side of the street, and was about to cross to the other side when Star starting barking." Thea was panting as she walked, nearly dragging Star who kept turning back to the car.

"Head home. I'll call you when I get the report. Do you still see the car?"

"Yes, but I'm about a block away now."

"Did you see anyone in the car, or standing near it?"

"No. I didn't see anyone."

"Right. Are you near your car?"

Thea had no plans to leave before the police arrived.

"Where are you now?" Tim said, after a few minutes.

"I'm a block from the garage," she lied, standing behind a sidewalk display in front of a drug store, looking down Cambridge Street at the black car. "When are the police coming?"

"They should be there momentarily. Thea, are you at a safe distance away?"

"I'm at the garage now." *Not.*

"Good. Look around before you go in. Make sure no one's following you, then get into your car and lock the door."

"Right. Wait! Someone's coming. A woman's getting into the car. Oh no! Tim, the car's pulling out."

"You're still there?"

"It's coming this way. . . I'll be able to see the driver in a second. It's a woman. I can only see her profile. She has blond hair. I think she's older. I can't be sure." Thea could feel disappointment deflate her. It wasn't *him.*

Tim told her they would check it out anyway. She could hear a siren in the distance. The patrol car was too late, but she wouldn't give up hope. She had trust in Tim. He would follow up. The woman could be involved. Someone had to drive the car when Emily was kidnapped. It could have been this woman.

For several miles after she drove away, Star sat at attention, eyes alert, ears straight up, turning her head in different directions, like an antenna searching for a signal. Thea drove with the fingers of both hands tapping the steering wheel in time to the beat of her drumming heart. *Please God. Please God. Let it be the car.*

CHAPTER THIRTY EIGHT

I t wasn't a problem, after all. Katherine called a babysitter. She chided herself for panicking, but to see her daughter ill again with the possibility of Graft-Host disease was too much to bear. Though she was calmer once she worked out the solution, the wait until late afternoon had been trying.

An hour before she'd left to take Maddy to the doctor's, she'd given Emily a good dose of antihistamine to make her sleep. Then she carried her to Madison's bed.

A new woman from the child care agency she'd used before arrived right on time. Katherine told the woman, named Marcy, that her other daughter, Emma, was sound asleep, recovering from a serious respiratory infection.

The woman was older, and she flinched when she saw Madison's feverish face. When Katherine told her not to disturb Emma, it was clear the babysitter had no desire to go near her. Her instructions were to call Katherine if she heard the child cry.

The doctor had seen Madison right away. On the way back home, Katherine withdrew money at the drive-through kiosk at her bank. When they returned home, Marcy told her Emma hadn't awakened.

Katherine left Madison in front of the television, and went upstairs to move Emily back to the attic. The little girl was confused when she awoke in a strange room. "Where's mommy?" Emily struggled to sit up in bed. She looked around the room. "This isn't Nana's cottage," she said, beginning to cry.

Emily's tears deepened Katherine's guilt. "Sweetie, you're in Madison's bed. Remember her room, and her princess castle? Don't worry, everything is all right."

Emily cried harder, and Katherine couldn't take it anymore. "I *am* taking you home. I'm taking you home tomorrow. I promise." How that would happen, she didn't know.

Katherine led Emily by the hand back to the attic room, as she chattered in her joy. "I'm going home tomorrow. Mommy wants to see me. Is Nana going to come, too?"

As Katherine closed the door, Emily was packing her scant belongings once again.

"But I want to go now!" Emily said, stomping her foot. "I don't want to eat dinner here. I want to go home!" She began to cry.

"Oh Emmie, stop it. I can't stand it anymore," Auntie Kay said, walking fast around her room, throwing her arms up in frustration.

Emily wouldn't stop; she wouldn't eat or drink anything Auntie brought her. "You said!"

"Yes. And I will. You *are* going home. I just can't take you right now. You know Maddy is sick, and I can't leave her."

Emily rolled over on her bed so she couldn't see Auntie Kay then sobbed as loud as she could. Her mommy missed her and she had to go home. Auntie told her she was going home, but then she didn't take her. Emily kicked her feet as hard as she could against the mattress. She heard the door close, so she wailed louder.

"Be patient, little sweetheart," Nana whispered in her ear. "Don't cry anymore."

Emily rolled over to her back. She closed her eyes because it felt so good when Nana's cool fingers brushed her hair off her forehead.

"I want to go with you, Nana."

Her grandmother chuckled. "Your mommy has a surprise for you when you get home. She's waiting for you."

Emily sat up. "Now, Nana? Will you take me?"

"Soon, Em. But you need to be ready when it's time. How about you eat your sandwich and drink your milk? Then we can play Red Rover. You love Red Rover."

Emily wiped her eyes. When she looked again, Nana was gone. Emily walked over to the little table to eat her sandwich. She wasn't worried. Nana would be back to play with her when it was time to go.

When the officer who handled the call on Cambridge Street came in, Tim was nearly finished typing a report on another case. He looked longingly at Emily's file and sighed. Another interruption. "What did you find out?"

"The car was gone. The hardware store salesclerk said an elderly woman with blond hair, maybe in her late sixties, paid cash for a set of wrenches. A gift for her son," the officer said. "Nothing out of the ordinary."

"Okay. Follow up on the plate information, and let me know what you find."

The hours of the day kept ticking away. Tim had started the morning conducting an interview of a witness on another case. Every time he returned to his office, thinking he could get to Emily's file, there was another fire to put out.

He didn't hold out much hope for the car Thea saw, knowing that every Mercury Marquis in Boston and the surrounding area had already been vetted. But the dog's reaction was strange.

Finally, he opened Emily's file and began to sort through reports. He checked his watch. Maybe this time he could make a little headway before his four o'clock team meeting.

He received information that the Mercury Marquis Thea had seen was registered to Arthur and Dolores Reyes. It was one of the cars they had checked out early in the investigation. He pulled the report from the file and read the officer's interview of the retired couple. Their alibi was solid. The man was handicapped, walked with a cane, and had graying hair.

The couple lived across the Mystic River in Chelsea. It wouldn't be strange to see their car around Boston. Was it worth rechecking? On what basis? Because of a dog's reaction? He could leave out that little item. But something told him to gather more information on the Reyes couple. Recheck their alibi. Tim knew an alibi based on the statement of an eye witness could not be considered as entirely solid.

The next morning, one of the beat officers knocked on the wall near the opening of Tim's cubicle. "I came across something you might be interested in. The name came up linked to a kidnapping you're working on."

Tim read it. His hand tightened on the paper. "Thanks. Good work," he said to the young officer, who went off with a smile.

He grabbed Emily's file and opened it to the interview he'd had with Katherine Anderson, John Warren's ex-wife. They had verified her alibi with phone records, showing she was home at the time of the abduction. He closed the file and pushed it away.

According to the report the officer handed him, a neighbor called the police when she saw lights in the Anderson house after a long absence of the residents. So, Anderson and her daughter were gone for some time. Maybe they took a long vacation. He had to check the child's age. School had already started. That nagging missing-something feeling started up again. He sat still, gazing at his file cabinet, lost in thought.

Tim stood up so fast his desk chair rolled back, banging against the opposite wall of his office. He retrieved the chair and sat back down. In an adrenaline rush, he pulled Emily's file in front of him again and began flipping through the pages. He knew exactly what he was looking for. They'd received several tips from airline personnel, none of which had panned out. But there was one flight attendant he'd spoken with whose story sounded credible enough to raise his hopes. When he'd shown her Emily's picture, though, she'd shaken her head. She couldn't identify either of the two children she saw as Emily.

What if the flight attendant could identify one of the children as Anderson's daughter? Emily had probably been disguised, but there would be no reason to hide—he checked his notes—*Madison.*

When he found the flight attendant's contact information, it took several calls to locate Ms. Santos-Cook. She was en route from an overseas flight. Her ETA was four-twenty this afternoon. The airline would ask her to meet with Tim as soon as she deplaned.

A Red Carpet Club employee brought Tim coffee and a sandwich. A tropical storm was making its way up the east coast, bringing gusty winds and warm humid temperatures. Bands of thunder storms were expected later, along with stronger winds. The gusts were already wreaking havoc with the scheduled landings at Logan Airport. He'd waited through several delays before Ms. Santos-Cook's flight had finally touched down at five-thirty. In her mid-thirties, a slender woman with dark curly hair and green eyes walked into the room at ten of six.

"Ms. Santos-Cook, I'm Detective McIntyre with the Boston Police," Tim said before they sat down in comfortable chairs stationed in a private area of the lounge. "We spoke a couple months ago, after you called in on the Emily Connor kidnapping tip line."

"Yes, I remember you," she said, tucking a lock of her dark hair behind her ear.

"You called because you were concerned about two children on your flight."

"Yes, but neither one looked like the picture of the little girl you showed me."

"I think it had been a few weeks earlier when they were on your flight."

"Yes. I'd missed all the news about the kidnapping initially because I was getting married. It was only because my friends were talking about seeing the mother on TV later that I started to wonder about the kids I saw and called the police. Did you ever find her?"

"Not yet."

"Oh, I'm so sorry for her and her family. But why did you want to see me again?"

"Some information recently came in. I know it's been a while, but would you take a look at this child?" Tim showed her the picture of Madison Warren.

"Oh my gosh! Yes. This is the one who was sitting in the middle. The other child was sleeping practically the entire trip. Now I remember, the woman told me the sleepy child had recently lost her mother."

Tim clamped his jaw. Her mother had lost her, was more like it. He felt as if an engine was revving up inside him. "You seem pretty certain that this is the child you saw?"

"No doubt. She looks just like this picture. Her skin is very white, and with her blond hair, well, you couldn't help but notice her."

"This is very important, Ms. Santos-Cook. I need the exact flight number and the date you saw her."

"You can call me Gloria," she said, as she began to forage in her flight bag. "I'm still not used to my new last name."

She took an iPad out and turned it on. "I know it was one of my last trips before my wedding, so it shouldn't be too hard to locate the date on my schedule."

It seemed to take forever. It was difficult for Tim to sit still. He leaned forward, anxious.

"Brazil," she finally said. "I'm pretty sure that was the one. It was on the way out. We had a three-day layover, and then I flew back." She turned the tablet toward him. "Here it is, the third of July." She looked up at Tim and smiled. "I hope this helps. Do you think you can find her now?"

"Gloria, you've been a huge help. I can't say if it will lead to finding Emily, but I'm optimistic. Thanks." He stood up to leave.

"So the little sleepy girl was Emily. I'll be watching the news. It would make me happy to have helped find her. I hope she's all right."

Rain began to fall, pounding the windshield with gusto. Wind rocked the car as it crawled in rush hour traffic, made worse than usual by the bad weather. He called in the flight information Santos-Cook had given him to Officer Kip Johnson. "Shake up anybody you have to. I need the manifest and the passports of every passenger on that flight."

CHAPTER THIRTY NINE

Thea had taken dinner to an elderly neighbor who was ill. She'd stayed with her for a couple hours and kept her company. As she walked to her car, the wind caught her hair and flung it over her face. She held the loose strands back as she looked up at the sky. There would be no stars tonight. Storm clouds were hanging so low she imagined she could reach up and stick her finger into their puffy, gray bellies. October was one of the most beautiful months on the Cape, but the weather could be fickle.

She was upbeat; certain Tim would be calling her with good news about the car she and Star had seen in Boston. A gust of wind buffeted her. She felt so light with optimism she knew if she spread her arms wide, she'd be able to fly away on the wind.

On the way from the garage to the house, she looked up at the swaying lilac tree and stopped. On a branch about eight feet up, a solitary bouquet of pure white lilacs had bloomed. In October! Thea stared at this wonder until light raindrops began to penetrate her denim jacket. She went back into the garage and pulled out a ladder then dragged it over to the lilac tree. She cut the flowers to bring inside to savor this little miracle. Star—who was no doubt watching her out the window—was barking inside the house, as if warning her to be careful. She put the ladder away, and carried the lilacs into the house. Somehow, she believed the off-season lilac blooms must have a special meaning. She smiled, hearing her mother's voice in her mind saying, "There are no coincidences."

Thea wondered if the grand old tree was heralding Emily's return. Her heart filled with hope as she set the flowers on the kitchen counter.

She gave Star a quick hug then let her outside, knowing she'd be quick in the rain. She arranged the lilacs in a vase. When Star came back inside, shaking the raindrops from her coat, Thea carried the flowers to her sacred space. She set the vase in the center of the round table with celebratory fanfare. Then she sat in the rocker and stared in awe at the lilacs. After a few minutes, she stood up and pulled out a book from one of the shelves. The book remained closed on her lap as she rocked absently in the old chair.

Tim was giving a tired-looking Haddon—dressed in a damp, wrinkled pair of sweats and a rain-soaked blue jacket—a status report as they stood on the small front porch of the Reyes' residence.

"It looks like Katherine Anderson took Emily out of the country." He told Haddon about his interview with the flight attendant. "I'm waiting for confirmation. Johnson's getting the flight manifest and the passengers' passport docs. He's brought the FBI up to speed.

"When Thea saw the Mercury Marquis, I had a hunch I should dig a little deeper. According to Anderson's neighbors' statements today, Dolores Reyes has been her housekeeper for years."

"Son of a bitch," Haddon said, shaking raindrops from his black hair. "The old couple with the Merc kidnapped Emily? Jeez. Why? What's the motive?"

"I don't know yet."

"So we have the who, where, when, and how, but not the why," Haddon summarized.

"Right. That's the big question we'll soon be asking Ms. Anderson. Or so I hope," Tim added, peering through a window into the dark, apparently empty house. "Looks like they're gone for good. There's a realtor's sold sign lying against the side of the house. I put a BOLO out on the Reyes' car." He straightened. "Head back to the station and wait for the flight manifest and passports. Call me as soon as you hear anything. I've already called the lieutenant to authorize the overtime, and sent a car over to watch the Anderson place. I'm going for warrants. I hope to God we're going to find Emily Connor safe and sound tonight."

Emily wasn't afraid of the storm, but she thought Maddy was frightened because she could hear her crying over the barking dog and the wind outside. Emily began to call out to her, cupping her hands and pressing her mouth close to the floor. "Maddy, don't be scared, the wind won't hurt you." She tried shouting her message several times, but Maddy continued to cry.

When the door opened, Emily bolted upright. Auntie Kay stood inside her room. "Emmie, stop yelling up here. What's wrong?"

"I was telling Maddy not to be afraid," Emily said, crab-walking toward her bed.

"She's not afraid, she's sick. Are you sick?" Auntie asked her. Her face looked white, like the scary ghost in one of Emily's books. She shivered, and couldn't answer, just shook her head. She didn't want to say anything anyway. She hated Auntie Kay.

"Fine then, sulk. I have to go back to Maddy. Be quiet up here. I'm trying to get her to sleep." Auntie turned and left.

Emily heard the door lock.

She pushed off the bed and padded to the window. She'd made the hole in the black paint bigger, so now she was able to see the lightning flashing. Since Nana taught her about thunder storms, Emily wasn't afraid. She counted between the lightning and the thunder. Seven.

Maddy must have stopped crying. Emily couldn't hear her anymore.

Thea checked her watch. It was eight-thirty. Still no call from Tim. He wouldn't forget to call her. He must not have an answer about the car. It *had* to be the kidnapper's car. Not because it was a similar black car, or the way Star had reacted to it. It was as if she could *feel* her daughter near her.

After a few minutes, she stood up. But she didn't know what to do next. Call Tim? But he would call when he had something. Wouldn't he? If only she could talk to him.

The wind had picked up outside; rain pelted the windows, making her sense of urgency greater.

She waited until nine then went to the kitchen to call Tim. She had to hear his voice or she'd go crazy.

She punched in the numbers she knew by heart, but each time, Tim's message came on. She hung up and called the station. Tim wasn't in, as she'd expected, but when she told the officer who she was, he didn't seem to know what to say. He cleared his throat, and Thea's knees turned to jelly. She sat. It had to be bad news.

"We're working on something that came up late today." He cleared his throat again. "Detective—"

"What's wrong? Is it Emily? What? Is it bad?"

"No. No. Nothing bad. I'm sorry. It's confusing right now. Nothing for you to worry about. I'll get a hold of Detective McIntyre and have him call you."

It was about Emily. And it wasn't bad! Something was going on and she had to be a part of it. She ran upstairs to dress in jeans, a sweatshirt, and sneakers. She pulled her hair into a ponytail. She was going to Boston.

When she was ready to leave, zipped up in her rain slicker, Star was standing at the back door with her tail wagging.

"Oh no. Not now. You have to go out?" Thea threw up her hands. "Okay, okay, go, Star," she said, holding open the door. "Hurry!"

But the dog ran into the garage and stood at the back door of the car with her nose pointing at the handle.

Thea followed her, laughing, and gave the dog a quick hug. "I get it. You feel it, too, don't you?" She opened the back door. Star jumped in and shook the rain from her furry coat. Thea placed the cell phone on the passenger seat, ready for Tim's call.

Her heart was beating as fast as a humming bird's wings; her spirit was soaring as high as an eagle's flight.

CHAPTER FORTY

Katherine sat by her daughter's bedside, mesmerized by the rapid flickering of Maddy's eyelids. She had vomited her dinner. Katherine had bathed her, managed to get her medicine down, and put her to bed. Then she'd read to her until she finally fell asleep. Now, Maddy was dreaming, happy dreams, she hoped. Her daughter's cheeks were pink from the slight fever, the cause of which they wouldn't know until the tests results were back. The doctor had calmed Katherine with his quiet manner and soft voice, but her nerves remained in tatters.

She stood up with a sigh. Madison had been distraught over the visit to the doctor. Once she'd been so carefree, smiled all the time, danced like an angel. Now she was a child full of fears. Would she ever recover her joie de vie? Could Katherine's unbounded love for her daughter bring her joy back?

Katherine was exhausted, rarely slept for more than an hour at a time. And now, she had another worry. She would have to wait to find out the cause of Madison's new illness. With a last look at her daughter, she left the room. As she stood in the hall, she thought she could hear Emily. No surprise that the child wasn't sleeping, she'd slept away hours of the afternoon. For a moment, she imagined how much Emily's mother must be missing her daughter, but she couldn't allow these thoughts to take hold. She had enough to worry about.

On her way back to her bedroom, the phone rang. She rushed to answer it before Madison woke up, swearing at whoever was calling. It was John.

"Katherine, I'll be over to pick up Maddy on the early side tomorrow. I'm planning to take her to our house for a backyard picnic with Sondra."

"You absolutely cannot. She's sick, John."

"What do you mean, sick?"

Katherine heard the concern in John's voice. Why would he choose to live up to his promise to see more of Madison right now? She had to stall him. "It seems to be just a cold, but you know how vulnerable she is to strep. I don't think she should go out. We saw the doctor yesterday. He ran some tests. And yes, he ruled out strep, for the moment. We'll see what he thinks tomorrow."

"Oh. Well, I'll bring her some ice cream then."

"No, John, you can't come over. I just told—"

"Katherine. What's going on?"

"Nothing. I'm taking care of our daughter. Can I call you when she's better?"

A rush of air filled the phone. "There's something you're not telling me. I'll be there at ten a.m. tomorrow." He hung up.

Now what? What else could happen? How could she cope with one assault after another on her attempt at establishing some normalcy?

She went downstairs to the bar in the conservatory. She poured herself a snifter of Courvoisier. On the way to a chair, she took a gulp of the amber liquid and felt the burn all the way to her stomach. Lightning was flashing simultaneously with cracks of thunder. Tree branches were slapping at the high glass walls. She sat on a cushioned sea-grass chair, set the brandy on the table beside her, and watched the storm rage. Then, with her eyes closed, she envisioned a cliff in front of her feet. A huge drop off, and she was right on the edge. She took another large swallow of brandy, coughed a little at the harsh burn of it.

John was finally becoming suspicious of her lies. Oh God, why now? If he came, he'd surely discover Emily, who continued to act out. After all Katherine had been through to save her daughter, she could end up in jail. No life. No daughter.

Katherine felt the press of tears, but they were locked behind the thick wall she'd grown as a shell to protect her sanity. She couldn't cry. So much trouble. So much work. So many lies.

She could not let a four-year-old child ruin everything at this point. There was only one way. Katherine must return the child to her mother. Emily had to go. And it had to be tonight. She noticed her hands were shaking. She refilled her snifter then sipped while she considered her options.

She could drive Emily to somewhere on the South shore, leave her in a remote place. Not too remote, just enough to give Katherine time to get away before someone saw her. But what if Maddy woke up? What if she needed her mother? What if she got sicker?

She crossed the room, picked up the phone and dialed Dee's cell number. For the first time in what seemed like a hundred attempts, Artie answered.

Katherine was so relieved she laughed. "Oh, thank God. Artie, I need your help. Dee isn't answering the phone. I need her."

"Look, she can't help you anymore. You have to do it yourself. Don't call again, ever, do you hear me?"

Who did these people think they were? Ire sharpened Katherine's wit. "I need help. You must help me. Besides, Artie, I have Dee's bonus money. Seven thousand dollars of it. All you have to do is take Emily when you pick up the money. Drop her off on your way home. Please."

The call was disconnected.

Katherine sat back down in the chair, calm now. She flipped through a magazine while she waited for them to come.

mily heard some noise. She'd finished watching the DVD movie a few minutes ago. Now she was reading a book in bed. She leaned over and turned off the lamp.

The storm was still raging outside, but the noise she heard was at her door. Someone was jiggling the key in the lock.

She quickly dropped her book, pulled the covers up under her chin. Emily squeezed her eyes closed; she didn't want to see Auntie's scary face.

When she heard the door creak, she opened her eyes a slit to peek. She could only see a shadow against the distant light from downstairs. But she could see the shadow was too small to be Auntie.

"Emmie?"

It was Madison. Emily threw off the covers and sat up. "What are you doing here?"

She was frightened. Madison had never come to her room before. Auntie would be so angry with her.

"Turn on your light."

She did. Madison was standing at the door, still holding the handle. "Hurry up, close the door," Emily whispered. "Auntie Kay will see you.

"Mommy's downstairs. Something's wrong with her," Madison said, walking over to Emily's bed.

It made sense to her. Auntie's face was different, her eyes were scary. "Are you going to call nine-one-one?"

"No. I don't think she's sick. I don't know. I think I'll call my grandmother."

"Oh," was all Emily said.

"First, you have to go home."

She froze. For so long she'd wanted to go home. She wanted to see her mommy so bad. Why was she afraid? "How can I?"

"Can you call your mommy?"

"Yes. I could!"

"Okay. I'm going to take you to the phone in the kitchen. But you have to be very quiet. Just follow me, and don't talk until I tell you."

Emily slid off the bed. "Should I get dressed?"

"No. Just come. You can do that when your mommy's here."

They tiptoed down the attic stairs. They passed Madison's room, but Emily couldn't see inside because the lights were off. There was a Hello

Kitty nightlight casting its dim light in the hall, so they could see to walk. Madison turned to her at the top of the next set of stairs, holding a finger against her lips to remind Emily to be quiet. She pointed down the stairs and whispered, "She's in the conservatory. Be super quiet."

Emily didn't know what a conservatory was, but she would be very quiet.

Madison led her faster down the stairs, then through big, pretty rooms and into the kitchen. She closed the kitchen door softly behind them, and went across the room to the phone on a desk. The cold hard floor chilled Emily's feet as she followed.

Madison handed her the receiver. "Go ahead. Call her."

"How will she know to come here?"

"I'll tell her my address after you talk to her. Hurry up. My mommy could come in any minute." She gave Emily's shoulder a little push.

Emily carefully pressed the ten buttons of her mommy's phone number. "It's making a funny noise," she said too loud.

Madison shushed her, glancing at the kitchen door. "Be quieter. What's wrong?"

"I don't know. A lady said I couldn't call."

Madison bent her head in thought.

"Don't you know your phone number?" Madison said, looking toward the kitchen door.

"Yes. I do." She repeated the number to Madison.

"Do you have to add the one? I have to push number one first to call Mimi."

"Oh," Emily said. She picked up the phone and pushed in the "one" button, then her phone number. Emily felt like crickets were hopping around in her tummy. The phone kept ringing. Finally, she heard a mechanical voice telling her to leave a message."

Emily held the handset out to Madison. "I have to leave a message."

Madison spoke into it. "Emma is—"

"No. Emily!"

Madison nodded. "Emily is at my house. You have to come and get her." She started to give her address when the beep sounded.

"You have to call—"

Emily's eyes widened. She heard it, too. "What's that?"

"My mother's coming. Come this way, quick!" Madison opened a narrow door, and Emily followed her up the stairs to the hall outside Maddy's bedroom.

"You have two stairs?"

"These are the back stairs."

"Is my mommy going to come now?"

"I don't know. We didn't finish, but she knows you called her. She can find you now, I think."

"She can find me?" Emily was trying not to cry.

Madison put an arm around her shoulders. "We have to hide you until she comes. I have a lot of good hiding places in my house. Come on."

CHAPTER FORTY TWO

Thea pulled up her hood and made a dash for the front door of
the police station. Breaking every speed record, she'd arrived in
Boston in less than two hours. Tim had not called. Inside, she told
the surprised officer at the desk that she needed to see Detective McIntyre
immediately.

Before she knew it, Officer Haddon, dressed as if he were home on the
couch watching television, came out to meet her. He brought her back to
his office.

"What are you doing here so late?" Thea said.

"Isn't that the question I should be asking you?"

She took a breath. "I tried several times to get through to Tim's phone
numbers. He's still not answering. I had to know. . . ."

He nodded. "Mac's working late, too, but he's out of the office. Let's
see if I can reach him." Haddon gave her a rare smile as he dialed Tim's
cell for her.

Thea's eyes were wide. Officers were buzzing around like it was two
o'clock in the afternoon. Static electricity seemed to fill the air, and it ran
through her, energizing her hope. Something was happening. She was sure
it was something good.

"What are you doing there?" Tim said. She could imagine the grimace
on his face.

How do I make this sound reasonable? "I—I just had to come. I have
this overwhelming feeling. I know we're going to find Emily tonight." She
swallowed. "I can imagine what you're thinking." She bit her lip, held her
breath.

The line remained silent for a few moments. "Did someone get in
touch with you? Call you? How do you know this?" Tim finally said. His
voice sounded angry.

"You didn't call about the car. I called into the station and when I
identified myself to the duty officer, he tripped over his words. I thought
you must have found the owner of the car or come across something."

After more silence, she tried again. "Tim, I can't explain it. I just felt
so sure."

"Sit tight, Thea. Stay right there. Put Haddon on the line." Thea
handed Detective Haddon the phone.

She felt as if she was in some quirky dimension, where nothing made sense. Tim didn't even seem to think she was acting strange.

Haddon listened, nodding. "I will." Pause. "I will as soon as I hear anything." Pause. "Yeah, I'll tell her."

"Okay," Haddon now said to her, "Detective McIntyre wants me to fill you in." He rubbed his beard as he arranged his thoughts. "First, a call came in about a possible break-in. The caller was concerned because the house had been empty for some time, and then she saw lights on in the middle of the night. Turned out to be Katherine Anderson's house. She told the officer she'd been away and had just returned. Katherine Anderson is—"

"I know who she is." Her eyes felt as if they might pop out of her head.

"Yes, okay. The officer who took the call notified our department. One thing led to another, and Tim re-interviewed a flight attendant who had previously called the tip line about two little girls on her flight. She couldn't identify Emily's picture earlier, but this time, she made a clean ID of Ms. Anderson's daughter. There were two children on that flight. We're waiting for passport and manifest confirmation right now. Are you with me?"

She couldn't speak; she could only manage to nod.

"We also found out the car plate you called in belonged to Arthur and Dolores Reyes. An officer had already interviewed them when their Mercury Marquis came up earlier in the investigation. Their alibi had checked out, but Tim had a hunch, and we checked them out again. This time we asked their neighbors some further questions, and we hit on a connection. Dolores Reyes is Katherine Anderson's housekeeper—has been for years.

"McIntyre and I went to question the Reyeses, but they were gone. We're looking for them now."

Thea knew her mouth was open. But after so long, breaks in the case were impossible to believe. "Do you think the Reyes couple took Emily away again?" The thought made her want to burst into tears. How could they be so close, and yet, too late?

"It's a possibility."

Thea raised her fist to her mouth while she wondered how to tell the detective what she knew in her heart. "Detective Haddon, I don't know about this housekeeper, but you *have* to go to Katherine Anderson's home. She might still have Emily there."

Haddon smiled. "It's done. Hang in there. Once we have the airline confirmation, we'll be visiting Ms. Anderson, don't worry."

Thea bent her head and cried. The first happy tears she could remember in a long time.

A few minutes later, an officer handed Haddon a fax. "Already faxed it to the judge."

Haddon studied the image then looked up at her with a sad smile. He handed her the picture he was holding.

"This is your daughter's enlarged passport picture under the name of Emma Cruickshank. It's the confirmation we needed to secure the arrest warrant."

The photo shook in her hands. *Emily.* Her hair was short, blond. She looked into her daughter's eyes, absorbed every pixel of her child's expression. She felt light-headed. Had they hurt her? Emily's face told her nothing. She'd seen that blank stare in pictures of other children who had been abducted. Could Emily ever recover from her experience? Could she ever giggle with joy again? The edges of the picture crumpled in Thea's hands, as if she were holding herself up with the strength of the paper alone.

Haddon leaned over, wide-eyed. "Are you all right? Not going to faint, are you?"

"I . . . I'm okay. Or I will be." She attempted a smile. "How soon can Tim get the warrant? What if she leaves again?"

"Don't worry. Everything's under control. We have the Anderson house surrounded. The FBI will be joining us in force. No one inside is going anywhere. Tim said he'll call you back when he knows something." He looked at her with narrowed eyes. "Really, are you all right? You're so pale. I know this is a shock."

Please God, please let Emily be there. "I just can't believe, after all this time—" Then an incomprehensible thought staggered her: *We are going to find Emily tonight.* She had to climb through the suffocating weight of emotion to stand upright. She pressed a hand over her chest. "I . . . can . . . hardly breathe."

Officer Haddon stood beside her, his face creased in concern. He placed his hands gently on her shoulders. "You'll be all right in a minute. It's so much to take in. Just sit down and breathe slowly with me. In. Out. In. Out." His hands were warm on her shoulders as he pressed her back into the chair. When she began to get a grip on her emotions, Haddon must have seen it on her face. He removed his hands and also sat down.

"Feel better now? Maybe a glass of water?"

Thea nodded. The deep breathing helped, but she still couldn't arrange her thoughts logically. The police were so close to finding Emily. She dropped her head, closed her eyes. She would be here when they did.

A flush of euphoria filled her. She could almost feel herself hugging Emily. She already knew when she came to headquarters that Emily was alive. The police hoped to confirm that. But Thea knew with certainty she would soon hold her daughter in her arms again.

Katherine looked at the clock. She'd been waiting nearly an hour. Where were Dee and Arthur? They should have arrived by now.

She tried not to panic. God, her nerves were so bad. She took a breath and forced a smile. Everything would be all right. Maybe the storm had delayed them. They would be here any minute. And Maddy was fine.

Just to be sure, she went upstairs to check on her daughter. She pushed the door open and walked to the bed. Madison was snoring a little-girl-with-a-cold snore. Katherine felt the tension in her shoulders ease. It was just a cold, nothing more.

Madison had pushed her comforter into a heap at the bottom of the bed. Katherine put a hand on Madison's forehead. Still a little warm.

On the way back to her own room, she looked up the attic stairs. Emily was quiet. She was an amazingly resilient child. How sweet that she'd worried about Madison's fear of the storm.

Katherine narrowed her eyes at the attic door she'd been staring at, but without seeing. She raised her hand to her throat. Was it ajar? She slowly climbed the stairs. A sense of horror was turning her blood into icy slush as she ascended. At the top of the stairs, she peered into the dark room. She moved like a robot over to the bed and leaned over. Even though she knew Emily wasn't there, she patted the covers. She turned the lamp on then stooped down to look under the bed. More quickly now, she went to the closet, pushing hangers laden with little girl clothing this way and that; kicking aside shoes. She rushed back to the bed, throwing off the covers, then to the shelves, sweeping off all the untouched toys.

Emily wasn't in her room!

She ran all over the house looking for the child. She could not have gone outside, or the security alarm would have sounded. Katherine had to find her. Dee and Arthur had to take her away tonight.

"Emily, where are you?" Katherine sang out, as if she were playing a game of hide and seek. She did the same on every floor, walking through every room, fighting the fear that kept bubbling to the surface. Emily didn't answer. That didn't mean she wasn't here, it was part of the game.

By her second round of calling, Katherine was losing her patience. "Emily! You come out right now, young lady. Where are you? Auntie is very angry, Emmie. Come out now. The game is over. No more hiding."

She searched the kitchen, the pantry, and the cabinets while she continued to call out. Emily didn't answer her. Katherine began to panic. She had to find Emily before Dee and Arthur were here, or they would just take the money and leave.

CHAPTER FORTY THREE

The wait for Tim's call back was excruciating, as if she were clinging by her fingers to the ledge of a high building. By the time he called, her shoulder muscles felt twisted like rope.

Tim said, "I'm on my way to Anderson's house to make the arrest."

"Wait," Thea said. "Let me come, please. I have to be there."

"No, Thea. I can't allow it. Wait there. I'll call as soon I can."

"Please, listen to me. I have to come. I promise not to interfere. Just let me come along. I need to see Emily, hold her in my arms." Her voice was breaking. "She's going to be so frightened."

"She may not be there."

"She's there, Tim. I know it."

He must have heard something telling in her voice. "Okay. Tell Haddon to bring you with him. But you will stay in the car until I ask for you. And remember, she may not be there. There's a good chance the Reyes couple have her. I don't want you to fall apart if I tell you Emily's not in the house."

"She's there," Thea said again.

Tim sped past impressive homes in Katherine Anderson's neighborhood, set well apart on lush lots, with mature landscaping. Street lights along one side of the road created circular oases of dim light, filled with the silvery spikes of slanted rain.

He could hear distant sirens, howling louder than the wind, heralding more police, ambulances, and FBI on the way. He noted DCF was already there.

As he swung into the drive, he waved to the officers on stake-out to come with him. He threw open the car door and jumped out.

Lights were on in the house. As Tim approached the front door, a woman began screaming inside. He tried the door knob, but found it was locked. "Bring the enforcer," Tim told the officers approaching behind him.

Once the door was forced open, Tim entered with his hand raised, holding up his gold detective badge. "Police! Detective Timothy McIntyre."

The house security alarm was screeching as the officers began clearing the house, room by room. Tim went to the bottom of the stairs, gun in hand. The woman standing at the top, Katherine Anderson, had stopped screaming. Her child, dressed in a nightgown, was crying, holding tight with both hands to her mother's arm.

"Katherine Anderson, I have a warrant for your arrest for the abduction of Emily Connor."

Katherine stared at him with glazed eyes. "Emily?" she said, looking around.

Tim started up the stairs, stopped two steps below her. "Ms. Anderson," he paused until her eyes focused on him, "tell me where Emily Connor is."

Katherine's brows narrowed. "I don't know. I . . . don't know where she is."

As Tim turned to motion to one of the DCF case officers standing in the hall below, he saw that the floodgates had opened and all kinds of law enforcement was streaming in. The social worker stood beside him.

"Take the child into a bedroom so the EMTs can check her," Tim said.

She stepped up and reached for Madison's hand.

"Let's go downstairs and talk," he said to Katherine, gently taking her hand from her daughter's. "Madison will be in her room for a few minutes."

She followed him down the stairs and into the living room. He indicated the couch, and she sat down, a dazed look on her face.

"Your daughter seems ill," Tim said, stooping in front of her.

Katherine looked blankly at him. "Oh, no. She's all better. She's all better. She won't ever be sick again."

Sam Lyons, an FBI special agent Tim had worked with on Emily's case, walked into the room. He put a hand on Tim's shoulder. "I see you have everything under control."

Tim rose. "Take over, Sam. See if you can get her to tell you where Emily Connor is. I'm going to help with the search."

It seemed like Thea had been waiting in Haddon's car for hours. She couldn't stand another minute. She'd taken her cell from her car before they left. Could she call Tim and see what was happening? If not, she would go crazy.

She pulled the phone from her pocket and noticed the number one on the voice mail symbol. She touched it then held the phone to her ear, expecting that Annie had called for an update. She'd called and talked to her on the ride to Boston, sharing her hope with her friend and keeping herself sane.

"Oh God! Emily! Emily!" she shouted when she heard her daughter's voice. She hit the button to repeat the message. Two little voices, Emily's in the background. When did they call? How did she miss it? Thea was already climbing out of the car.

A uniformed officer was at the door. "Sorry, you can't come in here."

"I have a message on my phone from my daughter. I need to speak to Detective McIntyre, right away. He knows I'm out here, I'm Emily's mother. Please. Hurry!"

The officer left to pass on the message. Thea stood on the front landing, out of the way of the officers coming and going.

Tim stepped out. "What's wrong, Thea?"

"Listen." She handed him the phone.

His eyes stayed on hers as he heard the message. He checked the number and the time of the call. When he handed the phone back to her, his expression was grim. "The call came from this house, but it was almost two hours ago. We've looked everywhere, Thea. Emily isn't here.

"There's a good chance the Reyeses have her. We have a BOLO out on their car. It's only a matter of time before we find them."

Thea dropped down on the step and held her head in her hands. Two hours ago she was speeding toward Boston in her car. While she was talking to Annie, she'd missed the beep from Emily's call. What if that was her last chance to reach her little girl?

Tim sat down beside her. "Hey, don't give up on me now. We'll find her. We'll find the car."

Thea raised her head and stared in front of her as a new thought came to her mind: Could Emily still be hidden in the house?

"Tim, she might still be in the house. Maybe she was threatened, told not to make a sound. Think about it, all the noise and commotion. Everything that's happened to her would have made her so fearful. Let me try. Please, Tim. She called me, asked me to come and get her. If she hears my voice. . . ."

After specific instructions, a female FBI agent escorted Thea around the house.

They began in the kitchen, since no officers were working there. Thea, wearing gloves, opened any cabinet or closet big enough to hide her four-year-old. "Emily, mommy's here, where are you?" she called in a low voice. They moved into the dining room, looked inside the huge French buffet, the console cabinet, behind the draperies.

Next they climbed the two sets of stairs to the attic room where Emily had been confined. Thea stopped at the threshold, her hand pressed over her heart. She was looking at her daughter's prison cell. A rage filled her. She wanted to run down the stairs and beat the woman who had done this to Emily. Her fists tightened into hard balls.

There were not many places in the sparsely furnished room to hide. It didn't take them long to complete their search. Thea blindly followed the agent back down the stairs, fighting a growing sense of despair. Maybe she wasn't here. Maybe those people had taken her. How could she survive losing Emily a second time?

Agents were working in the master bedroom, but they stopped and stood quietly so Thea could call out, "Emily, mommy's here, come out." She repeated it twice, but her growing hopelessness sounded in her voice.

She allowed the agent to lead her to the next room. She had a vague sense of the large size of the room, but then she focused on the child who sat in the middle of a bed large enough for two adults. Her eyes were wide with terror and tears as the paramedics examined her. At once Thea felt both shock and pity because she was looking at a sad little girl who should be Emily. Thea's eyes filled with tears. Why was this child here and not her own? Where was Emily?

But Thea's heart broke for this little girl, too. It was clear she was sick. The little cap she wore made her hair loss evident. Innocent as she was, she would be punished as well. Her mother would be going to prison. Thea approached the bed.

"Don't be afraid, honey," Thea said. The child began to cry harder.

She turned to follow the agent out of the room. She had taken only a few steps when the girl said something. It was hard to hear because of the loud buzzing in Thea's ears. She walked back and looked at the girl, waiting. Her lips didn't move, but the comforter heaped at the bottom of the bed did. The word Thea had so longed to hear for months came again, muffled by a load of eider down.

"Mommy?"

Thea rushed to the bottom of the bed, tugged at the comforter. "Emily! Emily!"

Suddenly, her daughter's most beautiful face was visible. Thea pulled

Emily the rest of the way out and into her arms. She hugged her, rocked her, and kissed her. Thea was crying with joy. But Emily was *giggling!* It was the best sound in the whole world.

CHAPTER FORTY FOUR

The picture would remain with Tim his whole life. No master had ever painted a more beautiful Madonna and Child. Thea stood under the hallway arch, clinging to Emily, who had her arms wrapped tightly around her mother, with her head nestled in Thea's neck. Thea's one arm gripped Emily across her legs, while the other hand cradled her head with splayed fingers. But it was Thea's face that made Tim and everyone else in the room, stop and take a collective breath. It was glowing with awesome beauty, and it appeared to Tim a halo of frosty white light rested around her head. He knew it had nothing at all to do with the stinging in his eyes. She didn't say a word, but her beautiful blue eyes, glistening with tears, beamed at him. He couldn't help himself. He walked over and wrapped his arms around both of them.

Tim gave Thea the basics outlining why Katherine had taken Emily. Madison was lying on a stretcher near the door. She had an IV running into her small hand. Her face was blotchy, and her swollen eyes were bloodshot. She still had two round red circles on her cheeks. Two Department of Children and Families case workers stood beside her, waiting to accompany her to the hospital.

Tim watched as Emily pulled Thea closer to the child lying on the stretcher. She reached her free hand out to touch Madison's arm. "Maddy, why do you have to go to the hospital again? Do I have to go, too?" Emily asked the sick child.

Thea, standing beside Emily, holding her hand tightly, answered. "No, Emily. You don't have to go. Maddy will be better soon."

"Will she wear her sick mask?" Emily asked, peering up at Thea.

"I don't know, baby."

"But, Mommy, I made Maddy better before." Her voice didn't disguise her fear. Thea picked her up and cuddled her.

"You did, and I'm very proud of you. But this time Maddy will get better without you."

Tim asked the paramedics from another ambulance to examine Emily, since Thea refused to allow her to be taken to the hospital. She agreed to have them check her, and promised to have Emily's own pediatrician examine her tomorrow.

Tim walked out with them. He'd assigned Officer Dietz to drive Emily and Thea home to Orleans. Thea's car, with Star in it, was parked at the curb. An officer had driven the car from the police station and would follow Officer Dietz's car to Orleans. When Star saw Emily, she began to bark and frantically paw at the car window. Tim opened the door and released her, and Star nearly knocked Emily over with her exuberant welcome of jumping, whining, barking, and licking. Emily giggled at the dog's joyous welcome. When Star settled down, all three squeezed together on the back seat of the cruiser to go home to their Cape Cod cottage. Tim closed the door with a smile on his face.

Everyone but Officer Dietz was asleep when they arrived at Thea's cottage at nearly two a.m. They woke up when the officer opened the back door. Emily jumped out, and heedless of the darkness and rain, ran in circles on the lawn between the driveway and the house, with her arms extended, letting out jubilant cries. Star pranced at her heels, barking. Thea grabbed her daughter, hugged and kissed her as she carried her into the house. On the way, with her small hand on Thea's cheek, Emily asked, "Is Nana here, Mommy?"

"No, Em, Nana's in heaven, remember?"

"Yes, but she'll come to see me." Emily nodded in her certainty, as her silky curls bobbed.

With Thea beside her, Emily walked through every room in the cottage, never relinquishing her mother's hand. Though they'd often stayed in the house alone during the last month of Hannah's illness, for Emily, it was still her grandmother's house.

Upstairs, when Emily saw her new room, she released Thea's hand and ran in, touching every new item. "Mommy!" Gone was the princess bower and rosebuds, now the room of a nature explorer with binoculars, a small microscope, nets, and science books. In the middle of the room was a child's play tent. Inside was a pink flashlight and a sleeping bag covered with pink and green butterflies. Thea knew, when the lights were turned off, butterflies of all sizes would glow on the ceiling.

"Mommy! Mommy! Look at my room! Nana told me I'd have a good surprise." Star, acting as her personal bodyguard, followed as Emily crawled into the small tent.

A little later, over cups of cocoa, the two officers asked Emily several questions, while the events were still fresh in her mind. When her eyelids began to close, they left.

Thea carried Emily into the sacred space and held her in the rocker. The rain had stopped, but the wind still sang through the old windows. Before she fell asleep, Emily whispered, "Mommy, Nana's in heaven with the angels now." Thea felt a chill at Emily's words, in spite of the warm room. Thea sniffed the air. Though the flowers were still on the table, the heavy scent of lilacs was absent. She cuddled her daughter tighter.

As the chair swayed gently back and forth, she stared down at her daughter's face. *Sleeping beauty.* Thea's eyes traveled over Emily's faint brows, her long blond lashes, the curve of her cheek, her soft lips, and the tilt of her stubborn chin. Her strawberry blond roots had grown in about an inch. Thea touched a finger to a short, springy curl. It would grow back. She noticed Emily's fingernails were clean and clipped short. Someone had cared for her, but it was little solace for the months of heartbreak she and Emily had endured. Thea rocked her back and forth and back and forth. Every few minutes she tightened her arms around her daughter in a gentle embrace.

Emily was home again. *Thank you, God.*

One of Thea's happy tears fell onto Emily's hand. She jumped and cried out in a breathy voice, "Mommy?"

"I'm right here, honey. Mommy's holding you in her arms, and she's not going to let you go." Emily sighed and grew quiet.

When her eyes began to close, Thea carried her daughter, not to Emily's bed, but to her own. It would be a long time before she could let the child out of her sight.

Emily's pediatrician met them at his office early the next morning. He examined her from head to toe, keeping up a cheerful dialogue with Emily. A small gasp escaped Thea before she could stop it. The doctor looked up then followed her gaze.

"These are from the needle punctures made to obtain bone marrow for the transplant. They'll disappear over time."

Thea stared at the small scars. *Would they? Maybe from sight, but would Emily be haunted by her trauma for the rest of her life?* She struggled to tamp down the anger that nearly choked her. How could that woman steal her daughter and use her like that? Why hadn't she come to Thea and asked for her help?

What if she had asked her to have Emily tested? Would she have re-fused to put Emily through the process of marrow donation for Katherine Anderson's daughter? John's daughter?

She would never know what she would have done. The woman she was now cringed at the thought she might have denied a child a chance at life. But in the end, this complex compilation of occurrences had, she hoped, saved another little girl's life, despite the cost to her own little girl.

But Thea had her daughter back. That was all that mattered now. Some Higher Power had awarded her the second chance she'd prayed for. A sense of peace floated over her as soft and warm as sunlight.

"Emily," the doctor concluded, "we're all finished." He turned to Thea. "Physically she checks out well. When I get her medical records, I'll review them, and then we'll decide what follow-up we'll need. Meanwhile, I'll give you the name of a couple of good child psychiatrists. She'll need some therapy to overcome what's happened to her."

CHAPTER FORTY FIVE

Tim came to the cottage three days later. He got out of the car wearing jeans and a navy blue V-neck sweater over a gray t-shirt. No gold badge on his belt, no gun. Just a tall, handsome man. Star ran toward him in a happy gallop, barking her welcome.

When Star calmed down, Thea walked slowly toward Tim.

He watched her approach, studying her face. "Thea?"

She smiled at him. "This is the first time I've seen you when you don't look like a cop."

"It's my day off. I guess the first one I've had in a while."

"And you're here?"

"No place I'd rather be. I wish I could have come sooner. But I've been thinking of you both, about how much must have changed around here since I first came with the search team." He looked up at the house. "*Looks* the same."

"You're right. It's very different," she said. "Come see Emily."

Together they went into the kitchen where Emily was sitting at the table eating a peanut butter and marshmallow Fluff sandwich. A quick flash of fear was replaced with a shy smile when she recognized Tim. Thea knew it would take time for her daughter to recover her trust of people.

Tim pulled out a chair and sat down. "Hi, Emily. I bet you're happy to be home."

Emily looked at Thea then nodded at him before she took another bite of her sandwich.

"Can I get you something, Tim? It's noon, I'll bet you haven't eaten lunch yet."

"You're right, thanks. I think I'd like what Emily's having. It looks so good."

Thea made two sandwiches, one for herself. As they ate, she noticed Tim was wonderful with Emily, who was completely at ease now and laughing at his jokes. He must be a great father. And husband.

"Emily," Tim said, "I have a little boy, named JT."

"JT's not a name, it's letters," Emily said.

"You're right. It is letters. They stand for James Timothy. We call him JT for short."

Emily nodded. "Did you bring him?"

"No, he's home with his mommy. Just like you."

"Can he come play with me?"

Tim glanced at Thea. "I think he'd like that. He's going to be staying with me next weekend. Maybe we can come visit?"

She watched as Emily clapped hands sticky with Fluff, but Thea was thinking about what Tim had just said: 'weekend.' She turned to him.

He answered her unasked question. "I'm divorced. Have been for three years."

After lunch, Thea and Tim sat on the glider on the porch, while Emily and Star ran around the yard. The sky was blue heaven, and bright flowers fought for attention in the crowded flower box. The air was crisp and sharp with its ocean scent. A perfect Cape Cod early autumn day.

"Someday, you're going to tell me how you were so sure we'd find Emily that night, right?" Tim asked.

"There's not much to tell. I *felt* that she was close." She crossed her hands over her heart. "My mom never grew out of her flower child beliefs. I only thought it was endearing." She smiled at him. "Just the facts, for me. Lately, I've been reading some of her books, and I think I'm developing a little *intuition*." She chuckled.

"Maybe you can teach me that skill when this is all wrapped up?" Tim smiled.

"Yes, then," Thea answered, smiling back.

"I can wait," he said, holding her eyes for a few seconds. He stood up and leaned back against the porch railing, facing her. "You know why Katherine kidnapped your daughter. Here's what you may not know. John Warren had no idea Emily was born. But Katherine did. When she suspected John was having an affair, she hired a private detective. He found out who you were, and that you gave birth to a daughter. Katherine called and threatened you, but she never told John about any of it.

"She was sure you wouldn't agree to have Emily tested. When Madison began to show signs of escalating symptoms, she phoned your mother—"

"My mother?"

Tim nodded. "She hoped she would intercede. Your mother died before she could talk to you about it."

Thea shook her head. "If I had told John about Emily from the beginning, this horror would have been avoided. I mean, John would have asked to have Emily tested. I'm sure I would have agreed."

"You didn't cause any of this. Katherine Anderson committed the crime. There were other ways she could have handled her daughter's need for a transplant, but she chose kidnapping.

"She involved her housekeeper, Dee Reyes, and Dee's husband, first because she knew how much Dee loved the child, and second by offering them enough money to retire in comfort."

Emily brought over a sprig of mint from her garden. She crushed the leaves a little then held them out for Tim to smell. When she ran off again, with Star close on her heels, Tim continued. "From what I'm hearing, Emily is one strong little girl with a mind of her own. For the most part, she was treated, if not lovingly, at least with care."

The day was cool, but the still-strong sun was warming Thea's face. She knew not all the warmth was coming from the sun. Joy warmed her. Emily being home warmed her. Tim standing before her warmed her. "What will happen to Katherine?" Thea asked, her face still tilted up to the sun.

"She's being represented by a senior partner in her ex-husband's law's firm. But even with the best attorneys, I doubt she'll escape prison. Juries don't look kindly on child abduction."

"She could be a sympathetic defendant. A mother desperate to save her daughter's life."

"Maybe, but all the evidence points to premeditation."

"I feel so sorry for her. Now that I know what it's like to love a child and lose her, I've been asking myself, what I would have done in her place?"

"It's sad. I agree. I still don't think it will convince a jury to acquit her, but you never know. A lot of damning information will come out in court. We have the guy who hacked Emily's medical records, and the one who forged her other documents. I think they're both quite willing to assist us in this matter, if it will help save their own skin."

Thea stood and walked to the end of the porch where she could better see Emily. "Funny, when John came to see me after you told him Emily was his child, he said he didn't want another child. It was clear to me he meant *any* children. If Katherine's convicted, he'll have full custody of Madison. I hope he takes good care of her. After all she's been through, for her to also lose her mother is heartbreaking. At least her latest illness isn't serious. I was so relieved to hear she only had a virus.

"What about the Reyes couple?" She asked after a pause.

"Their car was found at the airport in Manchester, New Hampshire.

They were several hours ahead of us. They flew to Cape Verde. He holds dual citizenship. We don't have an extradition treaty with Cape Verde. The State Department will try diplomacy, but that takes time. One thing you can be sure of, they won't willingly step back onto American soil."

"I still don't understand how ordinary people could do such a horrible thing: kidnap a child," Thea said, her eyes still on her daughter.

Tim followed her gaze. "Emily seems to be doing fine."

"She's amazing." She turned and smiled at Tim. "She needs to hold my hand much of the time, and she wakes up crying in the night, but otherwise, she seems just like the old Emily. We've seen a psychiatrist. He told me because she was inventive enough to conjure up such a realistic image of her grandmother visiting her, she'd protected herself from the worst of the harm." Thea laughed. "Emily told me, too, that Nana came several times to see her. She says it with complete sincerity." Thea looked away before she added, "And you know, I think I believe her."

He shook his head. "Nothing would surprise me."

Thea smiled into his eyes. It was the right answer.

Tim stood to leave. "I'll be in touch."

CHAPTER FORTY SIX

"Mommy, Star wants a cookie. So do I." At the word cookie, Star's ears perked and she tilted her head.

Thea was sitting on the glider, filling herself with the elation of watching her daughter play with Star in their yard. "I think you both deserve cookies." She held up a finger. "Stay right there where mommy can see you. I'll be right back."

She returned with a handful of small dog biscuits for Star, who offered her paw, and a bag of Oreos, giving three to Emily, who said, "Thank you." Thea carried the bag back to the porch then took three cookies for herself. She laughed watching Emily, sitting cross-legged on the grass, split the first Oreo and lick off the sugary center first.

"Who taught you how to eat Oreos that way?"

"Annie."

Annie had driven down early that morning to see Emily. There had been tears and hugs all around. "Oh, so this isn't the first time you've had Oreos today? When did she give them to you?"

"For breakfast."

"Really? Where was I?"

"In the bathroom, Mommy."

"You must have eaten the cookies pretty fast."

"Annie told me to."

Thea laughed again, which elicited a giggle from Emily. Her daughter had been through so much, but she would recover. The only visible signs of how her ordeal had frightened her were her small hand clinging to Thea's, or her beautiful eyes keeping her mother in sight, though she'd managed to be apart from Thea long enough to chow down some cookies. But Thea was determined to hold her hand and stay by her side as long as Emily needed the attachment. Thea needed it, too.

"Three stories, Mommy?"

While Emily chose her bedtime stories, Thea realized her little girl had grown taller. She didn't want her to grow up so quickly. She would have to make every moment count from now on.

Emily handed the books to her, then climbed into Thea's bed and snuggled up next to her.

"Which one are we going to read first?"

If You Were Born a Kitten. Emily slid the book out and put her finger on it. "Mommy, can I have a kitten?"

"Not tonight, Em. We'll talk about it tomorrow."

Emily fell asleep before Thea finished reading the book.

Thea pulled the covers over her daughter, but stayed where she was, simply staring at Emily. She was sleeping on her side with her knees pulled up. Her mouth was slightly open and her breathing was slow and easy. Thea took a long last look before she tiptoed away.

She went back downstairs and into the sacred space. She sat in the rocker and looked out the window at the dark shadow of Lizzie's lilac tree. Soon it would drop its leaves and sleep through the winter. By the time the flowers bloomed next spring, Thea knew she and Emily would be fine.

She closed her eyes and felt her spirit fill with love and gratitude. She even caught a faint drift of the scent of lilac. At some point, she was going to research the family who lived in Knoll Cottage with a child named Lizzie.

But right now, it was all about Emily and their new life together.

GERRI LeCLERC
is a Pennsylvania native who received her Nursing Education
in Vermont. An RN, her medical background is reflected in
her stories. She is an avid bird watcher, an enthusiastic (so-so)
tennis player, and an occasional cook, who is touted for her
sumptuous Braciole. She lives on Cape Cod and insists it is
magical. She shares her Cape cottage with her husband Ron,
and Livia, her cat, who doubles as her muse.

She can be reached at www.gerrileclerc.com

Photograph by Kim Reilly
Studio K Photography. LLC PPA

Don't miss
the next inspiring
offering from
GERRI LeCLERC

Excerpt from

S I L E N T
GRACE

With sleet tapping at the window of her New Bedford, Massachusetts apartment, Beth Henson sat on the floor, packing a box of books.

The phone rang with her sister's unique ringtone and interrupted her off-key singing. Beth hesitated, pressing tape over the flaps of the box, and considered letting the call roll to voicemail. Instead, she wove her way through a maze of packed boxes, retrieved her phone and answered.

It was a video call from Grace.

"Mommy won't wake up," her niece said in her fragile voice, while she also signed at a frantic pace. "Scared."

"Is she breathing? Turn the phone so I can see Mommy," Beth said, signing the main words. Grace understood and switched the phone's camera to Patrice on the couch. Beth saw that she was breathing deeply.

"I'm coming now, sweetie. Stay on the phone with me." But the call ended. Beth must have signed wrong. She didn't take time to call back. She grabbed her purse from the table by the front door. "Keys. Keys," she said, dumping the contents on the floor. She scooped up the keys and left everything except her wallet where it landed. Grace had to be alarmed to use her voice. Beth was afraid she knew what it was; had seen it before.

Made in the USA
Charleston, SC
07 April 2016